SWERVE

The Little Bastards 2

S

Jim Lindsay

Hampton Press

Praise for

The

Little Bastards

"Set in the 1950s, Lindsay's coming-of-age novel tours the physical, emotional, and, most importantly the vehicular landscapes of young narrator Sonny. Lindsay ruminates repeatedly on the fun and freedom of being a hot-rodding, blue-collar boy in the '50s, a nostalgia close to his heart. The prose is breezy, and will interest readers who lived through the era."

—*Kirkus Reviews*

"Jim Lindsay's coming of age story is richly evocative of the life and times of small-town kids during the 1950s. I quickly was immersed in Sonny's tale as he and his friends graduate from frantic bike rides around town while reading all about hot rods to actually working on and riding in their own, while listening all the while to the latest rock and roll music on the radio. The descriptions of the environment, the cool foggy days of western Oregon and the clubhouse hidden in blackberry thickets where the kids hang out, smoking cigarettes and listening to 45s are fabulous. Equally fascinating is the way Lindsay's narrator walks the reader through the intricacies of modifying cars and conveys the excitement of the drag races held on Otto's farm and the formalities of challenging racers. Add in the local high school girls who are just starting to appreciate these kids from the wrong side of town, and you've got the combination for a great story—and it rides beautifully."

—**Readers' Favorites Book Reviews**

"The quintessential coming-of-age tale of five boys in a mid-'50s American small town, this is a Henry Gregor Felsen novel as might be told by J. D. Salinger. Not only is the story engaging and accurate but, thankfully for once, so is all of the hot rod and custom car terminology and action. Much like *American Graffiti* spread over five years instead of one night."

—Pat Ganahl, author and contributor

"This dose of nostalgia (not a good enough word) is a fun read, a visitation with a familiar past, even if not the immediate past of some of our younger trad hot rod and custom cousins. I think the protagonist in the book (is it actually Jim?) was cooler than I was (although I did wear motorcycle boots in elementary school). It goes fast, doesn't labor over every drag race and every rise in the Levis; it moves and gets us to a point where we are able to leave the guy . . . well, you'll just have to read it and find out for yourself."

—Mark Morton, *Hop Up* magazine

"*The Little Bastards* is a gritty, gripping, heart-stopping remembrance of growing up in a small Northwestern American town in the 1950's. *Little Bastards* will take you back and fill your heart and soul with the same sense of excitement and freedom that you once experienced. It will make you remember your own youthful trials and tribulations. It will make you feel alive."

—John Kelly, *Detroit Free Press*

"Few writers today can match the authenticity of that mysterious, challenging time as the coming of age—especially in the1950s—that Jim Lindsay brings to this slice of time and life. It is rich in content, plain spoken in narration, and offers us insight into young lads whose journey has just begun. Highly Recommended."

—Grady Harp, Amazon Top 50 Hall of Fame Reviewer

"*The Little Bastards* teleports the reader to the 1950s and immerses them in the warm glow and simple lives of kids just trying to have fun with girls, cars, and life. It's complete with triumphs and tragedies. A must read for all who want a nostalgic trip back in time."

**—Jess Todtfeld, former TV producer
FOX-TV, NBC, and ABC**

Cover design and interior by Tom Heffron
Cover illustration by James Owen
Cover photo by William Gedney

Published by Stamper Press
Manufactured in the United States of America.
ISBN 978-1-7326319-0-0

Published 2018

For my dad,
Grant Lindsay

Preface

Thank you for opening my second book in *The Little Bastards* series.

I made it all up, but it has good bones; it's the way it was. It was an era that experienced huge, exciting changes, and I was seeing the whole phenomenon over the handlebars of my Columbia bike with those big balloon tires that were good on gravel roads. These so-called improved roads surrounded our farm for several miles in all directions. My older brother, Bob, and his friends would take these corners sideways and drift through them in their jalopies.

Hot rod magazines were my link to the world of show cars and drag racing. I pored over them like they were important documents, not missing a word. When in Albany, a typical town of ten thousand souls, shopping with Mom or riding with Dad, I witnessed these older boys mimicking what I saw in those periodicals.

Hot rods and customs were driven by these creatures wearing bomber jackets and Elvis hair. The girls were there too, sitting close with lipstick and flirtation. They gathered at local service stations and would roar out with their pipes cackling. The police dogged them and wrote traffic tickets by the bookful but couldn't slow the enthusiasm.

The fifties gradually faded out as Detroit was getting into the fest with their muscle cars. You didn't have to build them anymore, which took away the individualism of a self-made road rocket. The music survived a little while longer, until the Beatles got off the plane, relieving us of our innocence and simplicity.

I have told this story through the eyes of Sonny Mitchell, the fictional main character, who you may identify with. He and his friends have matured from bicycles to cars with an air of cockiness and camaraderie; they walk with their shoulders back. At times, I became Sonny Mitchell as I rattled off this tale, and it about wore me out being a teenager in a seventy-year-old body.

I hope you love this book as much as I do. I can truthfully say, I loved writing it. So hang on and ride with Sonny Mitchell.

Hot Rod Driver Saves Trio!

A spectacular crash averted a deadly car – train collision on the Willamette Boulevard late Saturday night involving 4 Willamette youths.

Uninjured but shaken are Morton Johnson, 19, graduate of Willamette High driver of a newer Plymouth hardtop, and passengers, Susan Bell 17, and Marylyn Swanson 18, both Willamette seniors.

Driver of the other car, a modified Ford coupe, Sonny Mitchell, also a Willamette graduate appeared uninjured but hasn't been available for comment.

Police said Mitchell; in an attempt to save the three chased and intercepted Johnson's car before it could hit the 11 o'clock train.

see Hot Rod Driver on p. A10

Chapter 1

My parents looked at me like we'd never met.

"What's up?" I asked, folding into a kitchen chair.

Their eyes froze on me as Dad, a cigarette burning in his fingers, slid me the morning newspaper. I stared in shock at the headline.

Hot Rod Driver
Saves Trio!

The huge photo above the headline was a spectacle of chaos, a scene of pandemonium engulfed in smoke and illuminated by headlights and flashbulbs, with me holding Marylyn—*my heart pounded*—Marylyn! I was helping her over a pool of radiator coolant to my '40 Ford, its rear end all bashed to hell. Behind my car was the crushed front of Morton Johnson's Plymouth and a cop cuffing Morton.

I looked at my parents—their eyes were big. "Am I in trouble?"

"No," Mom said. "An officer called at 1:30 a.m. looking for you. I told him you were home. He said you've done nothing wrong."

That was a relief. Then I read the article—calling me a hero! That's a stretch, I thought. That's newspaper talk for you. When I put the paper down, they were still staring at me, Mom, standing with the coffee pot in her hand. Dad's cigarette had burnt out in the ashtray. They just stared at me, stunned, which was unusual in our house. My parents were solid and held their emotions close, but this was having an effect on them I hadn't seen before.

"Must have been quite a night you had, Sonny," Dad said in his usual dry and understated way.

"Yeah, it looks like it," I said.

"Are you okay, Sonny?" Mom asked with a tremble in her lips. "You look worn out. Did this really happen?"

"Yeah," I said. "They got it about right, I guess, except about the heroic part maybe."

"Well, this was all noble of you," said Dad, "but ..." He frowned at me. "You could have gotten yourself killed." He lit another cigarette. "How did you get involved? Do you know these kids?"

"Morton and I graduated together but we weren't friends or anything. He was drunk and driving the two girls around town. I heard about his scheme to beat the train on the Boulevard and knew that in his condition he was way over his head and probably would kill himself and the girls, so I intervened. I've always regretted not doing the same the night Miles was killed. I might have saved him."

Their eyes dropped at the mention of Miles. Miles was a friend and one of our group. He was the careful one who didn't like taking chances and then was killed in a car wreck when we were juniors. Like the other boys, he was close to my folks too.

"Weren't you awful scared?" asked Mom.

"The scary part was right at the end, and I didn't really have time to think about it."

"Who's the girl?" Mom asked.

"M-M-Marylyn Swanson," I stammered, surprised to hear her name come out of my mouth.

"Almost time to leave for church," said Dad. "I'll get our raincoats," and he stepped out of the room. They no longer made me go. It seemed I'd spent most of my life there trussed up in a suit and tie, counting off the minutes until freedom.

"She's the daughter," I continued to Mom, "of Mr. Swanson down at the bank."

"I didn't know he had a daughter. Is there something special about her?" The way Mom asked it, I knew she'd picked up on how I felt. A little sparkle pushed away the worry in her eyes and she sat next to me. "What's she like?"

Suddenly I was gushing. "Marylyn is special. She has it all. Lots of friends, and she's in the right clubs at school, and she's even a cheerleader. I'd figured she was way out of my league, impossible for me to meet her. But I found out that, up close, she has kindness in her eyes and she's fun."

Dad came back in with their raincoats, looking at his watch. "We'd better get going, Evelyn, or we'll be late and have to sit in front. Sonny, you can use the pickup until your car is fixed."

"Thanks, Dad."

Mom patted my shoulder as she slid me a plate of scrambled eggs and bacon.

Dad opened the back door.

Mom said to me, "I'd like to hear more about this," and then they passed through as Spooky, my cocker spaniel, came sniffing in.

Getting on in age, Spooky couldn't do a hell of a lot or hear anything, but her nose hadn't let her down yet, and she expected her portion of bacon. When it was just me, she enjoyed more freedoms around the house. I lifted her into the chair across the table from me and popped a piece of bacon in her mouth. She swallowed it and looked at me through her old eyes with the undying love she'd carried for me all her life. She was my dog since forever.

I too began with the bacon while showing her the photo on the front of the paper. She cocked her head, seeming somewhat intrigued, so I confided in her like when I was little. "That's Marylyn Swanson—I fell in love with her last night!"

I'd had no plan; it was just time to get Marylyn away from the cameras and the gawkers who were showing up. I'd helped Marylyn into my car and driven away, her leaning on me, clutching my red shop rag in her hands. Being an innocent player in Morton's game to beat the train had taken a toll on her. A contrast to when I'd seen her with her bubble-gumming cheerleader friends whipping the crowd into a frenzy, tuned to rock and roll bleating from a runaway high school band. Now, because of whims of violence, she'd slumped against me like a sleeping princess, totally exhausted.

I turned off the Boulevard, the motor belched and died, and I was coasting. Damn, I was out of gas. What if I'd run out a mile sooner? I couldn't have stopped Morton's Plymouth before it hit the train.

Still rolling, I swung into the alley behind the Greyhound depot and coasted to a stop.

What would she think of me running out of gas? She would be right to think I was poor, because poor people work off the bottom of their gas tanks. But I wasn't poor, just short on gas. My one chance to show Marylyn Swanson what I was made of and now we'd have to walk.

"What's wrong?" Marylyn whispered into my neck.

"We're out of gas." The first words I'd said since the crash and my voice sounded funny—kind of meek, like I was admitting running out of gas was irresponsible.

Her shoulders shook a little and she giggled. "I thought boys drove their girls around a while before running out of gas."

We busted out into a mutual fit of hysterical laughter, brought on, I guessed, by the sudden break from our overwhelming fear of dying. After attempts to overcome the fit, then losing it again, we got it all out. Marylyn blew her nose in the red shop rag and then stuffed it into her pocket, like saying, "That's enough of that."

"Brrr," she shivered, and I realized the temperature in the car had dropped from lack of a running motor.

I pulled Dad's army blanket from behind the seat and laid it in Marylyn's hands. She unfolded it and covered our legs and brought it up to our chins and then snuggled against me in our little tent.

This brought on an exhilarating feeling, being so close to someone I'd ogled with desire and awe through years of high school.

I'd been close to girls' bodies before, but this was different. I was getting worked up of course, but was reluctant to let my impulses run amuck since it would ruin the moment, which I hoped would never end. It wasn't every night a guy was going to get this close to Marylyn Swanson. She wiggled her left arm around my back and put her right hand on my chest like she was flattening out wrinkles on my Penney's t-shirt. It was hard for me to grasp the fact that this was happening. She was more than I imagined. She was everything I thought she was and also exciting and fun and affectionate. Just two days before, we'd been strangers, without even a nod or any other show of recognition. She probably hadn't even known who I was, even though we'd shared the same high school for three years.

Marylyn jerked up. "Oh my gosh, what time is it?"

I raised my left arm to see my watch in the beam from the streetlight behind us. "Nine minutes till twelve."

"Uh-oh, I've got to be home in nine minutes!" she said.

Dang. Why she did she have to leave now? "Where do you live?"

"Eighth and Maple."

"That's clear across town."

"I know." She sounded worried.

I couldn't get her home in nine minutes, even if we ran all the way. Then I caught sight of a bicycle leaning against the alley wall and said as I left the car, "Don't worry—I'll be right back." Grabbing the Schwinn by its freezing handlebars, I ran it back to the car. Damn, it was cold out there. I opened the door for her. "Bring the blanket. I'm biking you home."

She got out of the car holding the blanket for me. *My God*, I thought, *she's even more beautiful than I remembered.*

Recovering from that, I looked at the blanket in my hands. How was this going to work? Thinking fast, I pulled out my pocketknife and, as Marylyn looked on with interest, I cut a slit in the middle of the blanket, making it into a giant serape. "This will keep us warm," I said.

"Good," she said.

I tucked the blanket under my arm, held the bike for her, and said, "Jump on."

She backed up to the front of the bike with the wheel between her legs and lifted herself onto the handlebars with grace, like the athlete she was. I swung my leg over and steadied the bike while pulling the blanket over our heads. I peddled us out of the alley, wobbling at first, then our ride smoothed as I pumped the bike for the white-collar west side of town.

With our heads sticking out of the blanket, we could have been mistaken for a camel crossing the desert in the night, except for our giggles and curses as I swung around potholes, taking shortcuts on our mission for home. Leaning into the corners, our heads were almost touching. Her hair was like silk on my face on one side and then the other. Her tears from the cold wind ran from her eyes and off her cheeks and onto mine like little raindrops in a clearing-up shower.

I wanted to check my watch to see if we were going to make it in time, but I didn't dare take my hands off the bars for fear of losing my precious cargo. It was the second time that night that I was trying to beat the clock. The consequences of failing this time seemed nil, but still, a task I wasn't going to avoid. Meanwhile, I wanted to make it fun and let Marylyn know a blue-collar kid's blood was warm too, so I barked out landmarks important to a boy, like Smitty's bike shop and Jones's hobby shop, like a tour of the town.

As I pedaled past the old red-brick library, Marylyn chimed in, "And that's the library!"

I laughed, "I haven't spent a lot of time in there." *Why did I say that?* It sounded stupid.

"But I noticed you carrying books home from school," she said.

She noticed me?

I kept up the high-speed pedaling, braving away the urge to let on that I was winded. "I didn't know you ever gave me a look."

"Everyone looked at you, Sonny. You and your friends, all gallant and tough. You didn't really strut, but you were sure of yourselves, all masculine with hot cars and bomber jackets."

"I would have never guessed it. I'm not so clever when it comes to those things."

"No, you aren't, and that's a good thing. Now, your friend Gary might be clever."

"Yeah, the girls really go for him."

"He needs it," she said.

"I'm going to be carrying a lot more books next year."

"Really? What for?"

"I'm going to the university in the fall." Since graduating from high school the spring before, I'd been stowing money away from working in the sawmill. In fact, it was piling up downtown at Marylyn's father's bank. My parents were helping by giving me free rent, but I wasn't going to ask them for money, since I felt their financial obligation to me had finished at graduation.

"I'm impressed," she said. "You'll look good in a college sweater."

She's impressed! Did I hear that right?

We biked past the funeral home. Marylyn leaned back into me with a shiver. "This place gives me the heebie-jeebies."

I moved up close to give her a little warmth and security any normal hero would do, and she let me.

"I grew up just around the corner," she said, "and I still get the jitters when I walk by. It's so cold and final-like."

"You ought to spend Halloween night in there some time, like Joe and I did, and see how you like that," I said.

"I can't imagine! You really did that? I remember Joe. What's he like, anyway?"

"He's my best friend."

"Isn't it funny—we grew up in the same little town

and witnessed a lot of the same things and never knew each other."

"We know each other now," I said into her ear.

"I'm glad."

She's glad she knows me! Man, I'm loving this.

"Turn right here." Marylyn cocked her head, rolling another tear off her cheek and onto mine. I savored the moment.

"Then left up there," she continued, "and we're home."

And there stood the nicest house in town, big and white with green shutters and a brick sidewalk leading to a wide porch with a massive front door and a chandelier hanging from its ceiling. Her home was stately, like a place a senator would live. What the hell was I doing here?

We glided up to the front and stopped. I lifted the blanket off and checked my watch—11:59, one minute to spare.

"Brrr," she said as she climbed down from the handlebars. "I forgot how cold it was."

"Well, you haven't been doing the pedaling."

Laughing, we left the blanket on the bike at the curb and I walked her onto the porch. She turned and faced me with her arms inviting me.

Oh boy! This was good. I stepped into her embrace. As her red lips were coming towards me, a scraping noise from above blew the moment away. It sounded like a window opening.

"Darn," she said, stepping back. "What's that?"

Damn. I let her go.

"Mumby, is that you?" It was the voice of a child, full of sleep.

"Shush," she said to the voice, then whispered in my ear, "It's my little brother." She leaned out from under the porch roof, looking up. "Harold, go back to sleep—you'll wake the whole neighborhood."

"Who's that with you?" he demanded from above.

"A friend. Now go back to sleep."

I heard him pull the window down. Marylyn got that look again and came closer. I wasn't going to let her get away this time and moved in with my arms around her, looking down into those beautiful dark eyes.

The chandelier blinked on and off. *Damn.* Marylyn winced reluctance and her eyes dropped. Without a good-bye, she turned on her heel, entered the house, and without a glance back, shut the door.

A lonesomeness fell on me. I was sure she hadn't wanted to leave me. But at the same time, I wondered—would she be the same when I saw her again, or would she go on with her privileged life and forget me back to my blue-collar roots?

When I finished my scrambled eggs, Spooky was sound asleep, her chin holding down the newspaper. She came out of it as my last piece of bacon neared her nose. I watched her swallow it down, noticing she'd slobbered over the picture, making the ink run together. My car was a smudge. I realized I hadn't been without a car since my sixteenth birthday. The thought scared the hell out of me.

How was I going to see Marylyn without a car? My car was my brand. She'd never be impressed with an old pickup. So the best thing for me and for my car would be to fix it fast.

Which meant I had to get off my ass.

Chapter 2

I pulled on my bomber jacket and engineer boots, then Spooky and I stepped out the front door together to a typical Oregon Sunday morning in January—wet, cold, and gray. The street was deserted except for Dad's faded old red Chevy pickup and my dark blue '40 Ford in its normal parking place, but beat all to hell. Both taillights were broken and the trunk lid was smashed. The rear bumper was crunched into the crushed lower panel. Both back fenders were caved in and had rubbed on the rear tires, which were cut up and ruined. Oh God. It was a gloomy picture for sure.

I'd gotten the car a week before I'd turned sixteen. The previous owner had taken special care of it, so it was immaculate inside and out. With the help of my friends, especially Billy Wheeler, who was good at mechanics, we had transformed the '40 into a teenage rocket and a dream of the envious. We had even driven it to Mexico for upholstery the summer before we were seniors, then swapped the motor out for a big Olds, which modernized it and made it a legend. It was the fastest car in town.

What had been a wonderful example of Henry Ford's finest creation was now a wreck. Funny how it hadn't looked this bad when I'd pedaled back to it from Marylyn's last night. I'd left the Schwinn where I'd found it. Then, with some gas and a few revolutions, the motor had popped and fired up. I'd limped my old '40 home, the tires rubbing on the fenders, my mind shifting from ecstasy to the crash and back.

Now, in the drizzly gray light of day, the extent of the ruination made me shudder to think how fortunate we all were to have come through the wreck alive, especially Marylyn, who was such a beautiful example of a living being.

I needed to call Bruce at Zig's Towing right away. He worked Sundays so the married employees could be home with their families. From being friends with Bruce during high school, I'd spent time with him at the towing yard and knew they had a fenced-off area for storing wrecks until the insurance companies sent their inspectors.

Turning back to the house, I noticed a red Buick sedan coming down the street, new and big and expensive. Cars of that caliber rarely ventured into our neighborhood, and when one did, the driver was usually lost. It pulled right up behind my '40 Ford, which made my car look that much worse. Figuring the driver needed directions, I waited on the sidewalk to help him out.

The long door swung open and a man in a gray suit stepped out. He was Al Capone–looking, except maybe taller, with an air about him that reminded me of a leader, like a general or something. He stared at me across the roof of the sedan. His nose was red enough that he might have a cold or a taste for booze. He seemed familiar, but I couldn't place him. He slapped a rolled-up newspaper on the car like he was trying to get my attention. "Are you Sonny Mitchell?"

It was Marylyn's dad. I remembered his voice from the bank. I'd been putting my money in his bank since I was twelve. I wondered how he knew where to find me. "Yes, sir, I am."

He came around his car, his movements steady and forthright as if he was used to being in control and the owner of the biggest bank in town.

"Well," he said, pounding the newspaper on the fender like he was driving home a point, "first of all, I want to thank you for saving my daughter's life." I liked hearing that, especially from Marylyn Swanson's father, to me, the King of Willamette.

"I just came from the police station, and after talking with the two officers mentioned in this article, I'm damn sure if it hadn't been for your quick thinking and guts, my daughter would be down at the morgue right now. I remembered your name as a client at my bank, and commend you on your savings record. It is impressive for a person of your age."

"Thank you, sir. I'm saving up for—"

"Here's the problem, young man," he cut me off. "Her mom and I have high expectations for our daughter, and they don't include her ending up with a man who works in a sawmill." He aimed the newspaper at my house, which suddenly looked small and worn. "And lives in a house like that, where she's expected to toil and raise a whole passel of kids. If you have any romantic inclinations that include my daughter, get them out of your head."

I was stunned. I couldn't believe he'd said that. J. R. pulled a money clip from his pants pocket, and peeled off some hundred-dollar bills. "How much?"

"I don't want your money!" I heard myself say.

He leveled his eyes at me as if a little taken aback, but he recovered quickly and returned the roll of bills to his pocket. "You just remember what I told you. My daughter is off limits, and if you come trespassing, you'll regret it." He got in his car and left.

I felt weak. My knees buckled and I found myself sitting on the curb with my head in my hands. I'd let myself go and fallen hard for the daughter of that beast. Sure, we did look a little poverty stricken compared to the layout he had on the west side, but he hadn't let me explain my goals of a college degree and a career. By keeping my mouth shut, I felt I'd made a promise to him I was already beginning to regret.

For the first time in my life, I began to feel sorry for myself.

I got a wet lick on my wrist. Spooky was sitting next to me, trying to relieve the sadness she sensed. I put my arm around her and pulled her up close. It started to rain. I hugged onto her as the rain ran down our faces. We got soaked and then we felt foolish, so we got up and took a solemn walk to the house. Inside, Spooky lay down by my chair at the table, and I sat with my feet near her and lit a smoke and stared at the newspaper photo of Marylyn with deep longing, trying to think of a way out of this mess but getting nowhere fast.

Mom and Dad came in pulling off their coats. I'd never smoked in front of them before but didn't feel like hiding it. Mom took Dad's coat to hang along with hers, and Dad sat down across the table and slid his ashtray towards me. There was a first time for everything.

"You look like you just came out of the river," he said.

"Yeah. It took a while to look my car over. It's a mess."

Mom slid into the chair between us with a concerned look on her face, and we just sat there. I couldn't think of anything to say. Dad excused himself, saying he had an errand to run down at the mill and that he would be back after a while.

After he left, Mom said, "What's the matter?"

"I got a visit from John Swanson," I said.

"Marylyn's father! That's nice!" Then she got a closer look at my face and said, "Things didn't go so well, I take it?"

"Nope. He's forbidden me from seeing Marylyn."

"What in heavens for?"

"Well, I guess it's pretty much that I live on the wrong side of the tracks."

"Oh, phooey. Why, you're a fine, upstanding boy."

"It's not that, Mom. He doesn't want his daughter to have a life as a mill worker's wife, laboring and producing children."

She got that protective look she had whenever someone crossed us. "We've raised two kids and have this nice home all paid for and some money in the bank.

"Sonny, your dad and I grew up in the depression. Each year it got worse. Sometimes going to bed at night with empty stomachs. I saw my father cry because he couldn't feed us as well as he thought he should. It was 1940 before we really came out of it. It wasn't what the government did, but the war brought us out. Everyone went to work. It was in the shipyards in San Francisco where we met and married. Your dad got drafted and I stayed and drilled holes and welded steel together."

"You did that?" I tried to see her in a welding helmet.

"After the war, we came to Oregon."

"Why here? With all the rain?"

"That makes the trees grow. We came because of the timber industry. Your dad's been employed steady ever since. Most of all, we're happy, Sonny, and that's what it's all about. Old Mr. Swanson can take his big house and bank, and shove them where the sun doesn't shine for all I care."

I grinned. "Sounds like you learned more than just welding."

Smiling back, she said, "It wasn't all just work; we had a little fun along the way."

"I guess I could have told him off, but that wouldn't have helped my chances of seeing Marylyn any."

"You did the right thing. Remember, Sonny, when you start the university this fall, you won't be a mill rat anymore. You'll be a bona fide college student with a white collar and a golden future, and that's going to change things with John R. Swanson. Uh-oh," she said suddenly, "I just had a thought. I wonder if Marylyn knows her dad warned you to keep away from her?"

"That's right. Darn! I hadn't thought of that. She'll wonder why I'm not coming around. I'm in a tight spot."

Mom gave me one of those motherly smiles. "Don't worry. I have a feeling it will work out for you, Sonny."

"Thanks for caring, Mom."

"You're welcome," she said.

"Well." I pushed my chair back and headed for the phone in the hall. "I gotta call up Bruce and see if he'll come get my '40."

I dialed the phone. Bruce answered. "Well, if it isn't the town hero."

"I don't feel like much of a hero now," I said. "I've been looking my car over, and it ain't good." I asked him if he could bring the truck over and tow the '40 back to the yard. He said to give him a few minutes to finish up a job he was doing and then he'd be over in the wrecker.

There was a knock on the front door. I opened it.

"So what about it, big shot?" ribbed Joe, his red hair wet from the rain. "You're the first Little Bastard that ever hit the front page." He grinned at me with the soft blue eyes that redheads have.

Things were looking up.

Gary followed him in, combing the water out of his hair. He was always combing his hair. He gave me a loving shove that about tipped me over. Then there was Billy coming in last. He was the oldest and had been our leader growing up. Billy was smart and in college already, home for winter break.

Now they were all talking at the same time and wearing shit-eating grins in anticipation of a report about the previous night. Joe, Gary, Billy, and I were the core of our club, which went back to our early grade-school years. We had been known as the Little Bastards, the toughs from the east side. Before I could say boo, they shed their bomber jackets and took places around the kitchen table, which was familiar to them from dinners and sleepovers of the past.

"I see you've been drooling over your picture here," Joe said, pointing at the wet paper.

"Spooky was reading it," I said.

"Yeah, sure," said Joe.

Mom was at the stove, stirring away on a large pot of soup, which filled the room with the smell of cooking tomatoes. She always had soup going this time of year. "Why don't you make the boys some Kool-Aid," she said. She liked my friends and made them feel welcome.

I pulled the large glass pitcher from the shelf and filled the thing with water from the sink, then dumped in a cup of sugar. "What'll it be?" I asked, fanning out the Kool-Aid packages of different flavors like a hand of cards.

"Red!" "Green!" "Red!" came their answers all at once.

"Strawberry it is." I stirred the red powder into the concoction.

"That tomato soup sure smells good," said Joe, eyeing the pot. He'd grown up poor, really poor, without a dad, and he hadn't seen his mom much because she was a cocktail waitress at night and slept through the day. It had made him self-reliant and dependable and tough. I'd always loved him for it.

"Yeah," said Gary, wiping his comb on his pants. "I like that stuff, Mrs. Mitchell."

Mom handed over a stack of bowls and they found their way around the table, along with big spoons that were embossed with navy insignia. Everyone was using stuff left over from the war.

In the middle of the table, she set a plate of sliced Wonder Bread and a cube of butter and a knife.

A freckled hand shot out from Joe's sleeve and one slice was gone. Mom doled out the soup with a ladle. I poured the Kool-Aid into jelly glasses and took a seat. The feast was on.

There was another knock on the door and Bruce came in wearing his jacket with Zig's Towing above the chest pocket. Bruce was stout and could have played football, but we'd saved him from trouble. He'd come to us later during high school, and he shared our interest in cars, so we'd included him in our outfit.

I got him a folding chair from the closet and poured him a Kool-Aid while Mom ladled up another bowl of soup.

"So let's hear about it," Billy said, motioning to the paper.

Mom started wringing her hands in her apron and left the kitchen. I heard her bedroom door close. She'd heard the version for Mom, but I didn't think she wanted to hear the more graphic story the boys expected.

With some prodding from the boys, I came out with what led up to the wreck and how close it was to a disaster. When I finished the story, it was stone-ass quiet.

Gary broke the silence. "What about the girl? Wasn't that Marylyn Swanson? The picture showed her with you. What did you do with her, anyway?" He was a little guy but smooth and good with girls, somehow knowing what they wanted.

I told them about running out of gas down by the bus depot and how Marylyn was on a curfew and needed to get right home so I borrowed a bicycle and rode her home on the handlebars.

Their eyes got big. They knew she was out of our league.

"Ooh," breathed Gary, "how was it to be that close to Marylyn Swanson?"

"It was all business, boys," I said with a wink. I wasn't going to get into my love life and how it had gotten complicated.

"Well," said Joe, "that was a shitload to accomplish all in one night."

"What made you try to stop Morton?" asked Billy.

"Well, like I just told Mom, I've always wished I'd tried to stop Miles from getting killed that night. I just wasn't going to let it happen again."

"Here's to Miles," Joe toasted with his glass of Kool-Aid.

"Cheers!" all around.

"Hey, Sonny," said Gary, "remember when you and me saved Miles from falling off Simpson's warehouse that night?"

It seemed that any time we all got together again we started talking about Miles. Any one of us would have said Miles was the one who should have lived. "Yeah, sure do. I still can't believe he crawled out on the roof after those pigeons."

"I got left out of that escapade, but I don't remember why," said Joe.

"You were home with the mumps," I said.

"I remember, you gave me half your pigeons," said Joe.

"You did that?" Gary said, surprised.

"Hell yes," I said. "We're all Little Bastards, you know."

"I wanna hear about the pigeons!" said Bruce.

Chapter 3

"It all started when Sonny saw this sign," said Gary.

I jumped in, "Yeah, it advertised for pigeons and they were paying money for them." The memory came buzzing back. As I started recounting the adventure to the boys, dramatics came out and we got to laughing and crying at the same time.

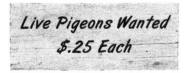

"Look at that sign!" I slammed on my coaster brake and pointed at it across the street in the window of Elmo's Sporting Goods store. "They're giving away real money for pigeons."

Gary stopped behind me and Miles pulled up alongside.

"So what," said Miles, leaning over his handlebars. "We don't have any pigeons." Miles was short, making it difficult for him to reach the ground with his feet. He teetered there, staring at the sign. Miles's dad had the Mobil station where there were tools and free air for our tires. That's how Miles got in with us, despite his innocence and naivety. Then we began to like him simply for who he was.

It was 1952. Even though we lived on the down-trodden side, we were twelve and didn't know any better, so every day was a new opportunity. With expenses like candy, pop, and an occasional smoke, we were always looking for ways to make a buck. Even more so now because it was midwinter and our usual sources of income, picking crops and turning in lost golf balls, had dried up. There was nothing to pick but empty beer bottles. We were nearly penniless and vulnerable. It was bad for a man to have nothing to jingle in his pocket.

"I'm taking a look." I rolled off my bike and pushed it across the street towards the sign, with Miles and Gary following. Being taller, I let them crowd their bikes in front of me since I could see the sign over their heads.

Miles flattened his nose against the window. "I can't see a darn thing."

"Dumbass," Gary said, combing his hair in the reflection in the window, "that's because you're fogging up the glass with your breath." He liked to torment Miles, a habit that I mostly kept a rein on.

Miles rubbed off the fog. "They're paying twenty-five cents each all right, but they gotta be alive."

"So how in the hell," Gary asked, "are we going to get our hands on a bunch of live pigeons?"

"Easy," I said. "We'll get 'em right off the top of Simpson's warehouse." The pigeons lived wild in a cupola at the top of Simpson's, flying in and out through broken-out windows. "My dad said when they fall asleep at dusk, they become docile and you can just pick 'em up."

"He wasn't shitting you, was he?" asked Gary.

"Nope," I said, "he was serious as a cry for help."

"What about Lucifer?" Miles shuddered.

"That old story about Lucifer is a crock," I said.

"I'm not so sure," said Gary.

Lucifer was a huge mythical rat whose legend was passed down through the hallways of Lincoln Grade School. The story was that Lucifer lived under Simpson's warehouse, actually a grain elevator, the tallest building in town and scary-looking since it was all boarded up. Bums had been found dead and mutilated close to the building. Something had gnawed into their necks.

I'd always thought it was bullshit, like fairies and ghosts, designed to scare the shit out of little boys.

To me, the sign in the window looked like a simple remedy to our financial problems. The temptation for money got my friends' attention too and, having read Hardy Boys, opportunities for adventure drove us all wild with anticipation. All I had to do was convince them that the reward for this adventure outweighed the risk.

Sitting with the boys on our bikes, staring at the sign, I started making my case by using their own weaknesses against them. "Looky here, Gary," I said, "you owe me money, right?"

"Yeah," Gary said meekly.

"You go and I'll relieve the debt, and you'll make a pile off your share to spend on the girls at the show."

"That would make some happy girls," he said.

"Come on, Miles. Think about all the candy and pop this represents. And it'll be a hell of an adventure, right?"

"That's what worries me." Miles was looking down. "The shit you lead us on can turn out pretty scary."

"You chicken, Miles?" said Gary.

"No!" said Miles, wrinkling his nose, "I just don't like rats."

He was scared of everything that we dragged him into. But at least he was honest about it. Gary was chicken too, but would deny it and then try to make us believe him.

"Well, you don't want to be left out, do ya?" I said. "Gary and I'll be living high off the hog, and you'll still be a pauper."

"So if we go, how're we gonna get at 'em way up there?" Gary asked.

"Look, you guys," I said. "It'll be easy. We know right where they are, and all we have to do is enter the building through that hole in the foundation on the river's side, scale the inside, reach the cupola, and simply scoop up the birds and drop them in a burlap bag." The summer before, we'd been playing across the river and noticed Simpson's foundation had a square hole in it, like the entrance to a mine shaft. My dad told us that back in the golden days of steam power, an auger had transferred grain through that hole to the cargo holds of big boats.

"But how," asked Miles, "are we going to get to Simpson's from the river side? It's a sheer drop to the water."

"We'll use the boat we've been borrowing and row us there."

"I'm going," said Gary. "Shit, I've already got the money spent."

Miles sighed, "Okay, I guess so."

"Good. It's settled then," I said.

"But I can't be late for dinner this time," Miles said. "My folks have been on my ass for that. I gotta be home by 6:30." His family led a regimented life. Luckily, dusk came plenty early this time of year. We planned to meet the following Saturday at 3:30, thinking it would give us enough time to bag the pigeons and get Miles home for dinner on time. And we'd meet up in the front of Simpson's because it was just a couple of blocks from the dock where the boat was moored and familiar to us from the million times we rode by it scavenging along the river. Simpson's was overgrown with brush and berry vines, offering a good place to stash our bikes.

Saturday came. I pedaled up to Simpson's holding my burlap bag under my arm, the first to arrive. There were two doors on the front of the building: a sliding truck door of corrugated metal, chained shut, and a man-door, locked from the inside. We'd always figured the man-door led into some kind of an office, but couldn't tell because the window next to it was boarded up from the inside, making it inviting and sinister-looking.

"Hey!" Gary yelled as he and Miles came chugging in on their bikes, sitting on burlap.

As Miles coasted up, his eyes went to the top of the building and his jaw dropped. "Jesus, that's a long way up there. A guy would be crazy to go up there!"

"Don't worry," I said, staring up at the scary height. "We'll be on the inside and probably taking the stairs like in a hotel or something." Then we saw the pigeons.

"There's hundreds of them all over the roof," Miles said, forgetting his fear for a moment.

"Let's check the door." Gary dumped his bike and walked to the door, confident, as if it would open.

"Go ahead," I said, "but it'll be locked like always."

He screwed on the knob hard as if that would help and said over his shoulder, "It's locked tighter than a whore's dream."

"Told you so," I said. "Now let's check our stuff and get going." We dumped the contents of our burlap bags onto the sidewalk. We had three flashlights, one compass, three Hersey's, and a wooden cane.

"What the hell is the cane for?" I asked Miles.

"I ain't going without a weapon," Miles said flatly.

Gary laughed, "You going to take on Lucifer with an old man's cane?"

Miles raised it like a golf club. "You'll be wishing you had one, big talker."

"Shit, Miles, sometimes I don't know about you," said Gary.

"Let's move," I said. "We're on a schedule."

We took off at a run upriver with the bags over our

shoulders, looking like robbers coming out of a bank. The river was scary-full and muddy with a swift current. I was used to playing in the river during summer when it was shallow and slow. To me it looked hairy, but I didn't let on.

Because of an upcoming storm blowing in from the coast, there was a muddle of people on the dock messing with their boats. They were checking the ropes, making sure they were safely moored. You would've thought it was a yacht club the way they strutted up and down purring over their little vessels. This was just fine, except it was offering a setback on our schedule. Even though we borrowed the boat on occasion, it wasn't exactly ours for the taking, so Gary and I paced back and forth while Miles fidgeted with his yo-yo, a thing he did when nervous, waiting for everyone to leave.

"Damn," said Gary. "I wish they would get the hell out of here."

"Yeah," I said, aching to get going. "We're running out of daylight."

After what seemed like an eternity, the yachters wandered off, leaving the dock and our boat to us.

We went for the boat. "It seems dangerous," Miles said, looking at the water.

"It's just wintertime," I said.

"I don't know," Miles whimpered.

"It's a good boat." I stretched, looking at the boat. It had seen better days. The paint was mostly peeled off, but the name it once proudly wore was still lettered on the back: *River Rat.*

Miles got in the bow and Gary got in the back. I pushed the boat away from the dock and jumped in the middle and began reefing on the oars.

The wind was picking up—cold, damp wind on the back of the coastal storm, slapping waves into the side of the boat. The cottonwood trees along both banks leaned with the wind, which gave off the smell of the coming rain.

Gary hunched down, shivering. "You didn't say it was going to be this goddamn cold, Sonny."

"Maybe you should have brought a coat like Miles and me. Or maybe, better yet, you ought to do the paddling—you don't see me shivering, do you?"

I navigated us under the old railroad bridge and out into the current. Over my shoulder, between strokes, I glimpsed the brooding silhouette of Simpson's warehouse looming towards the sky, breaking the lights of town, which flooded against the clouds over the river. It was eerie as hell, to say the least.

Crossing the current, I strained against the oars, paddling us in close to what looked like a deserted castle surrounded by a moat. In the dim light, Miles tethered us up by flipping the end of the rope over the ladder that ran from under the river's surface up the side of the building's foundation.

Gary and Miles gave me timid looks of reluctance, so I went first.

Clamoring up the crusty steel rungs, which were cold and slippery, gave me the feeling of scaling cliffs like in a movie. Miles climbed up next, so close behind me I kept stepping on his hands.

"You're hurting my hands!" he yelled.

"Slow down," I said. "Take it easy. We don't want to fall in the river, you know."

I pulled myself onto the concrete ledge at the top. When he caught up, his teeth were chattering. We watched Gary grunt his way to the top as the first drops of rain began to fall. Satisfied he was going to reach the ledge, I found the hole in the cement wall, and again, I went first. On my hands and knees, I squirmed through into darkness. I was hit with a smell no human had smelled in a while. It had that dead smell of dirt that hadn't seen light in a century. Flat on my stomach, I flicked on my flashlight. Waiting for my eyes to adjust, I yelled back. "Come on, Miles. It's warm in here."

"Is it real scary?"

"No, it's comfy," I said convincing-like. "Now get the hell in here."

Miles wiggled in next to me. I looked at him under my light. His eyes were as big as 45 records. "Is he in here?"

"Who?"

"Lucifer!"

"No," I said. "That's bullshit. Now follow me." It was really dark, not because of the time of day, but because the crawl space was sealed so tightly it didn't let in much light.

Our flashlights sent shaky cones of light bouncing around my scope of vision, revealing whiskey bottles, old shoes, and the like, brought in during the floods of a century.

Gary slipped in behind Miles, and I led, crawling towards the center of the building. Shinning along on all fours, we dragged our bags behind us through old, musty-smelling soil, teeming with things crawly. Our flashlights picked up the dust that we raised shuffling along, which made the whole scene look fuzzy, like sneaking a look into a smoky tavern downtown. A clicking and scampering noise stopped me.

"I hear something big," Miles whispered.

"Just a mouse," I said.

"Hell of a big mouse." Gary shuddered.

My partners were beginning to weaken. I was afraid that one more sound would send them screaming from under the building just to drown in the river. "Move!" I said and resumed wiggling ahead. "The pigeons are waiting for us."

As we dragged ourselves deeper under the building, a dim light appeared ahead of us, funneling down from overhead. It was good news. Someone had left a light turned on somewhere in the building. The faint light was illuminating the hole where the grain had dropped into the auger long ago. We had found a way into to the building. "Thank God," I said under my breath.

"What?" asked Miles.

"I just said we made it, that's all."

"Yeah," Miles breathed, "and without getting eaten by Lucifer."

I squeezed up and through the wooden cavity and rolled onto the floor inside the building, followed by Miles keeping in the middle, and then Gary.

I stood up in a mine-shaft-like hallway that had a low ceiling and walls made from lumber laminated together. Cobwebs illuminated by the distant light looked like ladies' lingerie hanging from a clothes line. The source of the light was inviting us from up ahead.

I led the way again, creeping down the hallway, past a coil of rope hanging on the wall and a lonely scoop shovel and other tools of the trade just waiting for the warmth of human hands. We found the light shining through the glass of a fruit jar–looking affair hooked to the ceiling.

Next to me was a man-lift—a box-looking thing similar in size to a phone booth, only made like an orange crate. I recognized it because I'd ridden one at the mill where Dad worked. The lift was really just an elevator—a one-man dumbwaiter that was suspended by a heavy rope that went up the wooden shaft to the top of the building, over a pulley, and down the other side, where it was attached to a concrete block weighing similar to an average man plus the lift. So by adding or taking off weights—lead-filled Maxwell House cans—a man could ride up or down by merely giving the rope a pull.

On one wall of the shaft was a wooden ladder. I peered up towards the daylight I could see entering through the cupola about a mile up. I could hear wind whistling through the broken windows and down the shaft—that made me shudder. It was scary in there. I was getting a little nervous, but I didn't let on about it.

"What the hell is that?" Gary asked.

"It's what's going to take us up to the top."

"I'm not getting into that," said Miles, giving off a worried look.

"People ride in these things every day," I assured him. "I rode one with my dad. It's easy. You just ride along up and down in this box between the rails, and that makes it steady and nice."

"Well," Gary said, "by the cobwebs growing all over it, I don't think this thing has traveled anywhere in a long time."

They stood there wagging their heads in doubt. I could see this was going to be like herding cats.

"Let's go find the stairs," said Gary.

"I'm with you," said Miles.

Gary crept off careful-like, hunching over, with Miles holding on his shirttail. I didn't have to wait long before Gary shouted. "We found a door!"

"Well, open it, ya dumb shit," I yelled back.

"It's pitch black in there!" Gary yelled.

They came back wrapped in cobwebs.

"There ain't no stairs like you promised, Sonny," Miles said.

"What I said was, 'There *probably* are stairs.'"

"Well, you didn't say 'probably' very loud then," Miles said.

"You sure you know about this?" Gary asked, looking at the man-lift.

"Oh yeah," I said with more confidence than I felt. "The trick is to get the right amount of weight on the other end of the rope to counterbalance us."

"So you're going to run the thing, right?" said Miles, who believed in me.

"Don't worry, I can handle it."

And so, because of my prior experience, I chose myself pilot. "But there's only room for two of us at a time."

"Don't leave me alone here," said Miles, hugging his cane.

I figured Miles and I combined would probably weigh more than an average man, so I removed a coffee can.

Grimacing, Miles stepped on with his bag and the damn cane.

"Shit, Miles," I said. "Every time you turn around you hook me with that thing."

"I ain't giving it up until we're out of this building—you'll be damn happy we have it if we come across that rat up there."

"It'll be safe where we're going. I guarantee it. And pull the goddamn cane in close so you don't hook it on the wall on the way up and get yanked out of the lift."

Miles relented, and I pulled the lever that released the brake, then gave the rope a pull, and we began edging north towards a small square patch of light in the cupola. I was grinning to myself on my newfound talent. It was a quiet sensation, and being almost dark, it was hard to tell how fast we were going. Up and up we went with just the noise of boards sliding against boards and Miles breathing in my ear. I began to smell something that had kind of a chicken house smell.

"What's that awful stink?" asked Miles.

"Money."

"Money doesn't smell like that."

"Pigeon shit, Miles. Gold-plated pigeon shit."

"You think you can get this thing stopped at the top?" asked a worried Miles.

"Yeah. No sweat. Don't worry about it, okay?"

"How many times have you been on one of these?"

"Once," I said. "Well, twice really. It was a round trip."

I could tell by the grimace on Miles's face he would have gotten off right then, but it was too late. He was in the scheme for the duration.

After about a minute of swishing along, we were getting close to the light, and I started applying the brake with my foot, and we came to a stop with a thud that jolted Miles. We were in the cupola, which, I could see now, was just a little shack built on top of the roof. And there were the pigeons, bivouacked for the night along the high sills of the glassless windows, seemingly undisturbed by our arrival.

Miles stepped off the lift grinning with excitement. I pulled the lever, setting the brake, got off, slipping in bird shit. Everything was covered in shit.

"Yuck," said Miles, wiping greasy stuff off his hands onto his jeans, making them look like a painter's clothes with white smudges all over them. "I've never seen this much shit in my life—even stealing duck eggs."

"Anything worth getting usually ain't easy."

"I know, Sonny; it will be worth it. Look at all these pigeons." He smiled big with shit smeared on his cheeks.

Gawking out the windows, we looked through the darkening sky at the lights and picked out familiar places like my house and Miles's dad's Mobil station. The scene was spectacular, like looking down at a toy train set that was alive with tracks and buildings and different colored cars that made motor sounds and an occasional honk from an impatient horn. Right below us the red neon sign over the American Legion blinked steadily on and off, luring guests off the street.

"What's taking so long up there?" Gary yelled from down below.

"Keep your pants on," I yelled down. "What do you think this is, Macy's?"

I lifted a couple of coffee can weights off the floor and put them on the lift to help me back to where Gary was waiting. I stepped on and let her go. The ballast I added must have been close to the right weight because by lightly riding the brake at times I was having a leisurely trip down. I flicked on my flashlight and watched as the thousands of boards went by, with occasional cross braces and darkened light bulbs hung together with vertical conduit and no one left to flip the switch.

The light in the fruit jar was getting brighter, along with another erratic beam bouncing off the walls. As I arrived at the ground floor, I could see it was Gary wearing out his flashlight battery.

"Well, you took long enough," Gary said.

I was feeling pretty cocky by then, with the successful round trip to my credit. "You could have taken the stairs," I pointed at the ladder.

"I'll ride along. You look like you know what you're doing."

"Throw off some weight and we'll be on our way," I said.

When Gary was on, I yanked on the lever and gave the rope a pull. We were having a pleasant trip and had gone up about halfway when Gary said, "I wonder how old this rope is that is between us and that cement floor down there."

I hadn't thought of that. "Oh well, don't sweat the small stuff."

"You know, Sonny, if we fall, we're going to break bones."

"If we fall from up here, you'll be deader than a hammer and so will I."

Gary went quiet.

We arrived at the top to a funny sight. Miles was grabbing birds like mad right off the windowsills, all the while counting quarters aloud: twenty-five, fifty, seventy-five, three dollars, twenty-five, fifty, seventy-five, four dollars, and so on. He didn't even acknowledge our arrival. I'd never seen Miles so enthusiastic about anything before.

Gary and I went to work. I reached for my first bird, careful-like, like I was going to crush it or something. It was pale blue and warm and fluffy, and its chest was almost fluid, like with its little heart in a buzz. It gave off little purrs and coos and chortles as I gently dropped it in my bag.

"Shit!" Miles hollered. "There's hundreds out on the peak of the roof—we're going to be rich. I'm going out after them."

And before I knew it, his tennis shoes disappeared through the opening. I smelled trouble right away and moved to his window, where I saw him straddling the peak of the roof like he was riding a giant cow. He was up to several dollars then, in his happy money lingo-thing. He wiggled along picking up pigeons. I couldn't believe my eyes. It was not like Miles to do something like that. He was careful almost to the ridiculous. But there he was, out on a roof a hundred feet off the ground scooping up birds like he was going for a walk in the park. He laughed, "My bag is full. I'm coming back in."

Then, trying to turn around, he just didn't have enough hands, and he began to juggle and lost his grip on the bag. Trying to catch it, he flipped one leg over the peak, putting him on his belly, one hand gripping the peak, the other grasping for the bag, but he missed it, and the pigeons went sliding and tumbling off the roof, and then Miles was sliding down after them, screaming, clawing the metal as he slid faster and faster towards the edge. His eyes were on me, pleading for his life. I was helpless as hell watching one of my best friends about to meet his maker. Just before his feet went over the edge, something caught him. He stopped sliding. Miles's screaming turned to moaning and then he was crying.

"Give me that cane," I yelled to Gary.

Gary handed me the cane. I reached it out the window and leaned as far as I could to try and hook Miles, but it was way too short.

"What are we going to do?" Gary asked. His face was white as a refrigerator.

"Here, take this thing. I saw a rope hanging in the hallway."

Gary grabbed for the cane with his pigeon shit–greasy hands, and it got away from him and went clattering down the roof, almost hitting Miles in the face, and then over the side to silence.

Miles groaned.

"Oh shit," said Gary. "I don't know what to do."

"Talk to him, Gary. I'm going for the rope. Tell him not to move."

I threw all the weights onto the lift to make it a quick trip, jumped on, kicked the brake loose, and plunged into the abyss, a black hole. I was dropping so fast I felt like I was flying. My body seemed weightless, and I had this feeling inside like I was on a carnival ride stuck in high gear.

Seeing the light rushing up at me brought me back to my senses. I jumped on the brake with both feet. Wood slammed against wood, squealing as the man-lift decelerated. I could feel the heat rising from the friction coming off the wooden brakes.

I stopped fast; slamming into the concrete floor took me to my knees. I shook off the shock of it, set the brake, and sprinted down the hallway for the rope, careening around objects, totally out of control. I grabbed the rope, stiff from age and heavy but manageable. I swung the coil over my shoulder and raced back to the man-lift on a dead-ass run, trying not to think of Miles but hoping I'd get to him in time.

I leaped on, kicked off all the weights, and released the brake. The acceleration pressed me to the floor, like riding a rocket ship, and I was heading for the moon. In a frantic attempt not to be catapulted out of the mill and into the river, I jumped on the brake. The screeching stopped with a smashing thud and a dust explosion that filled the cupola with a fog of grain dust and bird shit.

"Is he still alive?" I pleaded as I jumped from the lift.

Gary was at Miles's window, his arm stuck out towards me like a big hook, ready to take the rope. "He's hanging on!"

"Thank God." I reeled off a couple of loops and lassoed Gary's arm and then tied my end to a stout beam in the copula structure. "Fish it out to him, Gary, but take it easy, don't scare him with it."

Next to Gary then, I watched as, hand over hand, he let the rope slide down the roof towards Miles.

Miles wasn't looking up. Besides being caught by a nail or something, he'd found a bent-back piece of metal roofing that he was clamming on to. The rope was dangling right next to him.

"He won't take it," Gary said. "He won't let go so he can take it."

"Miles," I said. "Grab the rope. I tied it real good and we'll pull you up with it."

"I can't," he sobbed.

"Come on, Miles," I pleaded. "Please take hold of it so we can get you in here."

"I can't let go. I'll die."

"I'm coming to get you." The last thing I wanted to do was go out on that roof, but I couldn't give up on Miles. The good news was that I was wearing my tennis shoes and not my engineer boots. The bad news was that the wind was picking up, bringing with it a torrent of rain. The metal would be wet and slippery.

"Shit," Gary said. "What if you both get killed?"

"I guess you'll have all the pigeons for yourself then."

"That's not funny."

"Listen here, Gary, we all three are going to walk out of here together and that's that. Just be ready to pull him through the window when I get him close."

I slid through the window into the onslaught of weather. I grabbed on to the cold, wet rope and, hand over hand, let myself slide down on my stomach between the corrugations in the roof. When I arrived next to Miles, he was huddled in a fetal position next to the rope, soaked to the skin. His eyes were bloodshot and snot was running from his nose over his blue lips. He was breathing rapidly and shaking, seeming incoherent. He could let go any second.

I got a hellacious grip on the rope, wrapping it around my wrist and around one leg, and reached towards him.

"Don't touch me," he blubbered.

"Shut up," I said and grabbed the back of his belt and yanked him over beside me. He let go of the metal and grabbed on to me with his frozen hands and buried his face into my chest. Then, realizing he was loose, he seized the rope above me and, bless his heart, began pulling and digging in with his shoes, and with a push and encouragement from me, he climbed for the cupola, with Gary rooting him on and in. The bottom of his shoes disappeared into safety.

Now that Miles was taken care of, something inside me asked how close Miles had been to death. I took a peek over the edge. The burlap bag was a hundred feet below with lifeless pigeons scattered about. The roof started whirling around, making me dizzy, and nausea shot up from my gut to my throat.

"Get back in here!" Gary yelled. "You're going to fall off and kill your ass."

His hollering cleared my mind, and I started pulling myself up the rope to the cupola.

I entered the window and lowered myself to the floor, finding Miles hugging Gary in an uncontrolled shake.

"Knot the bags," I said. "We're going home."

As we did, Gary said, "I ain't staying alone this time."

Miles could only shake his head, so we all crammed into the man-lift together. It was a snug fit, like college kids in a phone booth. I could feel Miles's cold body still rattling with fear as he hooked on to us like we were saviors. With the three of us plus the pigeons, we way overweighted the man-lift, so I rode the brake all the way down, hoping the heat wouldn't ignite the wood. At the bottom, we jumped off and hustled for the escape route. Gary went down the hole first, dragging his bag through the opening, then Miles followed. I pulled mine through with me, which was a chore in such a tight place, but the pigeons were my reward and I hung on to them like nuggets from a gold mine.

On hands and knees again, Gary led the way, then Miles, then me. Suddenly, Gary stopped and Miles rammed into his ass and I ran into Miles's.

"Oh shit," said Gary. "It's Lucifer."

"You're full of shit," I said.

Gary and Miles wiggled past me backwards, asses up, raising dust in a hurry. We lay side by side. Through the haze, I saw red eyes blinking at us, and by judging where they were against the wall, they had to have been at least twenty inches off the ground. He was a giant, over two feet tall at least, if you counted his ears. *Oh God*, I thought, *is Lucifer really real?* Had I been wrong all this time?

"Sure would be nice to have that cane about now," croaked Miles.

Gary groaned. Miles began to shake again and I was getting the whirlies back. Lucifer was scaring us so bad we froze, which settled the dust. Then I noticed something about Lucifer that didn't seem right. He was too mechanical with the winking—almost methodical, like it was a machine. I could see the same red throbbing reflecting off the sweat on the side of Miles's face. It was in time with Lucifer's eyes. And it was coming from behind us. I craned my neck around. Behind us a red light was blinking through a ventilation grate in the wall of the foundation. I realized the wall faced town, and across from Simpson's sat the American Legion hall that sported that flashing red neon sign we'd seen from up in the cupola.

"What we got here," I whispered, "is some kind of reflection answering back as the sign flashes across the street. When the sign blinks, your rat here winks back at it."

"You're crazy," said Gary. "He's as real as I'm lying here."

"He's going to rip our throats out," Miles managed.

"I don't think so," I said. "I'm going to go and find out."

I crawled off towards Lucifer, leaving my unconvinced partners to monitor my progress from a distance.

"It's a pair of reflectors stuck in the cement!" I called back. "They must have broken off a truck when they were pouring the cement." Lucifer was a hoax, and I was happy to find out he was a phony, and I'd solved the mystery.

"Well, goddamn all mighty," said Gary.

Miles got out a nervous sounding "Son of a bitch."

Gary moved out first.

"You're not so tough after all, Mr. Rat," said Gary as he wiggled out past Lucifer.

"See you around campus," Miles said, slithering by.

I was feeling good. Things were looking up as I dragged my pigeons past the old imposter, leaving Simpson's and him blinking away for eternity for all we knew.

Following the boys, I slid out into the night and stood up with a satisfied air of accomplishment as the rain began to wash off the pigeon shit.

"You ain't going to like this," Miles said.

The boys were standing on the concrete ledge looking out at the river.

"What?" I asked.

"The boat's gone," said Gary.

I stared in disbelief into the darkness as a barrage of tree trunks floated by. Wind was whipping whitecaps into foam. And no boat. "How in the hell did that happen?"

"You tied it up, Sonny," Gary said, pointing at me.

"I thought you did it," I said.

"No. *You* did." Flatly.

"Well, it's gone," Miles got out, shaking again. "I'm gonna be late for supper."

"Well, shit," I said. "Maybe it's a blessing. We could drown out there."

"Now what the hell are we going to do?" asked Gary.

I thought for a minute. The river was out of the question. "We're gonna go back in and stroll out the front door," I said with confidence.

"I was hoping we wouldn't have to go back in," said Miles.

"It'll be okay, Miles," I said. "At least it ain't raining in there."

We grabbed the bags and crawled back into the warehouse. Unlike the first trip, we didn't give Lucifer a thought. After crawling up through the opening again, I led them past the man-lift, which still reeked of hot brakes.

"We're going through that door you guys found," I said. "It's got to lead somewhere and hopefully outside."

"God, I hope so." said Gary.

Lit up faintly by the light behind us, the door showed some paint, but it was worn. I swung it open. The room was inkwell-dark and eerie, and the smell of stale tobacco smoke and musty disuse hit me. And there was a faint buzzing sound.

"What's that buzzing?" squeaked Miles. "Did we set off a booby trap or something?"

Then I saw the eyes. Coming from the opposite wall not ten feet away—huge eyes with horns.

"Sh-sh-shit," stammered Gary. We plugged up halfway through the door where we couldn't run if we wanted to.

Then my eyes adjusted to the dim light. "It's a stuffed moose head, for crying out loud."

"Oh, good," whispered Gary.

"Whaddya whispering for?" I said. "You ain't going to wake him up."

Next to me, inside the door, was a large rolltop desk with one of those lamps with a green glass shade. I pulled the string and we had light. We stood there together looting the place with our eyes. It was full of masculinity: leather and oak and a cigar butt in a Firestone ashtray that looked like a tire. The next thing that caught my eye was a schoolroom clock on the wall that said 5:15. "Look at that." I pointed at it. "It's only a little past five!"

"Thank heavens!" Miles said, "I thought sure I was in trouble."

"And there's the way out." Gary pointed to the door under the moose head. Next to the door was the boarded-up window we'd seen from outside. It seemed a century ago.

I let my pigeon bag slip to my feet and stepped across the floor to the door, flipped the deadbolt, and turned the knob. The door swung in with the help of a heavy blast of wind and rain. I slammed it shut with a feeling I'd needed for a while. We could leave whenever we wanted to.

Miles sighed with relief.

Gary whooped a yahoo. "We have all the time in the world. Let's take some weight off." He plopped into the swivel desk chair, set his pigeons down, plucked a cigar butt from the ashtray, and began rummaging around in the drawers. Finding a wooden match, he raked it up the side of his Levi's like old farts did. After a few attempts, it caught fire. Puffing away, he said, "Smoke 'em if you got 'em." The room filled with a pleasant smell of sweet tobacco.

Miles and I pulled up a couple of chairs like they have in barbershops, upholstered green with chrome arms and legs spring-loaded for rocking. I noticed the buzzing again. Through the smoke, I saw Miles staring at one of those red Coke machines with the white embossed letters that made a mouth water on a hot day. We hadn't seen it before because it was hiding behind the office door.

The thought of swallowing a Coke sounded pretty good about then. But our pockets were empty as usual. So we just sat there looking poor and envious.

Miles was working his yo-yo, still shaking.

"The key is in the door," Gary said matter-of-factly.

And it was—the light from the desk lamp was reflecting off the brass key, twinkling at me with temptation.

Things were looking up again.

I dropped on my knees facing the key. A wonderful feeling came over me when I gave it a twist and the door popped open. Facing me were rows of Cokes standing at attention like a platoon of soldiers. I slid out the first three, and using the opener on the front of the machine, I relieved them of their caps. I handed them around, resumed my seat, and poured some down my throat. The soda popped and fizzed, detonating a rush in my throat glands. "Ahhh! The best Coke I ever drank."

"Might have something to do with earning it," said Gary.

Miles was nodding with agreement but still rattling so much he couldn't get his bottle lined up with his mouth long enough to take a swig.

"We got to do something for Miles," I told Gary, who was digging around in the desk again. "He's going to die of thirst before he ever gets a drink."

Gary pulled out a pint of Old Crow and grinned. "This might do the trick."

I grinned back. For some time we'd been sneaking whiskey swallows during our parents' social events at our homes. And we'd polished off a warm beer a time or two when we got lucky and they showed up in boxes of empties.

Screwing off the lid, Gary tilted his head towards Miles, who was quaking like a mental patient short his pills. "Give me your Coke bottle, Miles."

Miles splashed it over to him. Gary, not a man to waste, drank the Coke down halfway and filled it back up with the Crow.

"Here, take some of this," Gary recommended.

With both shaky hands holding the bottle, Miles upended the mixture and winced down a pretty fair shot. I had some room in my bottle by then and received a similar portion with a nod. Then Gary brought his Coke bottle to the top and we settled in to enjoy our cocktails. I took a healthy swig that instantly numbed my lips. Then I began to feel the pleasant softness of my upholstered chair.

"I can't wait to get to school Monday," said Gary, "and tell everyone about Lucifer and what he really is."

"The hell with them," Miles blurted. "If they want to find out about Lucifer, they should have to enjoy the task like we did. It wasn't all easy, you know, Gary."

"I'm with Miles," I said. "Why should we spoil their fun? I propose this toast to Lucifer." I lifted up my bottle. "Here's wishing he goes on forever scaring the piss out of every lucky son of a bitch who comes along."

"And here's to Lady Liquor," added Miles.

We clinked the Coke bottles together, then tipped them back like old sailors.

As the hooch uncoiled in our skulls, Gary started in about girls and which one he was going to take to the movies first and so on. Miles, a philosopher of sorts, set out on an alcohol-fueled ramble, in a grown-up sort of way, about loving his friends and other things important to a twelve-year-old.

Slouched there with two of my best friends, under a moose head, with our bags of sleeping pigeons at our feet, we were like generals toasting a victory. The warm glow I felt, and the relief of making it out alive, were truly ecstasy.

~ ~ ~

Joe poured us another round of red Kool-Aid and we drank to Miles again, wiping our tears of laughter and sadness away.

Chapter 4

With my '40 in tow in the pouring rain, I rode with Bruce while the rest followed in Joe's '50 Ford. I was a charioteer riding with an aide tending to his broken chariot, winding through the streets, waving back at the admirers and the envious, who were dodging the rain and waving and pointing at my '40, aware of what it had done the night before, and not ignorant of who did the driving either. All of us Little Bastards were pumped with pride to be seen with the car that had made the front page of the paper. All of the attention massaged away my aching muscles and renewed my energy, but I was still hurting like hell about my car, and the memory of my encounter with Marylyn's father kept crushing back.

Driving along with the wipers laboring against the rain, Bruce said, "We got a fella working at the shop that can make your car new again."

Perking up, I said, "That sounds good."

"Yeah, his name is Clayton, and he'll give you an estimate on the cost and so on."

"Let's do it," I said.

We drove along a high wooden fence holding up blackberry vines and covered with old signs advertising everything from Pennzoil to the circus that went through town last summer. We arrived at an open gate that featured a homemade Zig's Wrecking sign. Pulling my car through the gate was like carrying an old warrior into a field hospital, with crashed-up cars and forgotten dreams on both sides of us. Bruce continued into a smaller fenced-off area where cars like mine waited for the insurance adjusters.

"The bullpen," said Bruce, cutting the engine.

Joe and the boys took over the wrecking yard like curious cats, while I helped Bruce unhook my car, locked the gate behind it, and followed him into a corrugated metal building with the sign Office. And next to the office was the body shop I needed.

After filling out the paperwork, I crammed into the front seat of Joe's '50 next to Billy. Leaving, I shot a last look over my shoulder at my car. It looked awful sitting there in the rain, all beat to hell and jailed up like that. I whispered a quiet, "Good-bye, I'll be back."

"What was that?" Billy said.

"Nothing," I said.

As we motored away from the towing company, Joe, laid back in his usual cool "look at me" stance, fired up a cigarette. "Whatcha gonna drive now, Sonny?"

"My dad's old Chevy pickup." Thanks to Dad, at least I wouldn't be on foot. But, unfortunately, it wouldn't be the same as a kid in a cool-ass '40 Ford in the eyes of

Marylyn Swanson—as if it would matter anyway with the warning from her father.

"You always have it figured out, don't you, Sonny."

"I like to think ahead."

"Will it still run?"

"It will with a little pull from this car we're riding in."

There it was, parked in front, looking less than eager to take over my transportation. I got a log chain out of the garage, hooked Joe's car to the pickup's front, and jumped into the driver's seat. Ten feet later, I popped the clutch, the motor fired, I stepped on the brake, and it sat there belching smoke and carbon out of five cylinders. As it warmed, number six came in, and it smoothed out nice.

The boys gathered outside my window. "Joe," Billy said, "you better get me home now. My little brother and some friends are having a party at my folks' house."

"Are your parents gone or something?" I asked.

"Yeah," said Billy, "they went to the coast whale watching, so I got to stick around in case the kids start tearing the house up. Come on by for a beer later—I heard they got a keg."

The boys jumped into Joe's car. As he drove past, headed for Billy's house, Joe yelled, smiling, "See ya, hero boy!"

"See ya!" I said, returning his laugh.

I got out and stood there having a smoke, looking at the old pickup as I let it come up to temperature. Recollections came flooding back of the times I'd spent in it as a little kid with Dad, going to the dump and pheasant hunting and the like. At twelve I'd taken my first stint at driving, with the neighbor girls jumping up and down on the seat and egging me on as I hauled their young asses around the block.

Now I needed to make it roadworthy so I'd have wheels to take me to work, and for that I needed tools.

So I got in and lumped along on four square tires, from sitting so long, heading for the Mobil station owned by Frank Fletcher, Miles's father. Frank had been my friend all the way back to when Miles and the rest of us Little Bastards pumped our bike tires full out on the island. He was a great guy and took losing Miles awfully hard. Since then, most of us had worked there, sometimes for pay and sometimes not. Everything he had was ours and we loved him for it.

I wheeled around the pumps and right into the lube bay. Naturally, old Frank was inside working on a car. I bailed out and he nodded, not surprised to see me.

"Hey, Sonny," he said, "I was wondering what you were going terrorize the town with now, since you wrecked your coupe."

"I'm stepping down some, for sure."

"It was an awful good thing you saving those kids, Sonny." He began to tear up a little, the mention of the wreck bringing memories of the death of his only son. The thought wasn't lost on me either. Frank went on: "What you gonna do to the old truck here anyhow?"

"Just get it back on the road. Got to get to work, you know."

"Help yourself. I'll be leaving soon, but stay as long as you need to. You know how to close up."

"Thanks, Frank."

He left as I yanked the handle, raising the pickup on the rack until there was room to walk under. It was dripping water under there like it was raining. I pulled the oil plug and dropped the old oil into a bucket. While the old oil drained, I pumped up the tires and did a regular maintenance job with new filters and the grease it was longing for. Then I lowered it back down, took up the air hose, and blew everything out of the cab, sending old pheasant feathers, fishing licenses, and several empty brown paper bags all over the cement floor. The glove box yielded an empty Chesterfield carton and an Old Crow bottle not so dry. I put it back, thinking it might come in handy someday. I had a warm feeling the pickup was becoming mine.

I backed it out into the rain of an Oregon winter. Damn, it was already dark. I filled it with regular, getting soaking wet, put the gas money in the till, swept up the feathers and shit, and shut off the pumps.

I was about to lock up when I noticed a nice, clean red shop rag by the door. I could see that rag in Marylyn's hands. I'd developed a craving for her like I'd never experienced before, and along with it came the rebuke from her father, which was almost as strong. I still figured she'd be wondering why I wasn't calling or coming by. If I'd been born on the other side of town and hung out at the tennis court, I'd be having Sunday dinner at the Swansons' by now. I was in a hell of a jam, and for the first time in my life, I had no idea what to do. And that dropped me off the end of the world.

I grabbed the rag, jumped into the pickup, laid the folded rag over the steering column, yanked on the headlights, flipped on the windshield wipers, and drove for Billy's.

Chapter 5

Every light was on in Billy's house. Surrounding it were haphazardly parked hot rods and other cars, including Gary's Mercury backed up to the porch with the trunk open, revealing a half-empty case of Oly and assuring me there was a party going on. It was still Christmas vacation for students, a two-week stay in the monotonous sentence of academic prison.

Billy's place had been a destination for the Little Bastards since his dad built the garage in the backyard. In that modest wooden building, many a car had been relieved of its innocence, and more than one teenager had lost their naivety and nearly their chastity.

I parked the pickup, then took a running jump past Gary's car, landing on the porch. Two steps later and through the door, I was met with a blast of blaring rock 'n' roll coming from a hi-fi set turned on kill. Kids were everywhere, all talking at once. It was mayhem. The room was large and contained the dining room table, where Joe sprawled and Gary slouched, drinking Oly out of short brown bottles called stubbies.

"What's up?" I yelled to Joe. "What they all lit up about?"

"They got some hard stuff from somewhere," he yelled back, "and a keg on the porch."

"They over-pumped the keg," Gary yelled, "and all they're getting is foam, so they're getting jingled on cocktails. Wanna beer?" He popped a cap for me.

"Does a goat eat briers?" I asked, taking the bottle.

I spied Billy at the other end of the room, sitting in his dad's big leather chair amid a dozen younger boys and girls, about freshman age, I figured. His feet were up on the coffee table, and a cigar wobbled in his mouth as he talked into the phone cradled in one arm. "I came over to talk with Billy about my car!" I yelled and ambled off through the crowd with the beer.

"Good luck with that," I heard Joe holler.

I approached Billy, who seemed fascinated with the phone in his hand and the cigar and cocktail glass he balanced on his knee. I couldn't get his attention until, finally, he looked up and gave me one of those "shut up, I'm talking on the phone" looks. I gave up and sardined my way back to the table and dropped into a chair close to Joe and Gary, hoping we could talk over the racket.

"So what's with the telephone call?" I asked.

"Billy's trying to get through to the president." Gary was very matter-of-fact-like with his response, so I decided to go along with the ruse.

"Well, I'll be darned," I said. "Is he going to talk with old Ike?"

"Yep," said Joe. "That's the plan. He's been trying for an hour."

Nobody was laughing. "No shit," I said. "What's this all about?"

"He wants to talk to the president about some controversy he's having with his history professor about the war and all," said Gary. "Billy thinks his professor is trying to change history to meet his personal political agenda."

Billy was like that. He would go right to the top and get the real dope from the guy who was there. In this case, the president of the United States. "Yeah," I said. "I think the professor might find he took on the wrong man this time."

I watched Billy from my end of the room. He occasionally turned down the volume on the hi-fi wailing away next to his chair and waved everyone quiet while he talked into the receiver, and then would stop talking and crank up the volume again. Probably convincing his way up through the ranks of Washington.

The next time he turned the volume back up, I squatted next to him, hoping to ask about car parts before the next bureaucrat answered the phone. But before I could, Billy slurred, "No shit, Sonny. I'm talking to the White House." Jubilant as hell. I could tell he was on his third or fourth screwdriver.

"How did you do that?"

"I told them I was a doctor from Walter Reed hospital and that I'd been on the team that treated Ike after his heart attack. I told them I had to talk to Ike personally to advise him of his medical situation."

"So what did they say?"

"They said, 'How come?' So I told them because of recent studies, Ike was almost guaranteed to have a 'reoccurring coronary.' By adding up the days since his attack, it could be soon and final."

Billy told me that an aide was holding him back for security reasons and the fact that it was near midnight in Washington and the president was asleep.

I could tell by his grin that this did not deter him. I could see by the way his eyes were becoming soft and his eyelids were weighted that, as I'd concluded before, sobriety had left him. So I gave up trying to move the conversation to my car problems.

"Good luck, Billy," I said, squeezing his shoulder Then I crowded myself back to the table and tipped some Olys with Joe and Gary.

During Billy's phone call, the party heated up, the chaos in the room turning to a bedlam of roaring havoc. At least two revelers were little shithead braggers from Bridgeport, the next town to the west, a natural rival because of its proximity and similar size. Our high schools were in the same league and constantly battled in every sport, on and off the field. So I figured there was a wreck coming sooner or later, like fights did.

And sure enough, I saw a shove along with a remark, and at the very moment Billy shut down the music again, turning all faces towards him, a Bridgeport boy saw his chance and punched one of our Willamette boys in the side of the nose. Our boy fell backward over the coffee table; his foot got wrapped up in the phone cord and ripped it right out of the wall. Billy sat there for another second with the phone to his ear, then pulled it down and gaped; his connection to politics, a whole new world, had just gone dead.

At that historic moment, when Billy's dream of talking to Ike was yanked from the wall, the once cocky Bridgeport punk seemed to become aware of his error, because he made for the door.

Before he could get there, I intercepted him. With one hand on his shoulder and the other gripping the back of his belt, I guided him—easily, since the kid had momentum going—through the front door that Gary had left open on a beer trip to his car. Down the porch steps we went, and without slowing, I placed him in the car's trunk, which Gary then closed with a click.

I thumped on the trunk. "Hey, kid, we're going for a ride."

He got really remorseful then, with all this muffled "sorry" shit.

"Gary," I said, "we'll just take this kid for a little drive to mend his ways, and maybe he'll learn how to behave himself in Willamette."

"It's worth a try," Gary said, jumping behind the wheel.

We drove around, talking loudly over the constant wailing from our conscience-stricken passenger in the trunk.

"Hey, Sonny," Gary said, looking at himself in the mirror, "have you seen that new Impala in town?"

"No. What about it?"

"It just showed up Saturday. It's white with 'Crazy Horse' painted on the side, and sounds nasty as hell."

"Big motor, huh?"

"Yeah, and it has a four-speed and low gears," he said, combing his hair.

"Oh yeah?"

He filled me in some more on the new kid and his car, making a big deal out of it like Gary always did. He told me the word was that the kid was Indian and he came from down south somewhere, and that he was fast and he was looking for me.

"He'll have a wait on his hands, then." I wasn't liking not being ready.

"You better get your car fixed quick, Sonny. The kids around the drive-in are already betting on him, and the girls are all in love with him—he's good-looking they say."

"Is he running a 348?" I asked, knowing it was Chevy's biggest.

"Hell, I don't know," said Gary. "I'm mostly thinking about the way the girls are all goofy over him."

"Eddy will know," I said.

Eddy was a race car freak who hung out at Pop's Drive-In and knew everything about the fast cars coming and going around Willamette.

"Yeah, he'll know and tell you more than you want to know," Gary said, laughing.

"I think I've already heard more than I need," I said.

This chain of events wasn't new to me. It was always the same—a new kid with a hot car looking for a chance to race the fastest car in town. It was the gunslinger thing—the reputation and all that crap. Since I had swapped the big Olds motor into my '40, the challenge normally fell to me. Up until now, I had beat them all back, winning every race that came along.

Returning to the party, we helped the wide-eyed boy from the trunk and wobbled him up the porch and into the room. The Willamette kid, sporting a bloodied-up napkin wadded up in his nose, was waiting inside the door. The once tough guy from Bridgeport got all contrite, offering his hand out for a makeup shake. Our kid from Willamette gave him a look and then, to his credit, hit him in the mouth with everything he had. The boy slid down the front of Gary like a wet rag.

We helped him up and set him on the couch. The Willamette boy sat down beside him, and when the kid from Bridgeport woke up, he was with a new friend. Sometimes it was just better to let things play out. Instead of hating each other, these two kids made up and a friendship was born.

Billy stumbled up to our table and sat down in a tirade about missing his chance to speak to the president. "Damn, I was that close," he said, marking out an inch between his thumb and forefinger. "'This is the president,' Ike said before the whole episode was yanked from my life by that little snot. The words are stuck in my head like a 45 record going around. 'Hello, this is the president, this is the president,' and will be all my life, I'm afraid." Billy dropped his chin to the table and began to snore. I could see that I wasn't going to get anywhere with my car agenda.

Suddenly tired myself, I left.

When I got home, I staggered through the door, not from the alcohol but from sheer exhaustion. I reeled and tossed around in bed into the night, wondering how fast the Impala really was.

But, always, my thoughts came back to Marylyn Swanson.

Chapter 6

My feet hurt. Looking down, I noticed I was wearing shoes I hadn't seen since the eighth grade—my Sunday-best brogues cramped on my adult feet. *What's this all about?* I wondered. Wearing my bleached-white cords turned up just right, held up with a pencil-thin belt below a glitzy blue tuxedo jacket—I was looking good, and next to me stood my best friend, Joe, looking like Roy Rogers—tall, wearing fancy western dress dripping with fringe and a big ten-gallon raked on his head. He was way out of character, restless, twitching and itching all over like he was allergic. He was getting married and that's why we were there. I was happy for Joe, but troubled some, seeing him go.

Shoulder to shoulder, we stood there on the wine-colored carpet looking over a sanctuary with pews full of people. On our left, my family was in the front row dressed to the hilt, with happiness oozing out of every smile. Next to Mom sat Joe's mom, redheaded like Joe, wearing a low-cut cocktail dress, a cigarette dangling from her mouth. Her painted face hung as if she had just come straight from the White Goose Saloon, where she hawked drinks at night.

Abusing pew number two, a half-dozen boys squirmed like kids held inside on a sunny day. I couldn't make out their faces because they were blurred with the wiggling and giggling, but they were wearing bomber jackets, so I knew they were my Little Bastards.

Squinting, I peered through a dreamy fog, following the left-hand pews, stacked with people row after row, past big windows open to a June day with all its smells and sounds of nature waking up. The fresh breeze cleared the haze, revealing friends in the back pews that Joe and I had gathered up during our nineteen years of life. In the very last pew sat mill rats who made lumber with me down at the sawmill. They wore ill-fitted suit jackets over flannel shirts and suspenders, their tin logger hats off but rotating in their worn fingers, out of nervousness of the place, I figured.

On the right side of the aisle sat a collection of people who were strangers to me. The bride's family, I thought. They were better dressed and snooty-like and sneering at us through their gold teeth, as if we were the help or something. Oddly enough, they seemed unhappy with the event. In fact, the lady in the first pew was having a hard time of it, sobbing and going on like she'd lost her best friend, comforted by another lady sitting close and leaning over a young boy wriggling between them. I recognized him as Harold, Marylyn Swanson's little brother. At least *he* was having a good time, goggle-eyeing the works, including me. I flashed him a smile, which he returned as if he appreciated being in the show.

Suddenly, an organ blared behind me. I reared around to see Jerry Lee Lewis pounding out "Here Comes the Bride." Hair flying, he pulsated in an outfit that would make Liberace jealous. How nice it was for him to come play for Joe at his wedding.

Then the whole room lit up to sunshine, and I turned back around to see at the far end of the center aisle the Willamette High cheerleaders, the first of the wedding party, led by Susan Bell in her uniform, pom-poms and all.

Why was she there? Joe couldn't stand Susan—a snobby west-sider.

Jerry Lee switched to Willamette's fight song, and the cheerleaders paraded down the aisle doing spins and jumps like their team had just made a touchdown. With mouths bulging with bubble gum, they lined up on the other side of the podium and squiggled to attention facing the door.

Jerry Lee went back to "Here Comes the Bride," hushing the crowd. And there was the bride silhouetted in the doorway with the sun behind her. Dressed in white, she was stunning, even with her face masked by a veil. Joe must be very proud.

She walked towards us arm and arm with Al Capone, who wore a yellow wide-brimmed fedora. His bright double-breasted suit matched, and it bulged below the boutonniere he wore, giving away the clue that he might be carrying an iron. I hoped he wouldn't shoot up the place.

I could tell by his red face and eyes he'd been crying like a baby. Al was not a happy father. He glowered at everyone who dared look his way. But his daughter held her head high, as if she was the stronger of the two.

They arrived at the podium, where Al let go with a wary hand, and the bride took her place between Joe and me. The preacher, my high school vice principal, gave Joe and me a look like he was surprised to see us in a church. The feeling was mutual. Being his stern-ass self, he cleared his throat and asked who would be giving away the bride. Al Capone shot me a scowl.

Why is he pissed at me? I'm not the one marrying his daughter.

He turned and sat down with his grieving wife, a signal to the rest of the congregation to do the same. There was some shuffling and groaning as asses hit the wood.

"Is there anyone here who objects to this union?" the preacher boomed.

There was a buzz in the back row coming from some gangster-looking goons on the Capone side.

A boy's voice rang out from in front of me. "Let it happen, Big Al. He loves her more than you ever will."

I turned towards the voice and found it was Miles, who had been dead for two years, looking pale and ringing his hands in worry, sitting there in his bomber jacket with the other Little Bastards. I wanted to yell out to Miles, but my throat was clogged with emotion.

Al's face turned white as he looked at Miles. It was like he wondered, *Could others come back from the dead?*

Maybe he was haunted by a long list. Shaken, he raised his hand, offering a regretful blessing to the union.

We turned towards the preacher, who was peering at us over his glasses. "Do you, Sonny, take this woman to be your wife?"

What? Me? Why me? I was confused and in the wrong place. And Joe, knowing, stepped back and shoved me towards the bride. Close enough, I could smell a familiar scent, and then her face appeared behind the lace. Marylyn! Oh my God—it was my wedding all along. How did Miles know? How did everyone know? The most beautiful woman in the world and she was finally mine.

"Who has the ring?" the preacher broke in.

Joe's face turned brick red as he fidgeted around in his pocket. Joe's fumbling and the suddenness of the event produced a bead of sweat that skated down my forehead and lodged on the end of my nose. I was going crazy trying to rid myself of it, but I was frozen in agony, scared that if I made a move, Al might shoot me.

Joe came up with the ring and handed it to me like it was the great Orlov diamond. Marylyn was smiling through tears of love as I found her finger and slid on the washer from the throttle body of a Rochester carburetor. We were married.

The preacher announced I could kiss the bride.

Marylyn moved close with her arms out, raising her chin, smiling through the veil I was to lift. Her red lips said, "I love you," but I couldn't raise my arms to embrace her.

"Sonny," her lips said again. "Sonny … Sonny …"

A bell went off, like a school bell, and everyone was getting up from the pews and leaving like class was over.

My eyes opened; my alarm was going off and Mom was shaking me. "Sonny," she said. "Sonny, wake up. You're going to be late for work."

Chapter 7

The agony I felt as I woke from the dream was overwhelming. *Damn,* I thought, *every time I get close to that girl, she's taken away from me.* She was gone, my car was gone, and it was Monday, time to go back to work. I unwrapped my arms from the pillow and rolled out into reality.

Western Oregon was known for its rain, but it could get cold in the winter—damp, sometimes windy cold. So I pulled on my Levi's jacket over my sweatshirt as I grabbed a piece of toast off the table and Mom handed me lunch in a brown paper bag.

Outside, it was dark, even with the street light. The Chevy pickup looked like a ghost sitting there in the fog with the windows frosted over. I'd have to let it warm up. The pickup was cold inside, and I shivered as I rolled over the starter with a little choke and it fired up. I turned on the defroster and flipped the fan to high, blowing cold-ass air in my face.

As I sat there waiting for the engine to warm and the heat to clear the glass, I lit a smoke and thought about

Marylyn and my problem with her dad. It was the old class thing—what side of town you came from and what color your collar was. It seemed unfair to me, but it was a fact of life.

But living white-collar couldn't be that difficult, I was thinking. Some that wore them didn't seem especially smarter than a lot of folks I knew from our part of town. Since I wasn't born white-collar, it looked like I'd have to work into it. And the white-collar world would have to move over a little. The important thing for me was to do it. The sooner the better.

My cigarette short-burned my fingers and I realized I'd be late for work. Oh shit, I'd never been late to work before, and I wasn't planning on it then.

Peering through a half-frozen windshield, I headed east. There was no traffic that early, so I was goosing along pretty good, looking both ways while running all seven stop signs between me and the mill. I was probably going 40 when I disregarded the sign at Water Street that said to stop for everyone else. The cab was warm by then, clearing up the windows just in time for me to see a glow appear in the rear view mirror. It looked like the sun coming up through the fog, or like one of those weird moons, red with a circle around it, except this one was blinking. "Ah shit." Just what I needed was a ticket. Tickets weren't new to me; in fact, my '40's glove box was full of tickets I'd paid. Mostly, they were for speeding and racing, and there was even one for "car too low." But right then, I didn't have time to deal with getting another one.

I coasted the pickup over to the side and rolled down the window. The cold came rushing in as the officer approached the cab. I had my license ready, hoping I'd get written up quickly so I could beat the time clock. As luck would have it, he was a new guy, so he was going to take some time getting acquainted, when I didn't have any to spare.

"Good morning. I'm Officer Wilkinson with the Willamette Police Department." He was shivering a little and I could see the fog of his breath as he talked. He went on with the usual, keeping the important part for the last: the pinch. He took my license and, holding his flashlight with his other hand, began reading it. "Sonny Mitchell," he said. "Are you the same Sonny Mitchell who saved those teenagers on the Boulevard Saturday night?"

"That was me, sir," I said, tapping my fingers on the steering wheel, thinking, *Let's get on with it*. "And now I'm on my way to work. In fact," I chanced, "I'm going to be late maybe."

He handed back my license and reached for his ticket book, which he had tucked under his arm. *Here it comes*, I figured. But he snapped it shut. He started to say something, then just tipped his hat with a little smile and was gone. *Goddamn*, I thought. He let me go. That had never happened before.

As soon as he was around the corner, I stomped on the gas and made for the mill. I blew through the front gate and careened into the parking lot, bouncing over bark chips and through potholes, ending up at the man-gate. I grabbed my lunch bag, slammed the car door, and sprinted for the office. The mill was dead quiet—due to the lack of graveyard shift—but any second the whistle would blow. The men, some with tin hats, were at their workstations, ready for the chains to move, but most were watching me—differently from before—and I could tell by their looks they had read the Sunday paper. I about ripped the office door off its hinges getting to my time card, which I stuck into the time clock, punching it as it clicked 7:00 a.m. Just in time!

The whistle blew and the whole place roared alive. Oh shit, now the boards would be piling up at my post on the green chain. Out the door I ran like a madman, across the lot, jumping over mud puddles and around moving machinery, carrying my lunch bag like a football. When I arrived at my station, I couldn't believe it—men were slinging my boards for me. A rare moment around the sawmill. Usually, they would just let your boards run off the end and make a mess. But, apparently, because I'd become an over-the-weekend hero, they were covering for me.

I jumped in, slinging and stacking boards according to length and width, the job of a green chain worker.

At the first break in the day, the men surrounded me, pushing me around playful-like, with admiration and even some slight affection, also rare in the sawmill, asking questions like, "What was it like, Mitchell, when that Plymouth hit you in the ass?" and, "What about the girl? She's a real looker from the picture, I'd say." Many of the men had served in WWII and were *real* heroes compared to me. When they loaded the shit on me, I felt ashamed to take credit for what little I'd done compared with what they had done just a few years before.

Chapter 8

The shift-change whistle blew at 3:00 p.m. I worked day shift, so my time was over and my duties were about to go to the swing-shift worker with my job description. Nothing stopped. The swing-shift man, a big bearded guy with overalls, gave me a shove and grinned as he took my place. The chain bringing the water-heavy rough-cut lumber just kept coming, and around us, the peeler kept peeling and the grader kept right on grading. The screaming sound coming from the main saw, powered by several hundred horsepower and traveling 120 miles an hour, just kept torturing the human ears in its earnest interest of making lumber. My ears were still ringing when I jumped into the pickup and pulled out for Zig's Towing.

I was excited to see this guy named Clayton that Bruce had told me about and to find out what he thought about helping me fix my car. The Boulevard would take me right past Pop's Drive-In. It was way out of character for me to drive by without at least swinging through to see what was up, but today was different: I was on a mission to deal with my car. Also, being as Pop's was the local hangout, I knew I'd be mobbed as soon as I swung my door open. Honestly, I was beginning to tire from all the fuss over my actions of the previous Saturday. But the main reason I drove on by was there was a chance Marylyn would be there, and I was not looking forward to my first encounter with her since the visit from her dad, and she'd be with her friends, who I was not ready to share the moment with. I had no idea what that moment was going to be like, and I had no idea what I was going to do about it. Here I was trying to dodge the very person I wanted to see so badly. A double-edged sword: I wanted to see her, but I wasn't ready to deal with the outcome. What if she just ignored me?

The big accordion doors that fronted Zig's Towing were open and I could see a man I figured was Clayton, in coveralls, shooting paint on the front fender of a Dodge. You didn't want to bother a guy with a paint gun. It was bad timing, like butting in during surgery. I parked the pickup away from the painting, went looking for Bruce, and caught him ambling out of the towing office, wiping his hands with a red shop rag. The air compressor came alive with a roar, recharging Clayton's gun.

"Hi, Sonny," Bruce yelled over the noise.

"Howdy," I hollered back. "Your guy is busy, so I thought I'd wait around until he finishes up and see what he figured out about my '40."

"The insurance adjuster was here this morning and left your paperwork in the office."

I followed him in. Bruce closed the door, shutting off the God-awful noise. We sat at a desk under a light bulb, a basic office to say the least.

"Here's the dope from the insurance company." Bruce handed over the papers. They were copies of originals that must have gone with the adjuster. There was an estimate of damages, listing the particular panels and what each would cost in repair and painting. At the bottom was the total, which came to $317.81.

"Wow," I said. "That's a lot of money."

"It won't cost you that much if you use your head and help with the job."

"Will Clayton go for that?" I asked.

He lit a cigarette and shot a stream of smoke. "Yeah, maybe. If he thinks you've got grit." The compressor that had been laboring away gave out its last gasp and shut down. Through the window in the door that separated the two buildings, I could see Clayton coiling up the hose.

Not wanting to startle him, I went back out through the man-door and approached his area from the front.

He looked to be in his thirties; he was stout, dark skinned, and could grow a beard. He was wearing a baseball cap with the bill up like a mechanic. Clamped in his mouth was a cigarette without a filter, making it smoke he was breathing as if it was air. His nose looked like he could have been a boxer before he came to his senses.

"I'm Sonny Mitchell," I said. "I own the Ford there in the bullpen."

"You want it fixed?" he asked.

"That's right. I'd like to help if I could."

"You did a pretty good job of wrecking it."

"Yeah," I said. "It's the only car I've ever had, and I've got a lot into it, and not just money."

"What ya got in it for a mill?"

"A big motor; it's an Oldsmobile, sir."

"Fast, huh?"

"Yep, it really is." Good news—he was interested in my car.

"I'm from Tennessee." He smiled, showing what I figured was a new set of dentures. They looked too good for real teeth. "And your car here reminds me of the ones we used for business. We hauled stuff that needed to get somewhere in a hurry. They were Fords with hopped-up motors and stiff suspensions for heavy loads and cornering. Sometimes we'd get chased and drive for miles at night with no headlights. It was crazy fun and scary. Some went to the pen, and I decided to move west for some of this fresh air you got out here."

"Wow, that must have really been something! You're just the guy to work on my car."

"You got tools?"

"Small ones, but no body or fender stuff."

"Bring what you got, and for starters, you can pull off the bumper, trunk lid, and rear fenders. Then drop the gas tank so we can get in there below the trunk and pull out that panel that's smashed all to hell."

"I work at Dunlap's, so I won't get here before 3:30."

"That's okay. You'll have an hour or so before dark,

and when it's apart and you got the tin, we'll roll it in and finish her up. Oh, and by the way, you're going to need parts. Start sniffing around after some fenders and a deck lid and whatever else is crushed."

With that, he turned on his heel and went back to the Dodge. The meeting was over. Fixing my '40 was going to be a hell of a job and expensive, but with this Clayton guy helping, I felt confident I'd be back on the road, and soon.

I quickly returned to the pickup, grabbed up a couple of small wrenches Dad had left in it, and stepped through the gate to the bullpen with determination.

As I was removing the license plate off the trunk, Bruce walked into the bullpen, so I told him, "I'm looking for some '40 Ford parts."

Bruce ran his hand down the top of my car. He liked hot rods. "We ain't got anything like that here, but I'll put the word out."

"Clayton didn't say what it's going to cost me."

"That's a good sign. So he's going to let you help, huh?"

"Yep."

"He won't charge you a lot then. He's a pretty good old coot once you get to know him. Don't worry, Sonny. You'll have your car back good as new."

That was what I wanted to hear. Having my '40 back wouldn't get me a ticket to J. R.'s country club, but with it I carried a card to the exclusive club of Fastest Car in Town and the confidence that went with it. I wasn't giving up on Marylyn anytime soon.

Bruce went to clean up to go home, so I closed the gate to the bullpen and drove away. I needed to find some fenders, so planning to cast my net wide, I headed for Pop's, where I figured would be a logical place to begin my search. It was where the car guys lived after school or work. Maybe someone there would know or would know someone who did.

But I knew Marylyn might be there too—the thought made me shiver. But, I chanced, no one would know me in the pickup. I was driving incognito, under cover–like. Before I knew it, I was wheeling the pickup around Pop's parking lot out of habit. No one looked or gave me the time of day. I was finding out maybe my car was the famous one and not me. That was a rude awakening, going from a respected throttler to a nobody.

Eddy, always alert and nervous, saw me and jumped on my running board, clamming to the mirror as I circled the joint again. If anyone knew where '40 Ford parts were, Eddy knew. He stuck his head into the window, and before I could ask him about the parts I needed, he started right in about my '40, wanting to know how I was going to get it fixed and how long it would take. He enjoyed my car being fast and all, and I could tell by his angst that he was missing it already.

He was tall and skinny and jittery, and looked like a square and drove a little nerdy car. But he knew everything about performance cars. He tracked all the local iron and kept a list on who was winning and who was not. He liked to think he was my personal agent and could wrangle a race out of about any new, unsuspecting hot car that came to town. And he never shut up, managing to get under the skin of any guy who thought he was fast, taunting him until he was sucked in, and then it was my job to beat him out on the highway.

I pulled to a stop before reentering the Boulevard, giving Eddy a moment to hop into the cab with me, which he did without stopping the interrogation concerning my car. I turned left and chugged out towards Billie's Big Boy Burger. It was close to the freeway and frequented by patrons of outside areas. It was bigger and usually more crowded than Pop's, so it offered a respite from the usual crowd and offered a place to hide.

"Hey," I broke in, "I'm in need of some fenders and a trunk lid for the '40. Know where I could get some?"

Eddy let out a grin while he wiggled around in the cab. He had so much energy and it would ignite at the mention of something hot rod related. "As usual, you came to the right man," he said, proud as hell. "I know where there is a car, kind of a donor, that still had fenders as of last summer."

"How much?"

"They're free."

"Horseshit. There's got to be a catch."

"Well," he said, "they're free for the taking, but it won't be simple. The car is in a barn about ten miles south of town. It's on blocks held up by a creaky old wooden floor. The front fenders, doors, and hood are already gone, and the top is caved in, and all the glass is broken, and that's the good news."

I could hardly wait for what was coming. Eddy got way romantic with his stories because he watched too much TV. He wasn't a liar; he just liked making it interesting, and he liked stringing people along too. We had to pick out the parts of his story that might be true and discard the rest. "What's the bad news?"

"You have to go in at night because no one knows who owns the place.

"So what you're saying is, if I don't get them, someone else will, or they will just rust away with time?"

"Yeah, pretty much."

Eddy owed me a couple of favors, so I decided to call them in, along with a little interest. "Hey, Eddy," I said, "how about you coming over to the tow shop and helping me take off my fenders for practice?"

"Practice for what?"

"Practice for when you help me take off the fenders out at the barn."

"I guess I walked right into that," he said with a meek look on his face. "What's the plan then?"

"You get out of school about the same time as I get done working, so let's meet at the tow shop in the afternoons and we'll get the fenders off in a hurry."

By Thursday night, we had the parts removed and they were teetering on the top of Zig's Towing's scrap heap. We were ready to go parts hunting at the barn. So Friday we met up as usual, and within an hour, we'd managed to borrow the tools we needed for the nighttime escapade. All we needed then was some beer to accompany us. We didn't do things without beer, especially on Friday nights.

So, incognito again, we went to Pop's in search of

someone old enough to buy it for us. I parked in the shadows of the gravel lot with an eye out for Marylyn while we waited for one of our regular contacts, but to no avail. An up-and-down result; Marylyn didn't show and neither did a buyer. "No beer tonight, I guess," I said.

"I ain't going out to some creepy old barn," Eddy said, "without something to build some nerve."

I blew it off to his normal bullshit. "Okay, I guess we're down to Agnes."

She was our choice of last resort.

She had some kind of disability and lived on a meager check she got from the government, making her practically destitute, so she was always happy to help us out for a fee. But her fee was a six-pack, which was pretty high when we were only after a short case.

Eddy talked to her using the pay phone hanging on the wall outside of Pop's. He returned to the pickup, raising his eyebrows in accomplishment, signaling we were on for some beer.

"She'll have it at her place in fifteen minutes," he said as he loaded into the pickup. We pulled out just about the time the place was getting dark and warming up for a typical Friday night. Again, no one had noticed me in the pickup. I took the long way to Agnes's and parked in the alley behind her place, out of sight from the street. She lived in one of those big houses that was converted and chopped up and rented to poverty-stricken boarders. A flight of stairs was attached to the outside of the building. Eddy took two at a time and banged on the door, bringing on an outside light.

Good, she was back with the beer. By sliding low, I could see the whole deal go down from where I hunched in the pickup. He pulled the dollar bills out of his front pocket and handed them to her outstretched hand. Then he entered the room and a second later returned through the door carrying the short case with both hands. The thought of the cold beer made my taste buds tingle a little as Eddy bounced down the stairs, again two at a time.

Eddy slid into the pickup and carefully placed the box on the floor between us. Seeing Lucky Lager written all over it, I was horrified. Lucky Lager tasted like skunk piss. We all knew it, including Eddy. "What's this shit?" I demanded.

"It's Lucky Lager."

"I know what the hell it is. What's it doing in this pickup?"

"Agnes bought it because it was on sale."

"You got to be joking. Didn't you tell her Oly?"

"Yeah, but she said she just couldn't pass it up and that we should think about becoming better shoppers."

What's this world coming to, I thought.

Chapter 9

About six miles out of town, we hit gravel, a sign to pop a couple of caps. Over the years, we had become experts at opening beer bottles. There had to be at least sixteen different gadgets on a car that would take a cap off. One night, during a drinking session at the gravel pit, we made a rule that we couldn't use the same device twice. I remember Billy—he'd had a few—sitting in front of a headlight trying to pry a cap off with a hubcap.

Eddy flipped two caps with his pocketknife, letting the smelly foam run down his pants. The beer was putrid and I held my nose but got down a few gulps. I'd heard my dad say the way the government fixed bad government was more government. I wasn't sure what it meant, but that began to work with the awful beer. The more I drank, it seemed, the better it got.

With some lefts and rights, ever drifting south, the road led to the barn, silhouetted against a darkened sky. It was a God-awful sight, scary-as-shit-looking, backed by huge oak trees, naked for the winter. The moon, close to full, flashed at us as stormy clouds blew past it. The night would get dark and then light and dark again. Even with the bravado offered by the alcohol, the barn was a menacing sight, encircled by a tumbled-down wire fence and blackberry vines, with a wooden gate guarding the entrance. One end of the gate was wired to a wooden post that had a sign that read Keep Out scrawled on it, maybe by the man who owned the place, who might shoot me. The thought nagged at me. But "keep out" to us meant "come in if you dare."

We sat there in front of the gate finishing our beers, with the motor running, taking in the Edgar Allan Poe spirit of the scene. "I'm driving, so you open the gate," I said.

"Why me?"

"It's the rule," I said. "Man on the outside always opens the gate."

Eddy grunted the heavy gate out of our way, leaned it into the brush, then got back in with a shiver. We left it open and idled up the lane, which was overrun by blackberries. Last year's vines engulfed us as we putted along. The barn was smothered in them, with its top half rising above. Eddy, feeling no pain, seemed to enjoy the place as he pointed out imaginary sites like a tour guide, gawking around, pretending he had a microphone, and talking in monotone and all. "And to our left, ladies and gentlemen, is the Hitchcock barn, where an old man sacrificed sheep to the rain god but could never stop it from raining. His son was so distraught with the rain, he killed his dad with a shotgun, and it is said that he has been sitting out in the rain ever since, guarding the place."

"God, you're a morbid son of a bitch," I said, stopping near the barn. "Let's get out and get on with this before it starts raining again and the man with the gun gets really pissed off."

Eddy shot me a grinning look, like maybe I really believed his story, then got out, saying this would be as close as we could get with the pickup. I turned the pickup around in case we needed to leave in a hurry—like maybe dodging shotgun blasts. I backed up close and got out; brrr, it was cold and getting windy.

The sky opened to a flash from the moon. I looked up and was awed by the size of the barn, with boards running all the way up, still showing some white paint under the eaves but fading away down low where they were covered with moss. The whole structure leaned slightly away from us, assuring its time was almost over. I hoped it wouldn't fall down until after we looted it. With tools rattling in my arms, I followed Eddy as he thorned his way through the blackberry vines, up a dilapidated ramp, careful over rotted boards and between double sliding barn doors that appeared to have been left open for years. We clicked on our flashlights, sending an explosion of creepy beastly things disappearing through knotholes and cracks. The last things visible were long oily tails slithering to a point and then gone. These rats and such were the after-dead beings that had crawled in after the last living thing walked out to slaughter, and the cowman gave up and never came back. The smell was dead too, with rotting timbers and dirt that hadn't seen sun in years. I'd been in barns that were used daily before, with milk steaming as it hit the bucket and hungry cats loitering close, expecting their share. Baby calves nuzzling as their mothers consumed hay from the loft. Living barns have a smell of manure and stale milk with sounds of rubbing, chewing, and digestion. Life. Barns were supposed to be full of life, not morgue-like.

Eddy crept off towards a dark hulk near the cow pens. His light got there first and then mine, revealing what was left of a red '40 Ford. Someone's dream at one time but hard-looking now, and if it could talk, it would have a story for sure. Like Eddy said, no hood or front fenders, broken windows, and a caved-in roof, apparently from vandals jumping on it from the loft. The tires were gone and the car rested on blocks of cord wood. There was an inch of bird shit stuck on anything that would hold it up. The good news was the back fenders and trunk lid looked to be in good shape.

In hopes that we wouldn't have to come back and brave the place again, we propped up our lights, dropped to our knees, and began working like madmen. Eddie grabbed a squirt can of diesel we'd brought along and began soaking every nut and bolt, loosening the rusty fasteners, as I set out in a feverish rhythm busting nuts and dropping parts. For a time, as we were working around the top of the fenders, the moon was framed in the open hayloft door, with the clouds coming and going, blinking off and on some helpful light.

An enormous owl flew in the opening, giving off the sound of a kite flapping in the wind. The wingspan on that owl was wide, and when it came in with the wings set and claws open, it was like Halloween and fearful-scary. It landed in the peak of the barn, giving off warning hoots. We had invaded its sanctuary and it seemed pissed for it. The owl, along with everything else, gave me the incentive to hurry.

Flying out again, it used the big window in the end where loose hay had been brought in by a giant fork still hanging from a wooden beam that looked like a gallows running the length of the peak.

We had to have set a record peeling off those fenders. It took us half the time it had doing the same to my '40. The cage nuts held, and so we could buzz off those fender bolts like they were butter. The toughest part was the last. The bolts that held the fenders to the running boards just wouldn't give in. It was the final push, and we lay on our backs, side by side in the dirt, with rust and other filth falling into our eyes. The smell of the dirt and the wiggly, creepy feeling given off by the spiders and ants crawling around in my shorts got me itching and scratching like I was on fire.

The nuts and bolts finally relented, and we drug the parts through the door and out into the night, fighting the vines, to the safety of the pickup bed. Then we hurried back for the tools, glad it was over.

While we were bent over with our weakened lights searching for tools, headlights approached the barn, letting off slivers of light through the cracks in the siding and spooky cylinders blazing through the knotholes.

"Oh shit!" blurted Eddy. "Maybe it's the shotgun man?"

"Shut up," I shushed, worrying about bibbed overalls and a shotgun. But the motor put out a high-pitched buzz. "He'd be driving something he could haul cows in, but this thing sounds like some kind of dorky little car. It ain't him."

"It ain't a cop either," whispered Eddy.

He was right. Cop cars were built for speed and had a definite rumble coming from their dual pipes and solid lifters. This car was built for a shrewd penny-pincher bent on gas mileage. Whoever it was shut off the headlights and then the engine.

"Or it could be a guy delivering pizza," Eddy said, nervous-like.

"Whatever he's delivering, I don't want any of it."

"Whoever it is, he's in the driveway," Eddy warned, "and we gotta get around him to get out of here."

We grabbed up the wrenches and, flashlights off, felt our way out through the darkened barn and clawed our way through the vines again to the cab of the pickup, entering in a hurry but quietly as possible.

The motor caught on the first revolution and we were moving with our parking lights on towards the car blocking our escape route. My pickup, wrapped in vines, had to have looked monster-like to the little car—a Rambler. Good. I was relieved. No cowman with overalls and a gun would be caught dead in a Rambler. As I idled to a stop, face to face with it, I noticed the windows were fogged up and the car rocked back-and-forth as if someone was wiggling around inside.

"They're parkers!" Eddy said, kind of excited-like. He got really jumpy then, and in the moonlight, I could see a gleam in his eye, like the whole thing was turning him on or something. All I wanted to do was get the hell out of there with my fenders.

"Oh shit," I said. "We can't get by them."

"Good," Eddy said. "Pull up as close as you can and give them the brights." The headlights of the pickup were higher than the Rambler, and when I pulled the switch, the little car lit up like it was in a night game.

"Get out," said Eddy. "This is going to be fun."

Eddy was a little different—he got off on putting people on the spot. *Oh well*, I thought, and went along with it. Eddy strutted up to the driver's side, throwing his chest out, while I walked up to the passenger window behind my flashlight to conceal my identity and lack of importance.

In a voice that was not Eddy's, he growled, "Open up. This is the law."

After a moment of silence, the passenger-side window rolled down. I was staring at a girl, with an awkward look on her face, carrying a pair of bare tits with activated nipples. She screamed and then, as her eyes adjusted to the light, said, "You're not a cop."

"Undercover, ma'am," I said, enjoying her boobs.

"Like hell you are," she said. "I've seen you around town."

She sat there looking at me until she realized I was looking right at her breasts, which were there for the whole world to see. She covered herself with her sweater and then gave me a look like she kind of liked the way I was gawking at her.

I was curious who the lucky guy was, so I leaned down and peeked inside. The image that appeared in my flashlight was the face of an older guy with his head in her lap and a real case of guilt written all over his mug, and his pants down around his ankles. I could tell he was really bashful by the way he tried to cover his naked self with the young lady's undies.

As I watched, amused, he got himself untangled from the girl's underclothing in a hurry. He then wiggled his naked torso up behind the wheel. One move later, which I thought was extremely cool considering he was an older fart, he started the car, yanked the shifter to "R," and smashed on the throttle. Since his pants were still around his ankles, as he compressed the gas pedal, he was also pressing on the brake. The meek little car tried to back up but gave up and died. Not to be discouraged, the guy reached down with both hands to pull up his pants, hitting his head on the horn ring, which gave out a prissy little toot. He managed to get his pants up around his waist and then went through the car-starting ritual again. Backwards down the driveway they went, weaving into vines on the left and then on the right, and miraculously driving through the gateway without hitting either side. Off the little Rambler wobbled, dragging blackberry vines behind.

With Eddy and me back in the pickup and laughing, I cranked up the radio, let out the clutch, and we motored off down the road, singing along to "Alley Oop." We had half a tank of gas and eight beers left, so we didn't hurry back to town.

"Let's stay on the gravel for a while," suggested Eddy, "and enjoy the evening drive."

"Okay," I said, "we'll take the Champagne Flight home."

Driving on the gravel was soothing, with rocks tapping the underside as we putted down the road. The headlights showed big tree limbs stretching across from overhead, with eyes goggling back at us from time to time. I popped another beer and began to feel the glow of things warm and fuzzy racing through my veins.

It was nice sipping suds with a feeling of accomplishment from making the raid on the barn and hauling away my parts. It made for a wonderful state of mind, until Elvis started singing his new song, "Are You Lonesome Tonight?" It was the first time I'd heard it, and I went into a tailspin. My mind flew straight to Marylyn, wondering if she too was lonesome. My gut churned with the thought of her thinking I was a dick for not at least calling her to find out how she was or anything. Hopefully, her dad had told her of our visit and how he advised me not to be showing up around her. But I wasn't counting on it—I was expecting the worst.

I got quiet.

Eddy picked up on it and shut up for change. We silently consumed the Lucky Lager as the night turned uneventful, except when Eddy hammered a couple of signs and a mailbox with empties.

Chapter 10

After tossing and turning in misery all night, I got up at daybreak, and with the parts piled high in the back of the pickup, it was a new day. I headed eagerly for the body shop, as Clayton and I had planned.

He was sweeping the floor. The Dodge was gone, leaving a space that I hoped was for my car.

Clayton dropped the broom and came over to investigate my cargo. "You got 'em, I see."

"Is that empty space for me?"

"Yep! Wash them up." He pointed from the tin to the faucet behind the shop.

I unloaded the fenders and trunk lid next to the faucet and went to work with a hose, rag, and some dish soap. I rubbed and scraped the metal until I was looking at a fine coat of rust and some red paint that was still clinging to the tin. I carried the trunk lid inside and set it on some sawhorses, multicolored from thousands of paint jobs.

Clayton's hands went for the metal like a blind man, feeling for waves and divots. "You got this stuff just in

97

time, Sonny. The bird shit was beginning to affect the metal. They're going to be okay with a little work." He handed me an air sander. "Make 'em look like chrome and I'll see you Monday." He turned on his heel and left.

Compressor roaring, I leaned into the air-driven sander, which rained sparks as it ripped off the rust, leaving a surface shining at me. The work was good medicine. My mind slipped away into thoughts of cars and speed, and away from the agony of thinking about my problems with Marylyn, only to have her come flying back through the smoke, her face mirrored back at me from the chrome-like fenders.

Bruce was working the weekend shift, so he stopped by from time to time with advice and suggestions, always running his hands over the metal. Gasoline, oil, and metal were in our makeup. Our gears were always turning.

Once things got shiny, I moved to finer and finer sandpaper, until the tin had to be wearing thin, and I was too.

That night was the first time I slept well since the crash.

I returned first thing Sunday morning, fresh. By the middle of the afternoon, I'd skipped lunch but the fenders were bare, shiny metal. I was cleaning up when Joe showed up with a six-pack. After admiring my work, he sat down on the bench and opened us some beers, and I joined him as the compressor ground to a halt.

But Joe kept getting up and pacing around. I knew him pretty well from all we had been through together, so I could tell he wanted to talk about something and figured it was important, but couldn't guess what was on his mind. I didn't have to wait long.

He sat down again, tipped his bottle way back, letting the beer fill his mouth, and after a thoughtful moment, he swallowed hard. Looking out into space, he said, "Sonny, Angie and I are getting married."

"Wow," I said, stunned. I knew they were in love, but I'd had no idea it was that serious. He was moving on; our bunch was beginning to bust up—a fact that we'd all known was coming, but now it was getting scary.

His blue eyes questioned what my reaction was going to be.

I smiled and he looked relieved. We shook on it and I congratulated him with a slap on the back. I was happy for him. We had grown up together like the brothers we never had. I wasn't near ready to marry, let alone be a dad to a two-year-old, but he'd never had a real family life, so marriage and fatherhood probably appealed to him. He deserved a family life. He had eaten more peanut butter and jelly sandwiches than anyone should have to. We opened a couple more Olys with my pocketknife, then saluted and drank to his marriage and happiness.

"So when is the happy event?"

"Spring break—that way Billy will be home for it."

"Great, we can have a bachelor party."

"Yeah, about everyone should be around then, and the timing works for Angie's family. Oh, and there is one other thing. I was hoping that you would be my best man."

"You got it," I said without hesitation. "I'd be honored."

Then Joe turned serious. "Sonny," he said, "I'm taking on a lot of responsibility now. Working at Pop's is fine, but I'm needing a real job that pays a family wage. Could you get me on at Dunlap's?"

"I don't know, Joe. Things are slowing down out there; I can't even get overtime. But I'll find out and let you know tomorrow."

We sat there on the bench, leaning against the cool concrete wall, reminiscing about all the good times we'd had: raising hell down at the river, the Halloween we spent in the mortuary, our clubhouse in the blackberries.

"Hey," said Joe, leaning back, crossed feet up on a stool, making a "V" with his boots. He went to gleaming at me, and I knew this was gonna be good. "How 'bout that summer you lost your virginity!" he said, tossing an empty through the "V" at the trash can, an old Texaco grease barrel, missing.

I laughed. "Thanks to you! You're the one who raised the hoist."

"Yeah, I threw the lever," he said. "I wonder whatever happened to them cowgirls. You think they're still riding golf courses and roping boys?"

~ ~ ~

It was like thundering hooves in a Western, and the sound stopped me in my tracks. I looked up to see four horses galloping from around a blind corner, kicking up turf, riders hunkered down, pounding towards us down the eighth fairway. I froze, watching them come with my mouth open. They jumped the sand traps, then split up in twos, with a pair racing towards Gary and Miles and the others bearing down on Joe and me in a dead-ass gallop. It was too late to run. I watched dumbfounded as they came down on us— riders with blonde hair tied back, flashing in the evening sun, and in the closing distance, I could see their eyes; they were blue, piercing blue, the color of a glacier.

Circling with swinging ropes, they herded us like cattle to the center of the fairway and looped us together with lassos. They backed their ponies up until the ropes were taut.

Girls! They were girls and they had us surrounded, trussed up, and mortified.

Girls who looked like Scandinavians, a matched set with high cheekbones that could have been stolen from Norwegian goddesses. All tall or going to be tall, depending on which one you were gawking at—and I was gawking. My fifteen-year-old brain was reeling; were we to be found lynched in the golf course or were they gonna steal us away to another planet?

Without a sound, they slacked the ropes and let us meekly uncoil ourselves. Maybe we were going to live. My mind swung to other things as they rolled off the horses like they were born on them. Their legs were long and lean and their jeans tight, showing muscles and curves that sent my sex glands soaring.

Stepping up close with confidence, standing abreast undaunted, they threw these simper-ass grins at us, happy with themselves for scaring the piss out of us.

They'd caught us in the open on the fairway after a day of hunting golf balls we planned to turn in for money, one of many enterprises that kept us in walking-around money; that suddenly seemed far away and unimportant.

"Hi, y'all," said the tallest, "I'm Elsie Bonde." She was human, rolling up her rope with long, tan arms coming from a western-cut shirt over Wranglers. "And these are my sisters: Caren, Janna, and Trina." Elsie, the talker, looked like the oldest, and it appeared she had introduced the other three according to age. They were all knockouts; unapproachable to boys like us, except maybe in the dreams that came with puberty we'd been dealing with. I was blown away, speechless, and Miles had one of his blushy, red nervous smiles that he used when caught farting in class. Joe had a sweat going. And even Gary, who took himself to be a ladies' man, was spellbound.

But now the girls' expressions changed and they became all sweet and ladylike, with introductions as if they'd horsebacked it straight from finishing school.

"Nice to meet you," I heard my voice say, surprisingly steady. "I'm Sonny Mitchell and these are my friends: Joe, Gary, and Miles."

"How'd y'all get here?" asked Elsie. We were standing there still gaping.

"Sorry about the roping. Sometimes we can't help ourselves. You didn't get all this way out here on foot, did ya?"

"Nah," Gary said, "we got our bicycles stashed over at our hideout." He gave me a guilty look, realizing he'd just betrayed us. We'd taken an oath—a messy, bloody one—not to divulge our hideout's whereabouts to anyone. I had to give Gary a break. With all those blue eyes looking at me, I probably would have spilled the beans too, and everything else.

The girls mounted up, swinging legs like they'd done it a million times. I guess they were leaving us, like this thing was over. *Hey*, I was thinking, *don't run off just when we're getting to know you*. I didn't want them to go.

Elsie leaned over with her hands cupping the saddle horn. "We'll give you a ride over to your fort or whatever it is. There's no use walking if you can hitch a ride, right?"

"Right!" I said. Anything to keep it going now.

Caren's eyes fell on me as she stepped her horse towards me. I realized she was looking me over from horseback. She was looking into my eyes for some kind of intelligence. I looked back like I had some. She leaned over, offering her hand up like on TV.

I grabbed her hand. It wasn't pretty: me trying to get on her horse, even with her tugging. I had one foot in the stirrup and was hopping along on the other as the nervous beast circled away from me. It wasn't easy as Rowdy Yates made it look on *Rawhide*.

Finally, I was on behind Caren. "I ain't ever been on one of these before," I said, worried about being so far off the ground.

"Hang on around here, tenderfoot," Caren said, pulling my arms around her tiny waist. I moved up close, hooking on to her, my ticket for staying on the animal.

We were all loaded then: Joe behind Elsie, Gary

behind Janna, and Miles behind Trina. Miles's face was twisted with fear. He'd never recovered from the fear of nearly falling from the old mill by the river. Joe was okay, and I could tell by the way Gary was hanging on to Janna he was digging it already.

Elsie led the way, following Joe's directions. Caren turned her horse around to follow with a slight movement of the reins. She was in total command of the animal—calm now, the horse walked smooth-like, and I began to enjoy the ride. Then, with a muted click from Caren's mouth and a soft movement of her knees, she put the horse into a lope. A minute ago I'd been trudging along with my friends looking for golf balls, trying to make a buck, and now we were riding horses locked onto four girls from dreamland. The combination of riding a live animal and clinging to a woman brought out a lust that had been smoldering in me for some time. She had no perfume or glittery objects hanging off her, just a natural femininity that she let off like an erotic scent, and I was inhaling it.

I had enjoyed some close encounters and episodes in the theater balcony, but hadn't entered the "done it" column yet. In my world, there were two kinds of boys: the ones who'd done the deed and the ones who hadn't, and my end of the spectrum was diminishing rapidly. My friends had all sorts of claims and cover stories that were pretty unbelievable. Nevertheless, my condition was getting embarrassing, as well as physically and mentally agonizing.

There were two kinds of girls too. The ones who wore lots of makeup, advertising a need for growing up fast.

They hung around the theater and at the greasy spoons in our side of town. They were easily approached and accessible. Some were good-looking too, in a jaded sort of way. Then there were the girls from the west side of town, untouchable to my friends and me. They excelled in school, belonged to all the clubs and cliques. On a lucky day a guy might get a peek at them through the window of the soda fountain or in front of a clothing store, always in a group within telephone distance of their moms. They never acknowledged our existence. They offered a challenge that could only be achieved in a fantasy.

The problem for me was the girls who were available just didn't get me going, and the girls who did were way out of my league.

But Caren had it all. Graceful and beautiful, and by the way she acted, I could tell she'd been to a classy school. But she looked at me in a kind of sexy sort of way. It was like she was saying, "Anything is possible, hungry boy."

My hands felt her hips as she swayed with the lope of the horse. The back of the saddle was rubbing me in time with her movements. It was exciting and I was getting aroused, and she laughed over her shoulder like she knew it.

When we were almost to our hideout, Joe told Elsie to stop. I swung off, like they say in the Westerns—a long way down, but a hell of lot easier than getting on. Standing there looking up with the other boys, I was trying to think of something to keep the girls interest going—didn't have to.

"Hey," Elsie grinned down at us, "how about y'all showing us your fort?"

Gary threw me a hopeful look. He didn't want them to leave either.

This was my chance for more time with Caren. "Okay," I told Elsie, "but we'll have to blindfold you all first. It's for your own protection, you know. The boys and I are afraid if you get caught for something and you know of our hideout, you might give in under extreme interrogation or torture." This of course was a load of shit, but they went along with the charade in the interest of keeping the event going.

"Ooh," said Caren, "this is going to be fun." The girls slipped to the ground, tied the horses to some tree limbs, and giggled as we blindfolded them with the red shop rags that always dangled from our pockets.

Taking Caren by the hand, I led her through the twisting tunnel we'd hacked through tangled blackberry vines and brush. Even with eyesight, it was a challenging journey, the thorny climbers reaching out for you more and more as the summer went on. I held careful to Caren, not wanting her to tangle and go down. She wasn't minding it. One could call it a rain forest and not be real wrong. Vines of English ivy engulfed the giant oaks and hung to the forest floor, meeting up with waist-high ferns giving cover to all kinds of crawly animals that chattered and hurried as they disappeared in front of us.

The hideout looked different to me. I guessed it was because I was looking at it through the eyes of a host for the first time, worried how a stranger would take the hideout—it was like my first visit. With a lot of sweat, we had carved it out of briars and brambles, making a place naturally camouflaged for our ten-man army tent. We had backed the tent up on high ground between two huge oak trees and made it elaborate and homey with chairs and a couch and even a mirror so Gary could look at himself when he combed his hair. It was short a wall, so we'd covered the opening with a bamboo curtain from the Elks Club tiki bar. Joe had scored it from the alley before the garbage truck could get it. It protected our seating area, where we'd spent many an afternoon waiting out a shower or just lying back, smoking and jawing about life.

Now we had company: pilgrims—would they think it all silly and laugh at us? I hoped not. We unmasked our guests, and they blinked at their new surroundings.

"Wow, what is this?" Elsie smiled. "It looks like Robin Hood could live here."

"And his merry men," chimed in Joe, grinning. That was good. Joe could be funny.

"It's where we hide out," I said, "before we go searching for balls after the golfers get drunk and go home. The golf pro got tired of us out here all the time and threw us off, so now we do it sneaky-like, which is more fun anyway. We can be out there and cop a few balls and disappear back here before anyone is the wiser."

"Well, you're definitely upper crust to have a vacation home at the golf course," Elsie smiled, sliding into the couch, "and the bamboo gives it a Polynesian air."

"Yeah," Gary said. "Prime real estate and right on the fourth fairway facing the green."

Caren wiggled into the overstuffed chair with me. It was a big chair that I'd claimed for myself during episodes at the hideout. Caren was slim, but it was a tight fit and I could feel her chest expand as she breathed, surrounding me with her scent as she smiled at me. "This is cool," she said, looking around. "You make all this yourselves?"

"Yup," said Joe. "But we share it with a lot of little friends."

What? I wondered where Joe was going with this.

"Like who?" asked Janna, sitting up straight now.

"Like rabbits and coons. You know, forest animals, squirrels and—"

I shot him a warning look—*don't say snake!* If they heard the s-word, we might never see them again.

"—and frogs and such," he finished.

"I like it here," said the little one named Trina. "It's cozy and exciting here. Look at all those candles."

We had candlesticks and holders hidden safely from the wind in crevices and nooks of trees and surrounding our little realm. Made the place look Sherwood-like.

"Do you girls smoke?" asked Gary, reaching under the table.

"Only when we can get 'em," laughed Caren, taking my hand. I couldn't have said shit if my mouth was full of it. We were holding hands. Caren had beautiful hands, with long, graceful fingers with nails colored red. Under all that cowgirl stuff was a lady, and I was getting to like her.

Gary pulled out our stash of open packs of cigarettes and spread them out on the coffee table, an army footlocker we had brought over from our cannery clubhouse.

"Well, let's see here," said Joe. "We got Camels, L&M's, Pall Malls, and some Kools."

The sisters picked out a variety of weeds, one each according to their favorites, I supposed, and stuffed them between their lips.

Holding her hair back, Elsa leaned towards a candle to light up.

"Oh no," Gary said as he whipped out his Zippo, "allow me."

He fired it up and she took a drag; it wasn't her first cigarette. The smoke disappeared into the evening breeze.

Drawing and puffing like a platoon of marines, we lapped up the nicotine we craved like addicts enjoying a windfall. Trina got to coughing and choking, but never gave up as she impersonated her sisters, who were enjoying the smoke. She carried the one imperfection of the Bonde sisters, and that was only a temporary blemish. She had buckteeth. She rested her cigarette on her lower lip and cradled it down with those ivories in a vise, puffing and coughing like a cold motor.

With the coming of darkness, Joe lit the candles with an aura of a Masonic ritual. One after another he lit them up; the serious-as-shit ceremony set the girls giggling and making fun. Getting goofy over the candles on our table, making faces like creepy Halloween masks, going along with us—made me feel close to equals, even though they were a little older, except for Trina maybe.

"So how did you girls get to Willamette?" asked Miles, the first words I'd heard him say. "We ain't ever seen you here before."

"We're military brats," Elsie said. "We never stay in one place very long. Our dad is a colonel, serving a short stint out at the air force base. He's in intelligence, so we move around kind of quietly."

"Yeah," said Trina, "real sneaky-like."

"We've been to Europe and all over the Pacific," said Caren, "as well as in about every state in the Union. Niagara Falls, The Grand Ole Opry, and Mt. Rushmore have seen us drop-jawed and staring more than once. And we've crossed the Mississippi more times than I can count. It's fun seeing so much of the world, but it's not fun when we leave without really getting to know anyone." As she finished the sentence, she gave me a look that made me think she was hungry to know someone. It seemed to me the glue that held these sisters together was strong, probably because they hadn't had much chance to break out and latch on to something else.

When it was our turn, we laid out our account of what we had accomplished in a similar amount of lifetime. Our chronicle seemed boring compared with what we heard of their lives, but they seemed to take in every word like they were fascinated, especially the part about hot rods and partying. They seemed surprised about how we had found each other and become a group outside of family.

They had seen the world and carried accents with a flair for mobility, and we were a total contrast; our world beyond the Boulevard was only what we saw on TV.

Miles started fidgeting, looking at his watch. He still had a curfew, even in summertime. Sometimes Miles was a pain in the ass and scared of about everything. But sometimes he'd surprise us and pull off something brave, and we loved him for it.

Joe noticed too. "Hey," he asked, "do you have headlights on those nags?"

"Horses don't need lights," said Caren. "You just turn 'em loose and they head for the barn."

I didn't want to let her go. I loved being close to her and could have spent the whole night with her, protecting her from the boogieman. And the snakes.

It was ink-dark, so we didn't blindfold anybody, and of course we made a big deal out of that, to kind of put a cap on the evening. Joe blew out the candles, and I took Caren by the hand, and the rest followed as we grappled our way through the dark, with muffled talk and giggles, to the opening, which we closed behind us.

The horses seemed ready to go, circling in the dark as the girls mounted up for home. What now? Was this it? Were they just going to ride off and we wouldn't ever see them again? I was worried, needed to say something.

Elsie said, "Hey, you guys, we might be at the park along the river tomorrow about 2:00 if y'all are interested."

"We'll be there," Gary said.

Gary was anxious. But then, so was I, but I was trying not to show it so much. I couldn't wait to see Caren again.

"See you tomorrow," I hollered out as they rode their horses away in the night.

We pedaled for home. "Son of a bitch," Joe said, "I'm in love. I'm in love." He kept singing about Elsie as we approached the bridge.

"Janna loves me. I can just tell it by the way she coos at me," said Gary.

"You guys make me sick," said Miles.

"Hey, we gotta plan this out," I said. "We need to get these girls off their horses and into a car."

"Yeah," said Gary. "A beer-drinking party somewhere on our turf."

"Where we gonna find a car full of beer?" asked Miles.

"I'll talk to Billy," I said.

"We can't get everyone into that little Ford of his," said Miles, negative again.

"I'll get it figured out," I answered. "Tomorrow at 1:30, you guys meet me downtown under the bridge. That will give us enough time to make it to the park by 2:00 p.m. easy. See you after lunch tomorrow."

When the door closed behind me at home, I was still in high spirits. I had a bad case for Caren. She was just right: slim but curvy, and beautiful and fun—really fun.

The next morning, late, my ass hurt a little riding for the grocery where Billy worked. I'd heard of saddle sore but hadn't thought it was so easy to get. I wasn't my speedy self.

I wheeled up in the alley behind the store and leaned my bike on a garbage can reeking of rotting produce, home to flies waking to the morning sun. I entered through the back room, but Billy wasn't there, so I banged through the double swinging doors and headed for the produce department. Billy was unloading oranges from wooden crates, making a pyramid of the fruit being pawed over by beady-eyed shoppers.

"I got some good news," I said.

"Make it quick," he snapped. "The boss is here."

I told him about the girls. This old lady an aisle over stopped squeezing the melons and stretched her neck into our conversation.

Billy set down the orange he was holding and turned away from her. "You expect me to believe that shit?"

"Yeah! They're the most gorgeous girls ever, honest Indian—you gotta meet 'em."

"Okay," he said finally, "against my better judgment, I believe you. But how can I meet these dames of yours?"

"I got it all planned out. We're gonna need a car, and since you have one, you're invited to the party."

"Well that'll be nice of me. When's the party?"

"Not sure—but when I know, I'll call you."

I left the way I came in to find my bike covered with flies gnawing at my candy-green paint job. I rode off, leaving a swarm along the way. As I reached the end of the block, the last ones gave up, dropping off to return to their breakfast of rotting melons.

Running late, I coasted to a stop under the bridge, where I found the boys listening as some bums spun them a story. The boys didn't mention me being tardy or anything, as they were engrossed in a story coming from these guys sitting next to garbage cans with everything they owned scattered around them. It was hard to say how old they were. They were lean and hard, with whiskers and mustaches that hid gaps in their teeth.

Bums showed up every spring and spent the summer under the bridge and around the riverfront, disappearing in the fall, going south for the winter. They were like books with chapters about their adventures and how they'd gotten where they were and how it was always someone else's fault. We bartered with them—cigarettes and food when we had plenty, and they bought us beer using our money and their age. They never cheated us; they had a code they lived by, which meant that what they lacked in responsibility, they made up for in honesty.

"Well, if it isn't your leader," the tall one said, drawing on a homemade cigarette.

"Howdy, men. Did these guys tell you where we're off to today?"

"Sure did," the tall one said. "We don't believe any of it. You're as full of shit as a Christmas goose."

"No," I said, "it's the truth. We've really hit pay dirt."

"They must be some hard-up girls then," the short one said, showing a gap.

The clock across the street in front of the Oppenheimer Jewelry store broke into our conversation striking two o'clock. Time to meet the girls! We pedaled off, panting to the top of the bridge. Cresting, we let our bikes loose and coasted down the other side, then cut left onto a gravel road swallowed up by underbrush leaving bike room only, but it soon opened onto a wheel-rutted riverside park and boat launch that was underwater most winters. The lower branches of large cottonwood and willow trees held broken chairs and other human debris caught during the winter's flood. Close to the water were scattered picnic tables supporting people wasting away the summer. We rode on, with the river on our left, bouncing the ruts, looking for our girls. Instead, we found a family. We stopped.

Shaded by trees, a Pontiac sedan with faded blue paint was backed up to the brush with its hood and trunk up. A shirtless man and boy were working on the engine, six pistons and rods lined up on one of the front fenders. Streaks of oil ran from their red necks down to their skivvies, hiked above their pants. Next to the car, the mother, looking older than she probably was, stirred something bubbling in a large cast-iron pot over a fire. A boy about my age was stacking firewood, and a tiny boy, on his knees, scooted an old shoe around, making motor noises. A girl of maybe fourteen sat on a log, brushing her little sister's hair. The whole family had bowl cuts. Their clothing looked old and worn, but clean. Cotton dresses and overalls fluttered from a temporary clothesline running between trees. The family's whole life was exposed to God and us and everyone else to see. I figured they were migrant workers, in town for picking strawberries probably. I'd never seen migrants up close before.

The older girl saw us first and stopped brushing. The younger girl raised her head, looking annoyed that the brushing had stopped, and saw us too. Then the whole family was staring at us, as if sizing us up for potential trouble.

After a glance, the father went back to his task, which must have signaled to the rest that we weren't taken as a threat. The boy with the wood gave our bikes an envious look and the girl gave us a look too, but not at our bikes. Maybe she was older than I thought.

I wondered where Caren was. I was nervous at the thought of being with her, but I was terrified by the thought of not.

Gary read my thoughts. "Where are they? They're late."

"Maybe we just dreamed this up after all," Miles said. "Maybe we are full of shit like the bums said."

"Jesus, Miles, where do you come up with that shit?" Joe said. "I'm asking if they've seen 'em." He ambled over and struck up a conversation with the man about his motor. Joe was that way. He could adjust to any situation and to about anyone on a moment's notice. I heard him introduce himself, and the man stopped what he was doing, wiped his hands on his pants, and shook hands with Joe. He told Joe their family name was Arthur and they were pickers, like I'd guessed. The man told Joe the cowgirls had been there the day before about this time.

I was getting worried until I heard the distant clattering of hooves on pavement. Oh God, it sounded good—it had to be them; this wasn't exactly cowboy country. Then the hoofbeats sounded close, the horses and riders hidden by brush, coming down a dirt trail from the highway. A breeze coming down the river brought pieces of sentences drifting towards us—too far away to hear what they were saying, but they were definitely the girls' voices.

Everyone's attention swung in the direction of the sound in time to see horses—with our girls riding— clomping down the hill slowly, the horses setting the pace. Caren was second in line, and our eyes met. *She likes me.* What a feeling.

The Arthur girls sprang up with chatter in eager anticipation of the arrival, and the cowgirls rolled off, handing the reins to the Arthur girls, who were grinning with delight. All the while, the Bonde girls were throwing us boys looks like we were hoping.

Elsie was handling a burlap bag that held something alive. It wiggled and put out muffled clucking noises, not happy with the arrangement. She passed it off to Mrs. Arthur, who accepted it with a grin that showed she had teeth, a few anyway.

Passing her son at the woodpile, she said, "Bring the axe, Billy Jack," and headed for the river.

The chore was over with two whacks and some blood spurting as the birds flopped around on the riverbank, looking for their heads. In moments, the feathers and guts were gone and the carcasses were cooling in the river.

The girls turned to us, looking somber. I thought it was because of the chickens, but Elsie said, "We got some bad news."

Wondering what it could be, I looked at Caren, but she was staring at her boots.

"Sit down." Elsie motioned us to a picnic table.

I plopped down next to Caren. She took my hand.

Then Elsie dropped it on us: "We're leaving tomorrow."

The air rushed out of me. I'd known it was going to happen but not so soon.

"We got word this morning," Elsie continued. "When Dad is notified, we're to deploy somewhere. We have to move fast, so there's less chance of leaving a trail."

"Sneaky-like," Trina said.

"When you coming back?" I asked.

"We're not," said Caren, kinda bitter, I thought.

My face got hot—this wasn't fair. Caren and I were over already and we never had a chance to get to know each other.

"It's a beautiful day," said Janna, changing the subject. "Let's make the most of it. Let's take a ride."

She was right, but things had turned gloomy for me. Caren was staring at her boots, her lower lip out like I felt. She kicked the dirt with her boot, shrugged, and mounted her horse. She invited me with her arm, and I swung up behind her with my hands holding her like it might be the last time. The horse swung his head and sniffed me; maybe he'd miss me.

Joe climbed up behind Elsie, who took the lead, followed single file by Miles with Trina and Gary with Janna. I was where I wanted, close to Caren on her horse.

Leaving the park, Joe called out to Billy Jack. "Hey, kid, keep an eye on our bikes, would you?"

"You got it, mister. When are you coming back?"

"Who knows?" answered Joe. That was good for a laugh, changing the mood a little as we trotted up the road, heading for a meadow that paralleled the river where we could spread out. We rode along, Miles bitching about his sore ass and Joe looking at home on a horse, good enough that maybe he was born a hundred years late. And me, I was in a daze, sobering up from a love binge that hadn't happened.

Caren trotted us past Gary and Janna. I couldn't help noticing his arms were around her a little higher than needed for riding double.

A moment later, they passed by us in a full gallop. Gary grinned at me, going for her boobs. Without looking back, Janna gave him an elbow and Gary flew backwards with his feet up in the air and the most surprised look on his face. When he met dirt, he bounced and rolled with his arms flailing around him like a rag doll. I didn't have time to worry before he started pushing himself to his feet.

We reined in, enjoying the episode at Gary's expense as he wobbled from side to side.

He gave us a humble smile, no doubt hoping he wouldn't be walking back to the park.

Janna, bless her heart, must have figured he'd learned something. Turning, she walked her horse back and offered an arm up.

Elsie and Joe, on the lead horse, came to where the brush met the river. We couldn't go on, so I expected to turn and go back. Elsie reared around in her saddle and, over Joe's shoulder, hollered with an air of defiance, "Let's swim 'em across."

With that, she entered the river and began walking

the horse through shallow, smooth water where the river was wide and the current slow.

"I guess we're going," Caren said over her shoulder and reined the horse for the water. The horse didn't seem to care, and Caren was relaxed, so I shut up and hung on.

Near the middle, the river deepened. The cold water inched up our legs, over the saddle and my lap, until it was up to my waist. The horse began to swim across. Quivering in the middle of the cold river, I clung even closer to Caren's warm body.

She chattered with chopped words as she shivered them out to me. "When we find out we are about to leave somewhere, we seem to do crazy stuff," she laughed.

I laughed too. She was fun and it made me ache to think she would be leaving soon.

Joe and Elsie reached the opposite bank first. Our horse touched down and made a leap for land. My pockets gushed water, my wallet was wet, and my cigarettes were ruined, but I didn't care; I was loving this adventure with Caren. But how was Miles taking this? Engrossed in the adventure, I'd forgotten about him. He was out of the river then, wearing a relieved look. We moved on.

Sopping wet, our little caravan headed into town. I didn't know why and didn't care, just followed along with Caren after Joe and Elsie. Drivers slowed for us out of politeness and to have a look. Everyone who happened to be outside, even a mailman, stopped to take us in. An old lady who was bent over her small flower garden with her back to us must have heard our hoofbeats. She turned around and gave us a wave as she smiled like she could remember when the clatter of horseshoes was the norm.

Caren walked our horse along 5th Street, our legs swinging with the rhythm he put out, our clothes still wet from the river. Whenever a breeze hit, Caren shivered and leaned back for warmth, our bodies rubbing together. She stopped when we came to the Willamette County Courthouse, a stately brick building, the property covering a whole city block. The yard that wrapped around the building was roped off with bailing twine, protecting nearly an acre of sprouted baby grass, a brand new lawn still wet with the night's watering, beautiful like a rug, without a blemish on it.

Parked in front was the usual row of patrol cars—black and white Chevys with Willamette County on the doors. And today, parked in the lead, was an all-black Oldsmobile 88 sedan—badass-looking with a big gumball on top and a two-way radio antenna attached to the trunk—the pride and joy of my lifelong nemesis, city cop Duffy O'Malley. Since Duffy's office was in City Hall on 4th, I figured he was over on business, like a hot checkers game or something.

We'd been having run-ins with Duffy ever since he'd first found us flaunting our freedom, roaming downtown on our bikes, and he'd taken an immediate disliking to us. He'd stop us on the sidewalk and strut around in his starched uniform with his big blue cop hat cocked to one side. He liked his hat—we never saw him without it. He'd search our gunnysacks with his big hands, dumping out golf balls and empties we'd planned on selling. Then he'd shake a fat finger at us, ranting, "If I ever catch you breaking the law in my city, you'll rot in jail," or some such shit. I think he wanted to see us in reform school or a military academy where we could learn some discipline we surely lacked. We'd hover under his open office window, teetering on our bikes, listening to him pant and fume as dispatches came in. On occasion, we'd been lucky to be there when the dispatch was an emergency. Suddenly, all hell would break loose: The big double-doors would burst open, framing his bowling-pin figure. Taking two steps at a time, he'd reach his Olds and throw himself in. When the motor erupted, he'd yank it into gear, slam the throttle to the floor with one foot, and hold the brake with the other; a quick warmup for an car just waiting for action. Engine revving, the tires began to spin slowly, smoke curling out from the back wheel wells. Then he'd let up on the brake and burn rubber halfway to the intersection of 4th and Peterson streets, and turn either left or right, nailing the gas with the red light spinning and his siren wailing a high-pitched squealing sound particular to his car. I had to admit, his Olds was a cool car.

I felt Caren's body flinch and tighten. Then I saw the sign stuck in the middle of new lawn: Keep Off!

"Yee-haw," she yelled, and we were flying horseback through the air over the rope and onto the county's new lawn. To my terror, Caren bore straight ahead, leaping shrubs and jumping the front sidewalk with me hanging on for dear life, hearing pounding hooves behind me, comforted to know we weren't going to jail alone.

On the backstretch, Caren was flat out over the saddle horn, and I was clinging to her. Coming around the third corner, the horse slipped on the new grass, slick like owl shit, legs going everywhere. I was sure we were going down, but somehow he recovered with us still on. People were coming out the courthouse doors and some were wearing police uniforms, including, *oh shit*, Duffy O'Malley near his Olds, shaking his fat fists and yelling for us to stop. It didn't stop Caren. I dared a look back and saw Elsie lean over, lift Duffy's hat, and jam it down on her golden hair, which was flying in the wind. Joe ducked down behind her, hanging on.

They galloped past us at the same time I heard a siren wailing from behind; Duffy's siren—he was coming for us. Elsie reined her horse towards downtown, turf flying, pouring on the coal. Jumping the bushes that lined 4th Street, she entered an alley heading for the river, with Caren and me galloping close behind. I could hear Joe hollering at me over the sirens. He and I yelled back and forth now, making plans on the run while the other horses were close behind us. We wanted the safety of the golf course, but we'd have to cross the river, and the cops would be watching the bridge by now. I couldn't believe this was happening. It was like we were cowboy outlaws, but the law had cars and two-way radios. Not really fair, I was thinking.

But Duffy's siren was fading. Had we lost him? So we slowed, zigzagging our way at a trot, through alleys and side streets lined with gawking townspeople. We got ever closer to the river, walking here and trotting there, then stopping, peeking around corners for Duffy. Trina was sneaking her horse along behind us with Miles hanging on tight, his eyes slammed shut. He was scared shitless, but he was okay and still with us. When we came out on Water Street, nearly under the bridge, Duffy's siren got louder again and I saw the Olds careening around a corner at us, coming towards the bridge from the other side. He chose one of the openings to come under so Elsie chose the other, going the other way. As we passed Duffy, I could see he was driving with one hand and had the two-way mic in the other. I could have reached out and touched his nose, red as his gumball. The bums watched in awe, jumping and rooting us on.

I threw a look over my shoulder to see Duffy flip a 180 in the Moose Club parking lot to give chase. We galloped flat out behind Elsie and Joe, the rest behind us, hooves pounding the pavement, cars pulling off the street, letting us through. Down Water Street, we ran along the tops of ten-foot cliffs overlooking the river where it narrowed, making the water swift with scary rapids. Duffy was gaining on us, and red cop lights flashed ahead. We were had. We'd trapped ourselves; there was no way out. I expected Elsie to pull up anytime now, and we'd have to throw our hands in the air and give up.

Without slowing, Elsie veered and plunged the horse over the drop-off. I didn't have time to be scared. I held tight to Caren and we followed, arcing as we dove into the icy torrent. The impact tore me off the horse's back. All I could see was foaming water and bubbles exploding around me. I was sure I'd drown, but I came up choking and spitting river water. The horse was swimming nearby with only his head and saddle horn above the raging water. With strokes, I reached him, snagging his tail.

But where was Caren? Blinded by the swirling water and whitecaps lapping over me, I could hardly see the horse, let alone Caren. *Oh God*, I thought, *she's underwater somewhere, drowning by now.*

"Sonny!" It was Caren's voice. Thank God she was alive.

"Don't let go!" she shouted from the other side of the horse.

I caught hold of the stirrup and then the saddle horn. I pulled as close to her as I could and she did the same. Fear was in her eyes.

"We'll be okay!" I shouted. "The river calms up ahead!"

We clung to the horse like that, with our faces close as we washed through the narrows, rushing downriver with killer logs and limbs spinning at us, and whitecaps and whirlpools trying to drown us.

At last, we shot out into calm water.

"We're alive!" shouted Caren, swinging her leg over the saddle then. She rode like that, on the horse in the water, squealing encouragement back to the others.

We were all alive. We floated past the giant fir trees that guarded the golf course, then rounded a bend, finally out of sight of town and the bridge. And there was a beach ahead.

The horses snorted, blowing water and snot, and swam for the bank.

Moments later, we were all standing there in the gravel, shaking and shivering, when realization hit me. And it wasn't lost on just me. The fear of drowning was terrifying, and the thought of it clung to us as we stood there gaping at each other in silence.

"We're safe now," said Elsie.

It was good to hear. The horses, shaking water in the sun, went off towards some grass close by. We could relax now too, let the sun dry us while we calmed and returned to normal.

But then a siren wailed from across the river, bringing me back to reality. It sounded like it was on River Street, heading back into town—and the bridge? Shit. The cop with the siren might have seen us beach. If so, he knew exactly where we'd left the water and where we were now.

"I don't think this is over yet," I said. "We better get to the hideout!"

We saddled up and hurried the horses along the edge of the river until we came to a hole in the fence and the safety of golf course property. Taking an animal trail, we slipped through the brush into the shade of the fir trees that stood at the edge of the fairway on the back nine.

But across the fairway, three squad cars faced us like they were watching a drive-in movie.

Oh crap, I thought. We're had now for sure. Finally after all the shit we've pulled, we're caught and in trouble.

The driver doors opened and three officers leaned over them with their arms crossed. The one in the middle was Duffy, his head shining in the sun. He was as bald as Aunt Ina's sweet ass. No wonder he liked his hat so well.

It was a standoff, with us looking at them and them at us. The horses were fidgety, wanting to run.

"You wanna go for it?" asked Caren.

"They'd just catch us somewhere else," I said, holding her tight. "It would just make it worse on us. We're screwed."

It was a painful ride along our last stretch of freedom, on our way to meet our captors.

Getting closer, I could see Duffy rubbing his hands together, a satisfied look on his face.

"I don't think old Duffy took kindly to us embarrassing him in front of those county Mounties," said Joe, talking low.

"Yeah," I said. "I got a feeling he'll be looking for revenge."

The trio met us in front of Duffy's Olds.

We rolled off dripping wet.

Duffy stepped close to Elsie and grabbed his hat back he'd been missing. He shook some water out of it and jammed it on his head, cocking it like he was screwing it on.

"Well," Duffy swaggered, "what we got here are some genuine punk-ass juvenile delinquents. And it looks like our usual four Little Bastards picked up some friends along the way." Duffy's little eyes were beaming—he was having a good time. It was his usual threats but they weren't empty like normal. I wasn't liking what he had to say as he foamed out charges against us, like trespassing and some other shit, and how the judge was going to throw the book at us and we'd be locked away forever.

One of the deputies picked a small notebook from his pocket and started taking our names, addresses, and phone numbers, starting with Joe. Evidently this little chore was below Duffy's pay scale. When my turn came, the cold fact came down on me that I was giving over the code to the house I lived in with my folks. The phone would be ringing there shortly with some unpleasant news. I hated to think what the impact would be on my mom and dad.

When it came time for the girls and their information, Elsie merely pulled a card from the back pocket of her jeans, wet from the river, and handed it to the deputy.

"Well, what's up with this?" asked the deputy, "It isn't an Oregon number."

"It's the number we are to give out on occasions like this," said Elsie.

The deputy retreated to his cruiser and reached his mic to confer with the office downtown. Then got in and rolled up the window so we couldn't hear the conversation.

Duffy started getting pissy, saying something about this being his bust. His face reddened; the deputy had shut him out.

After some time, the deputy returned from his car. "Ya gotta let the girls go, Duffy."

"Why in the hell would I do that?" Duffy asked, redder.

"They got some kind of diplomatic immunity. The number is for a phone at the Pentagon."

Throwing spit, Duffy got out some more profanity, then pulled out his handkerchief and blew his nose. While he was wiping it he motioned the girls away. They were free to go.

The girls had long faces and seemed to regret their misdoings and what affect it was going to have on us. As they mounted up, bidding us farewell with little waves and good-byes, I wondered if I should attempt escaping with Caren and dying with three bullets in my back, or stay here and face Duffy with my buddies.

I was too young to die. With regret I decided to face the music.

Caren dropped back off her horse, ran to me with tears, and threw herself into my arms. "I love you, Sonny," she said into my shoulder, and before I could react she'd swung up and they were gone.

I just stood there, agape. She *loved* me?

I heard a muffled argument going on and turned to see Duffy pointing at us with those big fingers while the deputies calmly pressed their case, which was unknown to us. I cocked my ears in their direction, trying to pick up a hint of our immediate future, but only saw Duffy redden up, his chest getting bigger and bigger, until the county cops threw up their hands in exasperation and drove off across the golf course.

"This doesn't look good, boys," I said under my breath. "It looks like Duffy came out on top, and that's bad."

"Well, shit," said Joe. "I wonder what he's going to do to us."

"Maybe he's going to shoot us," shuddered Miles.

"Torture us," Gary said. "The old bag of shit is going to torture us."

"Nah," I said, pretending confidence, fearing they were both right.

Duffy opened his rear door, beckoned us close, then rubbed his hands together in gleeful anticipation, his small rodent eyes almost hidden by pudgy cheeks and scowling eyebrows.

He worried me, like he had some agenda other than just keeping the peace.

The handcuffs were cold. Once hooked together, he shoved us along until we were jammed into the backseat. You would have thought we were hardened criminals the way he slammed the doors on us. Duffy was way overdoing this. It was having an impact on me, and by the looks of the other boys' faces, I wasn't alone. We wouldn't be forgetting this for a while.

He started up the Olds and drove off, only to get lost in the maze of fairways and greens. We didn't let on that we were familiar with the layout. He would go to this dead end and that, making his face twist up as he pounded the steering wheel in frustration. He waved down a groundskeeper riding a mower and demanded to be led out of this "God-awful place."

Locked in the backseat as we rode over the bridge, I looked down at the water and wondered how we'd ever survived it. I wondered if I'd ever see Caren again.

~ ~ ~

"Why won't he let us have water?" Miles asked.

"He's torturing us just like I said he would," said Gary, leaning on his rake.

All day in the hot sun with no water made my tongue feel too big for my mouth. We were in the yard—not the prison yard, the courthouse yard, fixing what our horses tore up that day with Caren and her sisters. Duffy had been working us, making us wear jail uniforms in front of all passersby and keeping us from water.

"Goddamn, it's hot out here," said Miles, wiping his arm across his forehead.

"It usually is when you're out in the sun in July, ya dumbass," said Gary, still leaning on his rake.

"Shut up, Gary," said Joe.

"Cut the crap out there!" hollered Duffy from under a shade tree in front of the courthouse, his fat ass parked on a bench where he drank water from a tall glass, slurping like he wanted us to hear him. "This ain't no Boy Scout camp, you know."

We worked only on Sundays because that was Duffy's day off and we could be under his control full time. And this was our last Sunday of hell. We'd had three weeks of paying for our misdeeds. First, Duffy made us sit for an hour on a hard bench before processing us. Then some stone-faced female cop took our mug shots and fingerprints, grinding our fingers into the ink, just like we were going off to the big house or something—it was supposed to make us feel convict-like, but it couldn't make us feel like something we weren't. After a quick trial in Duffy's office, I wasn't laughing; I had a record all of a sudden. Then I had to make the call, tell Dad what I'd done. After a while, he came and got me in his pickup. It was a deaf and dumb trip home to a worried mother. All this was followed by a week at home feeling guilty and worrying what doing time would be like.

Civilians who entered the courthouse gave us little sneers and insults as they walked by, and some little boys lobbed rocks at us from the gravel parking lot to the west. We couldn't retaliate and had to hunker down and take the peppering, ducking and swaying as we worked like convicts. It was a wonder Duffy didn't make us drag those big iron balls around like in the movies.

"I hear horses," said Miles. "It's the girls. They're coming for us."

There weren't any horses.

"You're full of shit, Miles," said Gary.

"No, really, it's them."

I was worried about Miles. He was beginning to lose his mind in the heat. Joe was getting pissed like he might do something stupid. And I kept seeing Caren in the bouncing heat waves, waving at me while her horse drank from a fountain.

"I'm going to kill the son of a bitch," said Gary. "I'm going to ram this rake handle up his ass and twist it."

"Can't do that," I said. "They'd put you away forever for that."

"What are we going to do then?" Miles whispered through parched lips.

"We're going to get him for this," I said under my breath.

"How we going to do it?" Miles again.

"I'm working on it," I said. "It's got to be done right so he knows we did it to him, but we get away clean, 'cause I don't want to come back here or worse."

Finally, we were finished—it was all smoothed out good and seeded. Duffy turned on the garden sprinklers and we went for the water.

"Stop!" he yelled, cutting us back.

I never hated anyone in my life until that moment.

We headed for the tool shed with thirst on our minds.

Duffy puffed over to us, heading us off. "Where you think you're going?"

Now what? The son of a bitch.

"We got the yard done like you told us," Gary said, squinting into the sun.

"You're not done until I say you're done," Duffy said with a curled lip.

He marched us around front where his Olds was sitting next to a bucket of soapsuds.

The bonehead lying bastard—he'd said our sentence was just the lawn.

My eyes went to the hose wasting water on the sidewalk. I'd be drinking out of that soon even if I had to strangle the bastard.

"I know you fellas like my car, don't you?" Duffy grinned.

I hated that car now. Anything to do with him was a reason to hate.

We went to washing. He hovered over us like a helicopter, pointing and bitching at us, all the time bragging about his car. But he couldn't see all of us all of the time, so we were copping drinks when we could. God, it was good water.

Finally, he sat back on his bench in the shade.

A deputy I recognized as one of the ones who caught us in the golf course came walking out of the door of the courthouse. I wished he'd won the argument.

"The lawn's all done. Why are you washing Duffy's car?"

"He's making us," said Gary.

"I'll be seeing about this," the officer said. He turned and went back through the door.

Duffy got up from his bench, swaggered over to the car, and threw his foot up on the bumper. He leaned forward, squinting his tiny rodent eyes at us. "What was that all about?"

"He was wondering what washing your car had to do with fixing the lawn," Gary said.

"Oh, is that a fact?" Duffy said. With that, he raised the trunk lid and brought out a red can of Simonize car wax. "Now you can wax it," he said, throwing rags.

It was the shits: now we were polishing his car and his ego.

He stood over us as we leaned into the rubbing, offering his kind of advice and other abuse.

Then the deputy appeared at the door of the courthouse with Sheriff Stinson. "Come here, O'Malley," said the sheriff. Duffy turned and walked up the sidewalk and into the building, along with the two officers. When he returned, he announced with a snarl that we could go home. He was not a happy cop and was about to lay into us with some shit when the front door opened again, and that shut him up.

"Let's get the hell out of here," I yelled.

Before anyone could change their minds, we jumped on our bikes and lit out for home, letting off a couple of war whoops.

~ ~ ~

Sunday a week after Duffy had let us go, we were straddling our bikes across the street from his office where he was watching an inmate wash his Olds. From where we sat, he could see us too. I wanted him to know we hadn't forgotten about him and what he'd done to us.

"So what are we going to do about him?" asked Miles, picking at skin that was peeling from his face. He wore a fair complexion that was burnt to a crisp from raking in the sun.

"I'd like to scare the living shit out of him," said Gary.

"We could burn down City Hall," offered Joe. "That would get his attention."

"With him in it," said Gary.

"How about we rope him like the girls did to us and tie him to his car and push it in the river," Gary laughed. "What do you think, Sonny?"

"Well, boys," I said, "I think we could catch the prick by the bridge and roll tires down at him. I saw it happen on TV once and it was scary."

"Is that all?" asked Joe. "We got to get him more than just that."

I went on telling them of the plan I'd been concocting the past week. "We lure him away from his office, and as soon as he gets to the bridge, his motor blows up and then we get with the tires."

"How's that going to scare him?" asked Joe.

"Because the tires will be on fire," I said, "flaming gasoline that we're going fill 'em with. After dark, they'll be like flaming hoops."

"I'm liking this," said Gary.

I had their attention then. I told them about timing— everything was going to have to come down precisely on time.

"Well, just how are we going to get him to the bridge?" asked Miles. "And blow up his motor?"

"I'm coming to that part," I said. "This ain't all about just Duffy," I said. "Don't worry; we're going to take down his Olds too."

"I hate that car," said Miles.

"I wouldn't mind seeing the car destroyed either," said Gary. "How we going to do that?"

"You're going to do it, Gary."

"How's that?"

"You're going to slide under the Olds and drop the oil out of it."

"I am? Why do I have to do that part?"

"Because you're the littlest and can get under and back out of it. I'd get stuck under the car and Duffy would drag me all over town. How would you like that?"

"Okay," he said, "then what?"

"Then," I said, "you wind up your girly voice you use to coo that little harem of yours and give old Duffy a call from the phone booth across the street, acting like a maiden in distress. You're going to say you've been kidnapped, real scared-like, and you're over the bridge in North Willamette and you need help."

"I'm going to be kinda busy," Gary said. "What are you guys going to be doing all this time?"

"Well, first off, we'll have already stashed the tires and the gas near the bridge. Then we'll be up there waiting until we see the motor blow up, giving us a target. At that time, we'll fire off the tires, letting them loose for Duffy, giving him the scare of a lifetime."

"I don't know," whimpered Miles. "Something could go wrong. He might catch us and take us to the courthouse again."

"Don't worry. We'll watch the action, and as soon as we get done laughing we'll scoot for home using the railroad trestle," I said.

"Why do we have to use the trestle? I don't like the trestle," said Miles.

"We can't use the car bridge," I said, "because Duffy is going to be there, and he's going to be one pissed-off cop. Besides, we've walked the trestle lots of times. What could go wrong?"

Duffy worked nights on the weekend because that's when the action was, so we'd heard. Figuring he'd be there, we set the date for the following Friday, with zero hour at 11:00 p.m.

"I can't be out that late," said Miles.

"You're having a sleepover at Joe's," I said, "and the rest of us are saying we're going to the show and we'll be home a little late."

"Okay."

Tires were easy to find and gasoline easier. We borrowed a lawn mower can with gas from the station, along with a crescent wrench for Gary, and stashed the tires and gas can in the bushes on the other side of the bridge. On Friday night we met up in front of the theater at 9:00.

"Now what we going to do?" asked Joe. "We got a lot of time on our hands."

"Let's go in," said Gary. "It's Marilyn Monroe in *Some Like It Hot*."

Miles was so nervous he could hardly hold his popcorn bag. I was worried about how he would get through what we were about to do. As for me—Marilyn Monroe had me. She reminded me so much of Caren, with the blonde hair and blue eyes. It took my mind off worrying some.

Outside then, we checked our watches and lit up. We still had plenty of time. Gary was pacing.

"Five more minutes."

"Seems like an hour."

"Okay, Gary," I said, "let's move."

He pedaled off towards City Hall with the wrench sticking out his back pocket. I wondered what was going through his mind. He had the most important job of all: stalling the car before Duffy could get to us.

I swung my bike around and took off for the bridge behind Joe and Miles. Traffic was sparse: just a car or two with lights on dim. Good; the town was about to go to bed for the night. With a pale moon out now and the one lonely light of the bridge, we pedaled up and over to the other side of the river.

We dumped our bikes in the shadows of the bridge beams, and Joe rolled over the side into the berries after the tires and gasoline we'd stashed. From the darkness, he handed up the can and the three tires to Miles and me. Then, a tire each, we rolled them up to the crown of the bridge.

My watch said 10:48. "Almost time," I said.

Miles's teeth were chattering. It wasn't cold out—just a mild breeze carrying town noise towards us.

"Hand me the matches," I said to Joe.

"What matches?"

"Huh?" I looked at him like he was joking. "The matches to light gas with, for Christ's sake."

"You said you had 'em."

I looked at Miles. He was shaking his head. "Now what are we going to do?" he asked.

"How'd we light our smokes after the show?" I asked.

"Gary's Zippo."

I slammed my hand into my forehead. "So much for planning. Stay hidden," I said as I turned and sprinted for my bike, yelling back, "I'm going for the fort." I leaped on and jumped the cliff into the golf course and sped as fast as I could across the fairways, dodging trees and brush with the help of light from the moon. Off the bike, I tore open our gate of vines and ran headlong down the dark passage, tripping and falling in the thorny climbers as I went. I grabbed a book of matches off the table, looked to see if it was loaded, and returned to the bike scratched and bleeding. I reached the bridge, had to wait a second for a car, and then, to save time, pedaled right by where we'd ditched the other bikes, hoping I'd get there before Duffy made his heroic run.

Bent over there trying to catch my breath, I didn't have to wait long before shit began to happen.

I heard Duffy's twin pipes roar as he slammed the throttle to the floor. Then came the sound of screeching tires as he burned rubber up the block to Peterson Street. His headlights came into view as he ran the stop sign, turning left while stomping on the gas again, fishtailing his car to the left and then to the right. And then, straightening, he came roaring at us with smoke boiling out of both back wheel wells.

But instead of the motor seizing and blowing up like I'd figured by now, he kept coming faster. My heart began to pound. What if Gary hadn't got the plug out, chickened out on that part or got caught? Should I stay put with the plan or run like hell?

"I'm running!" hollered Miles.

I trusted Gary, and without oil the motor was doomed and couldn't last much longer. "Hold your ground," I yelled. "It'll blow before he gets us."

Duffy was almost to the bridge when his motor screeched out a horrid sound as hot metal scraped against hot metal, turning to a squall as the bearings welded themselves to the crankshaft, fataling the car. It stopped, with steam erupting from around the hood, turning to smoke as the motor melted. "We've done it now," I said to whoever was listening. "We might as well finish this off."

I aimed a tire, holding it between my hands as Miles sloshed it full of gas and leaned back. Joe flicked a match through the air. The tire went off with a *whop*, burning bluish red. I let it go. Flame boiled out as it began picking up speed, making wind that caught the fire, igniting the rubber, turning the tires into black, smoking infernos. Another tire was in my hands and gone and then the last one. I looked up. Our tires were flaming missiles heading straight for Duffy. Oh shit.

Unaware, Duffy climbed from his smoking car and kicked it out of frustration, then glanced our way just in time to see the tires flashing down the bridge towards him. He threw up his arms, jumped back into the safety of his car, and ducked down just as the first tire went flying by. The second tire hit a parking meter, bounced and wobbled over in the middle of the pavement, filling the street with smoke. The third hit a fire hydrant and became airborne, bouncing high, and then went crashing through the front window of the jewelry store, setting off the alarm. Oh my God, was this never going to end? The whole scene was like in a movie. It looked like a street a war had found.

"Oh shit," Joe yelled.

"Goddamn," hollered Miles.

"Let's get out of here," I yelled.

We pedaled like crazy off the bridge and bailed into the darkness of the golf course. From there, we watched in horror from across the river as downtown started to get lively with sirens blaring and gumballs flashing as police cars appeared from every direction in front of what looked like a jewelry heist. Then through the brush I could see two cop cars pop over the crown of the bridge behind us, stop, and throw on their searchlights, which lit up all around us.

"They're onto us," I said, leaning forward to go. We raced our bikes across the fairways, following the river, bouncing through the bunkers and over the greens, reaching the trestle that led to the safety of our side of town. We slung our bikes into the bushes and scaled the timbers three abreast to the rails and then began the sprint for the other side of the river. We were on the fly midway across when the searchlights caught us. The bridge in front of us lit up like a prison yard.

"Hit the dirt!" I tackled Miles, crashing our bodies into Joe, who went down in front of us. I froze with my face on the treated wood of the ties, sucking in the smell of creosote. Beams of light bounced around us, ricocheting off the support timbers and over the rails. They had us pinned down and we couldn't move. There was only about a hundred yards of open territory between us and safety, but in our predicament, it might as well have been ten miles. With the breeze out of the west, I could hear buzz and static spilling bits and pieces of conversation from the source of the lights: the police hunting us from the other bridge. Eerie red shadows given off by rotating gumballs from cop cars on Water Street flashed across the water at us.

Suddenly, I felt a vibration under me, then a ringing sound came through the rails. Son of a bitch, a train was coming! I had to think fast. If we got up and ran, it would give us away and we'd go to reform school. If we stayed hunkered down, we might live through it and keep our freedom.

"I told you so," moaned Miles. "We're going to die."

"Shut up," said Joe. "I'd rather die than go back to that courthouse."

I grabbed Miles's ankles. "If they catch us, we're going somewhere worse than that courthouse. Miles! Get hold of Joe's feet. Flatten out."

He clammed onto Joe's ankles. The bridge began to shudder under me and the train's roar got louder, charging towards us. Miles was blubbering and threatening to jump and run. But it was too late now.

The engine came first, crashing and booming like rolling thunder. Then the wind with it carried an ear-splitting howl, almost drowning out the horrendous racket of the diesel engine as the barrage of train cars came roaring over us with their steel wheels grinding away at the rails. My heart was pounding so hard it felt like it was throwing me around like a rag doll, threatening to heave me into the tons of steel above me, tearing me to shreds. I thought it was going to last forever. And then it was over.

We lay there a few moments, breathing hard.

"Are we alive?" Miles asked.

We ran for home, cutting across lawns and past barking dogs, taking shortcuts till we split up, panting good-byes. I got to our place out of breath, taking a minute to settle down with my head lowered and my hands on my knees and the ringing of the rails still in my head.

I slipped into bed quiet-like, not to wake a soul. Spooky gave me a goodnight lick on my cheek, but my eyes were wide open, staring at a ceiling I couldn't see. The whole incredible affair kept playing over and over in my mind, until, exhausted, I dropped off, worrying what trouble I'd be in come morning.

Daylight woke me from dreaming of tires crashing through the jewelry store window and giant pack rats running off with the diamonds as the place burned to the ground.

I rolled out with the premonition of a scene from hell inked on the front page of the paper. I wasn't to be disappointed.

Mom was alone in the kitchen working something in the sink. "Hi, Sonny," she said cheerfully, the sun from the window catching her smile.

"Good morning, Mom," I said.

"Oh," she said, changing to a frown, "someone robbed the jewelry store; it's in the paper there." She pointed to the table.

LOCAL JEWELRY STORE ROBBED—and below the giant headline was a page-sized picture of Duffy, standing in front of the broken-out window with his hands on his hips .... I began to breathe easier as I read the description of events. I was relieved enough that if Duffy didn't know it was us, I'd let it go.

Willamette city police officer Duffy O'Malley stated the intent of the criminals was obviously to rob the jewelry store, but because of his quick response, the crime was thwarted and the would-be thieves disappeared across the river to the north empty handed. He said that the burning tires were tools used by the robbers to break into the store and run off anyone in the mood to stop them. And he said: "I saw right through the ruse, and because of my experience as a lawman, I was able to dodge the barrage of missiles as they came flaming at me."

The paper went on to say that if O'Malley's car hadn't stalled at an inopportune time, he would have apprehended the crooks before they got away.

Thanks to Duffy and his pompous, self-absorbed way of describing the event, he took the spotlight off us as possible suspects in the case. We'd pulled it off. We had gotten away with it. I was smiling and eating toast.

A few weeks later, the Duffy escapade was still never far from our conversations. Sitting inside Pop's one day, we were reminiscing, just smoking away the day over Cokes.

"Man," said Joe sitting there in the booth, "I'll never forget the way Duffy dove back in his car when he saw the tires flaming at him."

"No shit," I said. "I could see his eyes get big from clear up on the bridge."

Gary, who was facing the Boulevard, jumped up and shouted, "They're back!"

"Who's back?" I asked. Gary was dramatic to the point that we didn't put much credence towards his outbursts of excitement.

"The cowgirls are back."

"You lying sack of shit," said Joe. "I wouldn't believe you if they walked right in and sat down with us."

Going for the door, he hollered back. "There goes their horse trailer."

I could tell by the look on Gary's face that he was serious. I chased him to the front door, sprinted across the parking lot to the highway, then weaved through speeding cars with blaring horns on my way to the middle of the Boulevard. Squinting into the sun, I could see a horse trailer and, just before it disappeared towards downtown, its license plate: US GOVERNMENT.

"It's them for sure!" I whooped. "They're on the way out to North Willamette."

"What are we going to do now?" asked Miles, standing close with Joe and Gary, who were trading shit-ass grins.

"First, let's see if we can get off the highway and back to Pop's without getting killed," I said.

"One thing for sure is, we can't catch them on bikes," said Gary.

"We don't know where they live even," said Miles. Horns honked around us.

"They can't be that hard to find," I said.

"Especially," said Joe, "if they're looking for us too."

The thought of Caren looking for me gave me a tingle I hadn't been feeling much lately.

Back in the booth, the boys looked at me like I'd know what to do.

"So what do you think, Sonny?" asked Gary. "How we going to find them?"

I picked up my still-burning cigarette and took a thoughtful drag. "Here's the plan," I said. "This is Wednesday, right? We'll give them a day to get settled and then scout the whole of North Willamette on our bikes if we have to. We'll find our girls. I'm sure of it."

"Sounds good," said Joe.

"Let's meet up under the bridge right after lunch on Friday," I said, "and we'll go hunting, see if the Arthurs are still there and if they've seen the girls, and from there, who knows."

The anticipation I had for getting my arms around Caren was rough on my sleep and filled the days with daydreams for two long days.

Friday finally. We pedaled up the bridge towards the park, riding on a surge of high expectations and testosterone. "Think they'll be there?" hollered Miles.

"I sure as hell hope so," I said with more hope than Miles would know.

I entered the park first, through brush and trees that were turning with the coming of fall. And then, single file, we were in the clearing where I could see the Arthurs and their old Pontiac. They were packing up. The rest of the park was deserted except for some picnic garbage and the like, strewn around in the ruts and weeds.

"Howdy there," Joe shouted to the family. They looked up and gave us a friendly wave.

"You boys got here just in time," said Mrs. Arthur. "We're fixing to leave for apple harvest in Hood River." The whole family was looking at us now.

"Have you seen the Bonde girls?" I asked with hope.

"Who?" she asked, cocking her head. "What was that name again?"

The whole family was looking at me like I was nuts.

I wanted to shake her. "Bonde," I said. "You know, those blondes we went horsebacking with."

"Come on," pleaded Gary, "you gotta remember them—we seen them the day before yesterday heading this way on the highway."

Still nothing. I looked at Joe, who looked as if he'd bitten into a lemon. I began to turn my bike when the little girl Arthur let out a giggle. Then they all burst out laughing. The old man and all got our goat good.

Mrs. Arthur handed me a small pink envelope with a wink. My heart leaped.

"Open it!" said Gary.

"Keep your shirt on," I said as the boys gathered around anxious-like.

I ripped open the envelope. I read it to myself.

We're back! Let's party! WA8-3486

"What does it say?" said Miles.

"They're back!" I shouted, throwing my arms around Mrs. Arthur grinning at me.

Gary whooped, ending with his rendition of "Back in the Saddle Again."

We yelled good-byes as we pedaled off for the phone booth at the restaurant north of the bridge. You could say we were jubilant.

"Anybody got a dime?" I closed the door of the phone booth behind me and dropped two nickels into the slot, getting a dial tone. I read the numbers off as I rotated the dial: "W-A-8-3-4-8-6." Miles's nose was pressing the glass.

A ring came from the other end of the line. My heart was pounding. What if the colonel answered? Then what? I'd deal with it.

"Bonde residence," a young feminine voice answered.

"H-h-hello," I stammered.

"Sonny?"

"Trina?"

"I'll get Caren."

My heart went from pounding to leaping.

"Hi, Sonny," came her voice. "You got the note."

"Sure did. When can I see you?"

"Tonight, I hope."

"Great, we'll come get you."

"Better not."

"Why?"

"We're in trouble with Dad right now. Best we meet you somewhere."

"You know the restaurant at the bottom of the bridge on the North Willamette side?"

"That would be good. We can walk to there. How about around 7:00, okay?"

"You betcha."

"I can't wait to see you again, Sonny."

I swung the door open. "Need another dime—gotta call Billy; we're on for tonight."

Glee all around.

After a plunge in the bathtub, I had just enough time to choke down some meatloaf and green beans with a pint of milk. I kissed Mom on the cheek and said good-bye to Dad and was out the door. Billy was waiting by the curb in his mom's big-ass four-door. He had made the trade for the night in high hopes of a large load. He had a good start with Johnny Smith already riding shotgun. Sliding in, I took over at the window, and Billy throttled off for Fletcher's Mobil to pick up Joe, Gary, and Miles, making six of us total.

We pooled our money together on our way downtown with the intent of finding the bums: we needed some suds.

In no time, we had two cases of Oly in the massive trunk, and the bums were into their share, tipping cool ones as we pulled out for North Willamette.

"This is the most beer we ever had at one time," said Gary.

"That's 4.8 beers apiece, providing everyone shows," said Billy, who was good with math.

"They'll show," I said, "and you won't believe how they look in them tight jeans."

"They dress real casual, like they might be a little casual about giving out, huh?" asked Billy.

"Well," I said, "Gary didn't get too far on his first try with Janna, but the jury is still out on the rest of 'em."

We chugged into the parking lot by the little restaurant to a shock—four young ladies in summer dresses sitting in the outside dining area. They were showing the same blonde hair but fashioned and big, with makeup and lipstick that brought out those white teeth when they smiled. And they were smiling at us as we unloaded, all dressed the same: Penney's t-shirts over Levi's, white socks, and loafers.

The girls weaved in with us as we lounged all over the big car, with its radio howling rock 'n' roll, with some of us, like me, leaning on a fender, and Joe on the roof, supporting his feet in the open window frame. We needed cars like they loved horses. A group of teenage boys with like interests wooing some sisters on a summer's eve. It would have made a picture.

"What is this?" asked Elsie. "A scene out of *Rebel Without a Cause?*"

"No, it's just us, and we're in the mood to party," said Gary. "We got some beer," he added, getting some of his bravado back.

"Let's get on with it then," said Caren, smiling and glomming on to me as we slid into the backseat. Squeezed there, we snuggled in the corner as the rest packed into the car with grunts and giggles. Janna let Gary sit next to her with a warning: "You're still on probation, you know, you little son of a bitch."

Trina was young and out of contention romantically, so she sat up front between Billy and Miles, who was having one of his pimple attacks.

Billy angled the big boat of a car out of the parking lot, scraping all four corners, until we leveled out on pavement. The scraping sound was funny, like we were in a clown car. Billy rapped the radio up and we motored over the bridge to our part of town.

"So what happened to you guys when we got let go and you got hauled off in the cop car?" asked Elsie.

"How did you know they took us away?" I asked.

"We hid in the bushes and watched until you were driven off in the squad car," said Caren with a little bump to my knee.

"You tell them, Sonny," Gary said. "You'll get it right."

"Okay," I said. "First off, Duffy was probably the wrong guy to borrow a hat from …"

After telling the girls about Duffy, I went on and filled the girls in on what took place after we were released and how we had to fix the damage to the lawn at the courthouse.

"Sorry about that," said Elsie. "Caren jumped the fence first. I just got caught up in the moment."

"Yeah, no kidding," added Caren.

"It's okay. We got him back real good, didn't we, Sonny?" said Miles.

"We sure did."

"More than we intended, as a matter of fact," I said.

I told them about the flaming tires and how Gary had dropped the oil out of Duffy's motor and then called City Hall pretending to be a damsel in distress and all that.

"Yeah. And the train ran over us on the railroad bridge. Don't forget to tell them about that," said Joe.

"Wow," said Elsie. "I can't believe you guys lived through all that."

"No kidding," said Caren. "I wish we could have gotten in on it—"

"Except the part about the yard work," added Janna.

"So what about you girls?" I asked. "Why did your dad haul you away just to come back?"

"We don't know," said Elsie. "We never know about those things and have quit asking. I'm not sure if Dad even knows. It's the Cold War, you know. It's about defending the continent against the Russians and their nuclear bombs. One minute we were settling into a place up north, and then all of a sudden, he was called back here to the base."

"That's the good news," said Janna. "The bad news is we could load up and leave at any moment. So anytime we want to do something, we get at it because it could be our last chance."

Caren elbowed me a bump.

Billy drove to Pop's to show off the girls. Swinging into the drive-in, he made a couple of revolutions, hoping our peers would get a look at all that hair we were hauling. It worked; the crowd looked at us, gawking like we were in a parade.

Back on the Boulevard, we scraped along, heading south, looking like a load of gypsies in a limo.

"So, where are we going to drink our trunkful of suds?" asked Johnny of anyone who could hear.

"In your dad's shop," answered Billy, cutting the radio.

"What?" said Johnny. "How's that going to work?"

"Hide and watch," grinned Billy. Billy had something up his sleeve.

"So what are we going to do?" said Miles, getting curious.

"We're going to pull in like we always do to use the shop," answered Billy. "Only, this time, we'll be lugging down beers instead of working on my car." Billy cruised us around to the back lot of the Ford garage, where Johnny got out to get the key that was hidden in the alley. He disappeared through the man-door, and suddenly, the garage door rolled up. With just the parking lights on, Billy eased the big car into the shop, and the garage door closed behind us. I'd been there lots of times, but it looked different now with the amber parking lights giving off a glow, making the dark room look exotic. He shut off the motor and switched the key to accessory and cranked up the radio.

The whole shop was long, with work bays lined up on the left, each with a vehicle in need of repair, with benches equipped with special tools and hoists for raising the cars off the ground.

At the end of the garage was an informal lounge space dimly illuminated by a single light bulb hanging from the ceiling. There was a leather couch, along with some office chairs that were probably hand-me-downs from the waiting room up front. This area was where the mechanics took their breaks and ate lunch.

We piled out into the dim light. I took Caren by the hand, and we worked our way to the lounge. Folding into our newfound surroundings made us a half-circle of thirsts, anticipating the two cases of Oly in the center. I sat at one end of the couch and Caren propped next to me on the overstuffed arm of the sofa, her arm around my neck for some "support," she'd said with a wink. With a handy screwdriver, Joe went to work prying off the bottle caps—a mood-changing event, with popping and fizzing marking the start of a party.

The cowgirls' enthusiasm for drinking matched their enthusiasm for life. Trina nursed her beer, but as for the rest, it was a guzzling affair. The empties piled up, replacing the full ones that were waiting. Pleasant conversation changed to chatter and the noise level notched up as the beer flowed and we were trying to compete with the rock 'n' roll music spilling out of the AM radio in the DeSoto.

Through the cigarette smoke, I could see a glow developing on the faces of our guests, and their feet bopping and beeping to the jolts given off by the tunes. There was a new station out of Portland that had been coming in good at night, and it was pumping out some favorites. We got to talking music and what we liked. The girls liked country-western and we had a one-track affiliation with rock 'n' roll. The girls talked about Porter Wagoner, George Jones, and others I'd never heard of. Elsie explained how some of our heroes, such as Elvis and Jerry Lee, were crossovers and could be heard on the country shows too.

"Hey, I got a good idea," said Caren. "Let's turn all the car radios in here to the same channel and see how it sounds."

She popped up and took me by the arm and we marched to the first car in line—a '50 Mercury. She opened the door, reached in, and switched the key to accessory, then spun the dial to KVLN in Portland. Then we did the same from car to car until we reached the last one, which happened to be on a hoist but only a short distance off the floor.

It was a turquoise 1956 Lincoln four-door sedan. The car was shiny new and dripping with chrome. The leather interior was massive and matched the color of the paint.

Caren reached the handle and said, "Allow me," as she opened the door. She crawled in the backseat, beckoning me with her blue eyes. I didn't need much encouragement.

I shut the door after me. She stretched out over the front seat and switched the key, showing white panties with little red hearts, and they were winking at me. She found the radio and tuned in; Elvis was singing; "Love Me Tender" filled the car with a mood I'd been carrying for a while. Turning, she was in my arms, wiggling in close, her lips finding mine. Something began to rise. The room was sinking.

"Going up," I heard Joe say with a chuckle near my steamed-up window. He'd pulled the hydraulic lever, raising the hoist.

As the car lifted towards the ceiling, things were happening. Elvis moved to "I Want You, I Need You, I Love You." Caren was on fire; she wanted me. Things started happening faster than I could plan ahead—and she was way out ahead of me. She led me along and I helped, as much as I knew how, which wasn't much.

And then it happened. My world was changed forever.

~ ~ ~

On and on Joe and I talked about growing up together until we came to Miles, who'd lost his life the summer before we were seniors. Joe laid his head on his arms and began to bawl. I put my arm around him and then I lost it too.

Chapter 11

So Joe was getting married—and I'd told him I'd try to get him a job at the mill.

The next morning, while pulling boards, I waved the foreman over to the chain for a talk. Raising my voice over the roar, I told him about Joe, his good character and talents, and so on. Then I sprung the question. "Have you got something for him out here?"

He had a bad-news look on his face. "Things aren't the same now," he said. "Something's going on here and everyone's got the jitters, including the owner. Tell your friend Joe I'll get his name on the list, but he better look somewhere else if he's in a hurry."

"I'll tell him. Thanks." *Damn*, I thought. I wasn't looking forward to dropping that on Joe. It was important, so I wanted to tell Joe personally, which meant catching him at work—which meant I had to go to Pop's. I dreaded going to Pop's since it was after school and the place would be humming with high school students off for the day. Like Marylyn and her friends.

It had been only a few days since I'd seen her, but it seemed like months. Doubts constantly buzzed around in my head about her. Maybe her old man had locked her in the basement or maybe she really didn't like me and she was avoiding me.

Wary, I swung into Pop's after work to tell Joe the bad news. His Ford was out in front and I caught him in the kitchen washing dishes. Angie was drying them and beaming. They were in love, and I hated to unload the bad news on them. And when I did, Angie's expression showed worry as she looked to Joe for support. Joe had heard a lot of bad in his life, so he went to smiling and swung his arm around Angie. They were survivors.

I walked out to my pickup feeling better about them but not so about my love life, if I could call it that. The torturing I was doing to myself was taking its toll. The only thing that seemed to help was staying busy, so I headed for the towing shop to work on my '40. Laboring on my car was like going to a shrink. It was reassuring like a friend and was something I could count on.

At the shop, Clayton was breathing a cigarette while massaging the shiny fenders I'd relieved from the barn like they were rare art. "Sonny," he drawled, "you got some nice straight fenders here." In body and fender language, straight meant good, really good.

That made me feel like a savior rather than a thief. I lit up a smoke. "So what do we do to these next?"

"Paint 'em. I'm gonna primer them and you're going to sand 'em, and when they're good enough, I'll shoot 'em blue."

"How we going to find the right color of blue?"

"Come here. I'll show ya."

I followed him into the office, where he pulled a dictionary-thick manual off a shelf and said, "Out of this book here."

I looked over his shoulder as he thumbed through the tattered pages printed in black and white, greasy from decades of use. According to the manual, '40 Fords came painted with two different blues, a light blue called Como and a dark blue called Lyon. Mine, obviously, was the latter, and it was lacquer.

"Being's it's lacquer," he said, "we'll just shoot it with a lacquer primer and then go on with the paint."

We carried all the tin to a room in the back for priming. He had sort of a makeshift paint booth that he had erected out of two-by-four studs and clear plastic, with a metal fan sealed into the door for ventilation. He had me wet down the floor to settle the dust while he was mixing primer, then he waved me out, and I left him to his painting.

As I walked towards the pickup I heard the air compressor come to life. It was exciting to me that my '40 was on its way to recovery.

It was dark then, and with headlights and wipers going, and the heater on kill, I drove for home, the rain and darkness bringing back my sour mood. The trip took me right by Pop's, and out of habit, I wheeled in under the cover of a hellacious rain shower. On the first circuit around the joint, Eddy jumped on my running board again, hanging on with one hand and holding his jacket over his head with the other. As we motored around the restaurant, he was jumping up and down rocking the pickup.

"Sonny," he yelled, "you gotta stop. I'm going to drown out here; besides, there's a new car in town."

I wasn't in any mood to talk cars and was sure he was all pumped about the damned Impala Gary had already told me about. Taking pity on him, I stopped, letting him in, his ass dripping water all over the army blanket I'd wrapped Marylyn in. So it was kinda personal to me.

"Park this heap," he said, shivering. "I got to tell you about this car."

Hungering for a burger anyway, I pulled in between a station wagon on my left—with a couple on a date, I figured, by the way they were using only half the front seat—and a four-door miniature Hudson on my right, filled with teenage boys with greasy hair. There was a full Coke glass on the window tray, a set of bongos propped on the back window ledge, and some fuzzy dice hanging from the mirror. The car was driven by a poser wearing a black leather biker's jacket with chrome stars all over it. The driver kid suddenly decided to get out of his car, and he swung his door wide, crashing it into the passenger side of my dad's Chevy pickup. It was a really bad time to irritate me. Maybe by the look on my face, he realized he'd made a mistake, because he closed his door and stayed in the car. I opened my door, and three steps later, I was at the little jerk's window as he was frantically trying to start the motor. Reaching over the tray, I took his keys, then dumped the Coke, ice and all, in his lap.

His eyes crossed when the ice found its mark. I grabbed him by the collar and yanked him half out the window. My fists pushed his cheeks up, beading his eyes in a contortion that made him look like a cornered pig.

"Look, you little prick," I said, "if you're going to come out here and play with the big dogs, you'd better grow some manners." That done, I shoved him back in his car and tossed the keys in after him. He and his scared-shitless buddies left with the tray still hanging on the door.

I got back into the pickup, careful not to hit the station wagon with my door. The lover couple's heads were so close together looking at me they could have been a four-eyed camel—eyes all big and worried-looking.

"Angie's going to kill me for that," I said as I started the pickup. "Maybe we should go for a little ride."

"Jeez, Sonny, are you feeling okay?" Eddy asked.

"Why," I snapped, "is there something wrong?"

"Here, have a smoke." He handed me a Lucky. It seemed the predicament with Marylyn was really getting to me.

I lit up and slipped the pickup out of the joint, heading north on the Boulevard towards Billie's Big Boy Burger.

At night the Boulevard was like a small-town parade—half the town coming one way waving at the other half going the other way. As Eddy began to inform me about the damn Impala, I noticed a lime-green bug approaching—the same Volkswagen that I'd hitched a ride in the night I met Marylyn. It had been raining that night too, and the windows had been foggy from steamed-up passengers, girls hot from cheering a high school basketball game.

As it passed now, the fogged windows kept me from seeing if Marylyn was in the car, but a hand with a hanky came down, wiping the driver's window, revealing Susan Bell. And in that moment I could see by the look on her face that she recognized me. Susan was one of Marylyn's closest friends, the same girl who was with Marylyn on the night of the crash. Looking back to see if maybe Marylyn was in the backseat, I saw the car's brake lights come on, and then it swerved into a parking lot, U-turning and coming after us. At that moment, I wasn't in any mood to have a meeting with Marylyn or to discuss my love life in front of her friends, so I darted into a side street on two wheels and hit the gas for downtown to get away and avoid a showdown. By the way Eddy was looking at me, he was afraid I'd lost my mind.

I decided I'd better confide in him, even though we'd never talked girls before. I thought it best to tell him before he had me committed or something. "Eddy, sorry about all this."

"What, ya got the clap or something?"

"No, nothing like that. You know that girl I rescued the other night?"

"Yeah. That good-looking daughter-of-a-banker girl."

"That's the one. Her name is Marylyn Swanson, and well, I've kind of fallen for her a little bit, but her old man ain't having anything to do with it, and well, it's pissing me off some," I said.

"Well, tell him to shove it—this is the twentieth century, you know. What's he think, he's a king?"

"The problem is, Eddy, I kinda promised him I wouldn't go near her, and now she probably thinks I'm a real dickhead for avoiding her."

"Doesn't she know about her dad warning you off?"

"That's the question. I don't know, and so I don't know how to act if we're thrown together out here somewhere."

"So, is that why you don't want a visit from the green Volkswagen?"

"Yeah. You know that car. Those girls are friends with Marylyn, and she might even be with them."

"I don't know anything about stuff like this, but for sure you got a problem."

"Up until a couple weeks ago, I didn't know much about these things either. I kind of envy you, Eddy."

"Sonny. All I know is about cars. Hot cars."

"So tell me about this new car," I said.

"It's a Chevy Impala. A 348 four-speed."

"So what's so special about that? We've put a couple of them away."

"This one's different. It has traction bars, slicks, and low gears. Those other Imps were just weekend warriors, but this guy is serious."

"What's he doing around here?"

"Well, for starters, he's kicking everyone's ass."

"Just whose ass are you talking about?"

"The word is he's beat everyone in Bridgeport."

That was impressive, I thought. There were some hot cars in Bridgeport.

"He must have an agenda," I said. "He isn't just traveling around the country racing everyone, is he?"

"I don't know, but he seems pretty well-heeled, because he doesn't seem to work or anything."

I wonder what that would be like, I was thinking. I was working my ass off and still lived at home.

I was caught by the red light that let the traffic off the bridge from North Willamette.

"There he is now!" Eddy pointed ahead. "He's coming off the bridge." It was the third car off, a white Chevrolet Impala like everyone said. I'd never seen a street-driven car like it before. It was seriously business-looking. The front wheels were black, wrapped with skinny whitewalls that sat in front of vertical exhaust dumps sporting large pipe plugs for quick removal. The back tires were slicks, like Eddy said, big enough that the wheel wells had been enlarged, and the tires were mounted on steel wheels painted with red pie shapes so a crew chief could monitor the tire spin. And if all that wasn't enough to make a guy shake in his boots, the rear fender had Crazy Horse painted across it.

The light turned green. I turned and followed a couple of cars behind him. But with nothing under me to challenge him with, I peeled off and cruised the gut downtown. Not for any reason. We drove to be driving—we didn't drive to get somewhere. The trip wouldn't take long. Small towns have small guts, so when we finished the loop downtown, there was nothing to do but to return to Pop's like always, but this time despite a premonition of dread.

I turned onto the slow lane of the four-lane boulevard and drove north in the direction of Pop's. I was beginning to relax, thinking since it was a school night and nearing the magic pumpkin hour, all the students would have curfewed home.

I was lying back in the driver's seat having a smoke with Eddy chattering when the whole rearview mirror was an image of the Impala. "Shit, he's on our tail," I said.

"Who's on our tail?" Eddy swung around in his seat. "How'd he get behind us like that?"

"Has to be coincidence. He knows my car by now for sure, but he sure as hell doesn't know we're in this old pickup." I was a little bit rattled because the Impala stayed close behind as I drove towards Pop's in the slow lane.

Up ahead, I saw the green Volkswagen pull out of Pop's heading right for us. *Damn*, I thought. *I'm tired of running from Marylyn. I'm gonna pull over and face the music.*

At that very moment, I heard peeling tires behind us and then the Impala came roaring by us in the fast lane. Then the Volkswagen passed us from the other direction. My mirror showed its brake lights come on. The little bug then spun around in the street and came after us. Must have recognized me.

The Impala slowed, staying a couple of car links ahead of us in the fast lane, and I pulled over behind it, signaling to turn left into Pop's for my encounter with Marylyn. I was getting rattled. The Volkswagen caught up with us, but instead of following us into Pop's, it sped up, chasing after the Impala. I was stunned. One minute I'm hiding from her and the next she's off after someone else.

"What the hell was that all about?" wondered Eddy.

"Hell if I know, but if I had to guess, I'd say they're a lot more interested in what's driving that Impala than they are in us."

I let Eddy out at his car. It was a meek drive home for sure. I tossed and turned all night, thinking of Marylyn and the ghost driving the Impala. By morning, I was sure they had fallen in love and were running off together, leaving me blue-collared, driving a worn-out pickup, spending my life in a mill, growing a beard, and drinking cheap beer.

Chapter 12

"Sonny," Clayton said from under my '40, "if you're going to keep roaring around chasing cars and getting chased, you need to do something about your suspension."

I was on my knees with my head near the concrete, watching him skate around lying face up on a creeper, giving me a verbal tour of my '40's undercarriage, illuminated by a droplight hooked to the frame. The car was held up by jack stands made from Ford axle housings, multicolored from past paint jobs. I could tell by the way Clayton handled my '40's parts with those big, worn hands of his that he had a love for old Fords. They weren't strangers to him.

"But I'm a drag racer," I said. "I race in a straight line."

It was a Saturday morning in mid-February, over a month since I'd seen Marylyn. The weather been miserable, and—I had to admit it—my mood had been even worse. I'd been suffering the doldrums of a lovesick boy. Fortunately, Clayton had asked me to come to the shop early, so we'd have the whole day to assemble and line up the tin, which would keep my mind busy and meant the job would be finished by the end of the day, which excited the hell out me. The thought of hitting the streets with my '40 and reentering the world of fast cars—the smell of gasoline and burning rubber—was pumping me.

"I read the article in the paper," he said. "You weren't just in a straight line the night you ran down the Plymouth."

"Yeah," I said, "it wants to roll coming in and out of the turns, and when I hit the brakes hard, it goes crazy. What can I do to make it corner better?"

"You need some new shocks—good aftermarket competition type that will stabilize and smooth out the ride. Even when you're drag racing, you'll be safer at those high speeds with stiffer suspension. And your traction bars need to be adjusted lower in front to take out more wheel hop. And it would help if you dropped the rear of the car more."

That sounded expensive, but then, nothing was too good for my '40 Ford and speed.

A few hours later, the phone rang in the office. I was under the trunk and Clayton was in it, tightening bolts. We'd been absorbed in the job, losing all sense of time.

"Get that, would you, Sonny?"

I rolled out from under the car and off the creeper, and hurried to the office. "Body shop," I said into the phone.

"It's Joe. You guys hungry? I've got some burgers here."

"I'm starving!" I said, then hollered out the door, "Hey Clayton! You want a burger?"

"Does a hobby horse have a wooden dick?"

Joe soon appeared with a paper bag full of burgers someone had ordered from Pop's but hadn't picked up. His other hand clutched a cardboard case of Olympia. A happy sight—twenty-four bottles—two dozen little maidens willing to spend the afternoon with us boys in the shop. Who knew where Joe came up with the beer? He was good that way. Because of Joe, I never lacked crucial supplies.

Clayton unfolded from the trunk, slid down the wall, and planted himself on the concrete floor across from my car. We joined him there, where Joe pawed at the sack. Moments later, we were jabbering and chomping away at the red meat and condiments, washing it down with beer.

"Well," said Joe, "it was nice of the son of a bitch to order the deluxe and everything."

"Damn right," I said, "but where's the fries?"

"Angie shit-canned 'em—they were cold."

Clayton grinned. "It would take a couple Yankees to complain about a high-end meal like this, free for the taking."

"Hey there," I said. "Hold on a minute. According to local history, this town was split right down the middle over that North/South deal."

"Yeah," said Joe, "but now the split is between 'them' and 'us,' and Sonny and I aren't exactly from the affluent group."

"We're blue-collar mill rats from the east side," I said. "We're not welcome over there." I pointed west and took a hard pull on the bottle. Marylyn might as well be a million miles away.

"I knew there was something I liked about you guys," Clayton said.

I balled up the paper bag carrying my onions and tomatoes, and flung it at the empty Shell oil drum in the corner, a futile attempt. Then we got serious about drinking beer, which fit my mood just fine. The alcohol began to ooze into my brain, making my cement chair soften a little.

"Clayton," I said, "you know a lot about these old Fords. How come?"

It was like no one had asked him before, the way he stared into space that was full of ghosts looking back.

Joe and I waited, suspenseful, while he took a long drink from the brown bottle, then lit a smoke.

With a draw off the cigarette, he began to talk, the smoke seeping from his lips. "Whisky tripping," he said. "I was brung up poor in the Appalachian Mountains, along with four brothers and three sisters. I fell in with a whiskey-making man who needed a driver."

We listened agog as he took us along through a life of excitement and danger, hauling moonshine, a stint in prison, and wrenching on airplanes in WWII.

"Wasn't there dirt-track racing down there during that time?" I asked. "What was that like?'

Clayton pulled another beer from the box and worked a screwdriver around the cap. "Most towns had fairgrounds with horse tracks," he said. "We used 'em for dirt-track racing, where we loosened up from the heart-hammerin' whiskey runnin' we'd done all week. The races offered small purses, but mostly we did it for God, glory, and country. No helmets or seat belts—we just drove the ruts, turning left with our doors strapped shut. Cars sometimes ended up three deep in the corners, maiming the unlucky and thrilling the rest. Meanwhile, the crowds were inching ever closer to the chicken wire and would sometimes catch a car tearing through the fence, putting some in the hospital and some in the morgue. It was an orgy of wild and crazy men, machines, and whiskey."

Goddamn, I thought, so engrossed in his story I could smell the hot motors and see the blood, and the dirt and dust were choking me. "It must have been crowded with all the cars on such a small track." I asked, "What happens if a guy won't let you by?"

"Well," Clayton said, "there's an equation for that. You ride on his tail a couple of laps, and if he don't get the idea, then you pull up to his right rear fender just as he's turning for the corner and give him a nudge with your bumper. Right in the sweet spot, we call it. This most likely will put him into a spin, and when he goes spiraling by on your left, you hammer the throttle and continue with the race."

That got me thinking. After an encounter like that, I bet some guys went to "fist city," which was fun for some.

"Did you ever wreck and get hurt?" Joe asked.

Clayton turned and faced us, smiling full-on. He

dropped an upper plate from his mouth, revealing an impressive vacancy. "I'm missing a score of teeth here. Given to me by God himself, just to be taken away by a pole on the third turn at Dalton in '47."

Chapter 13

My car was finished.

Bruce slid the big door of the shop open. Clayton, with his cap pushed back on his head in thought, watched as I climbed into the '40, which smelled new with the scent of lacquer drifting off its skin. My heart pounded like the first time I had the keys in my pocket. My being giddy with anticipation wasn't lost on Clayton, who said in that drawl of his, "Sonny, you're grinning like a tick on a fat dog."

He was right and I couldn't help it, but I wasn't grinning any harder than Bruce. We were all loving the moment.

I fired up the motor, which had been sleeping for weeks. The rush of air from the fan blew body shop dust from under the car. I hurried the car out before the dust could land on my new paint, parked under the yard light in front of the shop, and jumped out to see what it looked like out in the world. The three of us looked at it from every angle, admiring and commenting about how bitchin' it truly was.

And then, suddenly, my '40's coming-out party was over—Bruce closed the big door on my vision of Clayton rolling up the air hose. Clayton would be on to a new job in the morning and Bruce would go on with life. I was left alone with my thoughts. I gave the car one more look around and then climbed in, sprawling back in the driving form I was known for. With the motor at idle, I took in the ambiance of the world I'd created and had missed so much. A rolling trademark of who I was: the Stewart-Warner gauges, the louvers in the hood letting out the roar of the Oldsmobile V8, the painting on the dash that was surely a masterpiece done by a red wine–powered beatnik. Dumped in front with big tires in the back. Every item was available to any hot rodder with the lust for it, but the total concoction was mine, on my canvas, making it my personal rocket ship.

And then she came back again—Marylyn—rather, the vision of her on the night of the crash, sitting beside me, wringing her hands in the shop rag and shaking with fear. My mood tanked.

I wanted to drive to her house and show her my '40 and how it was okay now and like everything else it was going to be okay. But I couldn't.

To shake it off, I pulled out into the street and slammed the throttle down, lighting up the tires and fishtailing to the stop sign. It helped a little.

The night had turned dry—a common occurrence for the middle of February in my part of Oregon. It was chilly out, showing stars I hadn't seen for a while, and I was grateful for the respite from the constant drubbing we got from the rain.

I needed gas. By the time I had driven to Fletcher's Mobil, it had grown dark, but through the steamy windows, I could see someone working in the lube bay. I strolled through the door, getting a warm nod from Frank, who was hunched under the hood of a Studebaker Hawk. He was in his overalls, which had been washed a thousand times but still showed stains of a workingman. I swung my head under the hood and took a look around. It was a small V8, but it had a cylinder-shaped belt-driven pump mounted on the front. It looked like some sort of supercharger, or blower as I'd heard them called.

"Got your '40 back, huh?" Frank groaned as he straightened. Frank was getting older and his bones hurt from pumping gas in the cold rain.

"Yeah, Frank. It's good to drive it again."

"Speaking of driving, I'm a little worried about the kid who owns this car," he said.

"How's that?" I asked.

"Well, he has this wild streak in him kind of like Theodore had." Theodore was his nephew who was driving the night that Miles was killed.

According to Frank, the father of the kid whose car it was bought him the Studebaker without knowing that it was a high-performance model. By the way the car kept coming back for repairs, he could tell it was being used hard. Frank walked me around the little coupe and showed me the sides of the car, which were scraped and battered from slamming into objects. "I'm afraid he's going to have the big one anytime now, Sonny," he said.

"I think you're right. Maybe you should talk to his dad about it."

"I don't know if I should get involved—you know. Men like him don't take to getting told what to do very well. I just hope the boy comes out alive and learns something before it's too late."

I could see it pained him, so to change the subject, I got us a couple of Cokes out of the machine and lit up a smoke. I pointed to the blower. "What you got here?"

"It's a McCulloch supercharger, Sonny."

"How do those little things make power?"

Frank reached into a drawer in his tool chest and pulled out a pint of Old Grand-Dad bourbon. After pouring half the Coke into the floor drain, he brought it back to full with 114 proof. "Here's to you, Sonny," he said as he tipped it back. Ever since Miles got killed, I noticed Frank was drinking more and more.

After his cocktail began to settle, he leaned on the fender and began telling me about superchargers. "Blowers are nothing new." He told me they had been trying them one way or another since the invention of gasoline and air. Planes had them forever and McCulloch had been making centrifugal models like this one for use on production cars for some time. "Sonny, they make horsepower that will help a small motor tear up a big lazy one."

Just what I need, I thought, thinking of the new Impala in town.

Frank carefully shut the hood and wiped the fingerprints off the pale yellow paint with his red shop rag.

I gassed up and helped Frank close up the station, then headed for Pop's with mixed emotions. The return of my '40 would cause a stir for sure. I'd like that, of course, but not as much anymore, since I was plagued with the ups and downs of a love life without the lover. She might be at Pop's. The thought gave me a jolt.

The change of weather had brought out the mob of teenagers that used Pop's. Their expressions changed at seeing my car—eyes watching, hoping I'd land somewhere where they could surround me with curious envy. I kept moving, though, looping the joint, on guard for the Volkswagen. It wasn't there, so I parked in front by Joe's Ford, and as I shut off the motor, I heard something new—a loudspeaker sound coming over the normal hum and buzz of a parking lot full of youngsters loose for the night. To ward off the crowd that was soon to come, I hurried to the door and the safety of the restaurant. I slouched down in a booth where I could see the kitchen area. Joe had graduated from washing dishes to flipping burgers, which he did with his usual grinning good nature.

Angie was yakking away into a microphone mounted on the wall in the kitchen. It was her voice I'd heard outside. It was new and a great idea. The customers ordered and their voices came over a speaker so the cook as well as the carhops could hear. Next to the speaker was the mic that Angie was using to communicate with them about the details of the order.

Joe, who was now looking at me through the doorway, waving a spatula, had told me that system was also equipped with a volume control and a switch to alarm all the phones in case the restaurant wanted to make an announcement, such as, "We will be closing in 15 minutes," or some such thing.

"What are they going to think of next?" I asked. "How about cooking me a burger, Joe?"

I folded back into the booth where I could monitor the traffic coming off the Boulevard—an old habit from the days of watching for potential racers, but now included in my search was a green Volkswagen that didn't have power enough to pull the hat off a head. The usual locals were out in force, along with some strangers, and my '40 was engulfed by teenagers taking a peek. The yellow Studebaker Hawk I'd seen at Frank's came and went. I figured the young kid driving was the customer Frank was worried sick about, and with him was another about the same age. The place was rocking and, with the orders coming in on the new intercom and the clanging and banging going on in the kitchen, it was close to organized havoc.

Chewing away on my burger, I'd forgotten about the cars until I heard a loud motor idling into the lot. The windows in the building rattled with the vibration brought on by a wild-ass reground camshaft.

I reeled in my seat in time to see the back of a Chevy Impala roll by. The interest in my car dropped and eyes went to the new car in town. It was Crazy Horse, and directly behind it was the lime-green Volkswagen, windows down and packed full of big hair. A pang of excitement shot through me.

The little car was loaded as usual, but I couldn't tell if Marylyn was along or not. In one sudden second, all the hype and euphoria of being back in my '40 was gone, replaced by a sick feeling of despair and loneliness.

Soon, the Impala appeared on the other side of the drive-in. A guy was behind the wheel and the rest of the car was full of girls, one of which was for sure Susan Bell, the driver of the V-Dub, and there were two in the backseat who I assumed were Alice Johnson and Linda Nelson, the normal backseat occupiers. Evidently, they had left the Volkswagen and were riding in Crazy Horse's Impala.

Wow, I thought. Now this was a big development. It seemed I was getting old and out of the loop already.

I could tell Crazy Horse liked being noticed by the way he let his car rump as it idled towards the stop sign leading to the Boulevard. My car was sitting in front in plain sight, so I knew that he knew I was watching him from the inside of the drive-in. It was a big deal to him.

What he didn't know was that I was watching for Marylyn a lot more than for him. He pulled out, gently turning left, and when he got it straightened out, he made the hit. Rolling at twenty, he hammered the throttle, boiling the hides—a term for peeling out through first—and then let off of it and went on his way towards Billie's.

Over the racket of dishes rattling and the like, Angie told me that Susan Bell and the new kid, Crazy Horse, had become an item as of late.

Eddy blew the front door open and entered in a rush. "Hi, Sonny," he said, dropping into the booth. "Did you see Crazy Horse come through?"

"Yep. How could I miss it?"

"Pretty bitchin', huh?"

"Yeah, I guess."

"What's bugging you?" he asked. "It's that girl, isn't it?"

"Tell me what you know about the Impala."

"Well, from what I've found out, it, of course, has the big motor—a 348—a late GM high-performance block that isn't supposed to be available to the public until next year."

"How'd he get that?"

"The story is," said Eddy, "the kid is from a small town in Northern California, where his folks own the Chevrolet garage, and from being an insider, he was able to purchase the factory souped-up car made especially for racing, with lightened parts and competition suspension."

"You're talking a lot of money. How could a kid afford such a car?"

"He's full of Indian blood and his tribe sold off part of their reservation. That's what's been going around anyway.

"I gotta go," said Eddy.

"What's the hurry? You just got here."

"I have to be at work in a few minutes." The door slammed behind him.

The building started shaking again. It was like an earthquake rattling the place. *Will this be the car that brings me down?* I wondered.

I gave Joe a serious glance to see him standing in the kitchen holding the dishes back from falling off the shelves, confirming that Crazy Horse was a serious contender. It would be this one or the one after. It was the gunslinger thing and would happen sooner or later. He would have to work for it, though, like I did.

A blast came over the intercom from a female voice. "Is that sissy in there that drives the funny little '40 Ford that's supposed to be famous?"

What was that? The voice sounded like it came from Susan Bell.

Hearing it too, Angie whirled around from the cash register and gave me a "what the hell was that" look. Then she slapped the talk button on the mic.

"What?" she asked.

"Speak up," the voice said. "I can't hear you."

"I'm here to take your order," said Angie. "Can you hear that?"

"I said," the voice got louder, "I'm riding with Crazy Horse out here and he's now the fastest in town."

"You what?" asked Angie. Getting annoyed.

"I said, I couldn't hear you," came the voice.

Angie gave me a look again. This time Joe saw it and quit flipping and I stopped chewing.

Angie switched the speaker over to broadcast. "Now can you hear me?" The whole block was filled with Angie's voice. She had turned up the volume to high, and every speaker was tuned in to the conversation at hand. Then the voice again. "I'm here with Crazy Horse and his big Impala is the fastest car in town." By the way the voice cracked with enthusiasm, I could tell it was Susan.

"Well, there's a guy in here who might have something to say about that," Angie shot back through the mic. "His name is Sonny Mitchell, and up till now, nobody has even come close to beating him."

The whole town was hearing about my racing accomplishments thanks to Pop's new address system. I wondered what I'd hear next. I didn't have to wait long.

"Tell him to come on out here," Susan taunted, "if he ain't afraid to get his ass kicked by Crazy Horse."

"He's eating a meal, but I'll pass it on to him," said Angie.

"You call anything made in this greasy spoon a meal?" Susan said with a laugh.

Uh-oh, now she'd done it. Susan didn't know Angie very well.

"Listen here, you rich bitch," said Angie. "You wouldn't know what went into making a meal if you were swimming in it. And, by the way, you can take those pom-poms of yours and stick 'em where the sun don't shine—and tell Geronimo there, or whoever he is, Mr. Mitchell will be out when he's damn good and ready," Angie added with finality. With that, she flipped the switch back to normal.

Joe and I were gawking at Angie as she began taking orders like nothing had happened. The burgers were on fire by then, so Joe got back to business.

Suddenly, I was wishing Eddy was still there. He'd know how to get Crazy Horse worried. He'd bullshit him and get him on the defensive. And have an orgasm doing it. They'd want me to pick the track and I'd choose

Oakdale Road, the closest place, and all this would be over soon. A morbid thought entered my skull: I could lose.

I swallowed and left through the swinging door and headed for my car. All eyes were on me as the bystanders wagered whether or not I would race or just whimper out and go home.

I flashed my confident smile, piled into my '40, turned the key, and reached for the starter button. Before I could bump it, a trio of little devil-looking characters with pitchforks appeared on my dash, looking at me with their egging grins. My race demons. Since I was seventeen, they'd lived somewhere in my mind, breaking out to appear before and during the contests. At first I'd been able to blink them away. But with each race the naughty little devils had come back, whispering their gloomy warnings that I might lose.

I was pretty sure that it was just jitters I had. After all I'd been young – young to be as fast as I was. The competition was older and more experienced and intimidating. But I had Eddy, who rode with me when he could. He couldn't see my demons and I never told him about them. I never talked about them; not a soul knew of them. As far as everyone was concerned I was Superman—made of steel. Eddy had a mouth and he used it to goad the ones who'd come looking for me at Pop's. That's what they did; come looking for me, wanting a chance at the fast kid from Willamette. Those races would come and go—sometimes in an hour or two they'd show up, get beat and go back where they had come from. My demons' role would be short lived too. They would come out making me ache with apprehension and then root me on during the race, riding my shoulders and clinging to my hair. Then when the race was over they'd go back into hiding, waiting for the next hungry hot rod pilot to come to town.

With Crazy Horse it was different. It had been a pot of anticipation on slow burn rising in temperature ready to boil. He had his fans; some had been mine but now they'd crossed over to his camp. It was a perfect scenario to fuel my demons. They loved the drama of it all.

I pushed the starter button. The motor fired on the first revolution and roared crisp and powerful-like, blowing away the demons for now—a good omen, I thought.

I backed out and idled past the row of parked cars to where Crazy Horse was sitting in his car, surrounded by his teenage admirers. I swung around the end, which put me next to the passenger side of the Impala, blocking traffic, a mediocre foul in the game of street racing.

The passenger window rolled down, framing Susan Bell's face. Challenging and cocky-looking, her demeanor was different from the last time I'd seen her up close, which was after the crash at the railroad tracks just weeks before. At that time, she'd seemed thankful to see me. I'd just saved her young, sweet ass. *It's funny how things can change*, I thought as I leaned over to roll down my window.

"Well, what about it?" Susan asked. "You ready to run that pile of junk?"

"Follow me," I said. "We're going to race at Oakdale Road."

"Let me out," came a girl's voice from the Impala's backseat. "I'm riding with Sonny."

Susan opened her door and leaned forward to let the passenger sitting behind her out.

It was Linda Nelson, Marylyn's best friend, another one of the trio commonly seen in the Volkswagen. She was a dark-headed, fidgeting Betty Boop–looker.

Before I could say shit, she had wiggled in, making herself at home in my car.

"Why are we going to race at Oakdale?" she asked between popping bubbles.

Why do they have to chew bubble gum? I wondered. I didn't remember Marylyn chewing bubble gum. "It's the closest, and I want to get this over with."

I pulled out with a parade of cars behind me. Some were spectators lining up to follow us out of town, and some were merely trying to circle the establishment and look for a place to land. When I turned south onto the Boulevard, I noticed the Studebaker Hawk was following me, two cars behind. I took it easy, making sure the Impala was in the lineup, then passed where the train crossed the highway, bringing back the memory of the crash.

"This place always makes me shiver," said Linda.

"No kidding, " I said. "It was scary."

The Hawk kid pulled alongside on our right and revved his motor.

I asked Linda, "Do you know the anxious cat in the Studebaker?"

"Oh, that's Joey Thompson, and the guy with him is Freddy somebody. Joey is only sixteen and is wild and crazy with that car of his."

Joey romped on his throttle a couple more times, then backed off, letting us by with a grin on his face. *He's a show-off*, I thought, *but so am I, I guess.*

When the four lanes changed into two, Joey slowed and pulled in behind the Impala, which was followed by a few stragglers bent on spectating a good race, I figured. It was a ten-minute ride, so we settled in for the trip, with me worrying about the outcome of the race and its implications on my status as a local race car giant.

"So, what's with you and Marylyn?" Linda asked. "You've been avoiding her like the plague."

It shocked me. I hadn't heard Marylyn's name come from someone else for a while.

"Well," I said, recovering, "the morning after the wreck I was outside, looking to see how bad my car was damaged, when Marylyn's dad drove up in that big car of his and thanked me for saving his daughter's life. That was all great and everything, but then he told me not to come around and to leave Marylyn alone."

"Why's that?"

"Because he doesn't want his daughter marrying a blue-collar mill rat like me ..."

"So that's it," Linda said, cracking her gum. "Marylyn has been wondering if her dad contacted you."

My fears were justified. "You mean she doesn't know? He didn't tell her?"

"No, she doesn't know about that and is hurt as hell over you not calling or coming around or something."

Damn, I thought. "I was afraid of that."

"Is that why you have been ignoring her?"

"Damn," I said. "I've been in kind of a tight spot. If I tried to see Marylyn, I would prove I was a dishonest bastard to her dad, and if I didn't, I'd be a jerk in her eyes."

"Her dad is a real hard one. With her almost getting killed on the Boulevard, he's gone a little mad in my estimation. She's been almost a prisoner in that big old house since the crash. She's allowed to go to school, of course, and we can see her, but she's not permitted near that Volkswagen."

Shit, here I'd been thinking mostly about my hard luck and how I was feeling, and all the time Marylyn was the one paying.

Chapter 14

We arrived first; Linda was excited, but I was just here to do a job. I couldn't seem to get revved about it. Maybe I was outgrowing the hype and challenge of it.

The drag strip I'd used many times before was just an isolated patch of county highway that went straight as an arrow for a mile and wore black rubber marks, like stripes on a sleeve, proof it had seen battles. This night was cold and lonely with no traffic in sight, damp but it hadn't rained for hours, leaving the pavement dry-looking. But we'd had weeks of rain and, even with a dry night, moisture would be coming up through the cracks. It could be slippery. But I could handle it.

Up ahead by a power pole, the starting line was only a white line painted across the pavement. The finish line was the mailbox a quarter mile ahead on the left, where you would flash by at full speed, hopefully ahead of the sorry punk next to you. Behind the starting area where we'd pulled up, there was a triangle gravel lot, offering a place for parking in preparation for the race.

Cars pulled in, crowding the area, headlights on, illuminating the lot—a large bunch, maybe eight carloads of spectators along with us racers.

I did a 180-degree turn and came back along Crazy Horse's window. "We better get on with this," I said. "All these cars are going to get noticed."

"Okay with me," said Crazy Horse.

I pointed out the start and finish for him, then added, "You can't see it from here, but there's a church about a mile ahead with a parking lot where we can turn around."

"Sounds good to me," said Crazy Horse.

Agreeable son of a bitch, I thought.

"Get out," I said to Linda.

"Oh, why can't I ride?" she whined. "It would be fun, and besides, it's cold outside."

"I'm a little worried about the pavement. It might be dangerous and I'm not in the mood to get someone killed tonight. I know what you can do, though."

"What?" she said with hope.

I pulled my flashlight out of the glove box, flipped it on and off to check it, and handed it to Linda. "You're the starter. Take this flashlight and run up there and stand behind the power pole on the right. Our two cars will come up together and stop at the line. Then, when we gun our engines, flip on the light towards us."

"Okay, Sonny." Giggling, she fluttered off towards the starting line.

Bitching and moaning came from Crazy Horse's car as passengers steamed out into the cold. Through his open door I yelled, "We're going on the light," and motioned towards Linda by the pole.

He nodded back with a salute, as in a duel, a respect thing that I liked him for. Turning my '40, I idled towards the line in the right-hand lane and stopped short about ten feet back. Crazy Horse did a couple of hops, cleaning his tires and motor. The roar of his motor and the squeal of his tires brought my demons back, leaping and dancing across my dash. The little devils bounced up on my shoulders and began pulling my hair, anticipating another thrill ride. They brought me back out of the doldrums.

Crazy Horse stopped left of me; I slammed down on the throttle and laid two black smoky lines of rubber on the pavement. Backing up, I stopped next to Crazy Horse, then we both rolled in, fender to fender. Putting everything out of my head, I raised the rpm, keeping one eye on my tachometer and the other on Linda.

The light flashed and we were gone. I struggled for traction on the damp pavement. It was worse than I thought. With tires slipping and then catching, I had to feather the throttle going through first gear, and Crazy Horse was doing the same. With motors whining between shifts and getting in and out of the throttle, it wasn't pretty: two cars with big motors that we couldn't use because the road was way too wet for racing. I got into high just as Crazy Horse shifted, which unhooked his tires, and he began to drift into my lane. Side by side, we were going a hundred when he got smart and let up. I went by the mailbox two car lengths ahead of the Impala.

At the turnaround in the church parking lot we talked through our open windows.

"I'd of had you if my tires hadn't broke loose on the wet pavement," said Crazy Horse.

"Yeah, maybe," I said, lighting a cigarette. "That road is slicker than snot on a doorknob. I think we best postpone this until we get a dryer road to play on."

"That's okay with me," said Crazy Horse. "No use in killing ourselves."

The excuse of the wet pavement let me off the hook in a way. In a full-on blast, down a dry warm quarter mile, he would have beat my ass fair and square. This was not lost on my demons, who disappeared in the disappointment. They too knew I'd been outmatched, which was something new. On the good side, the outcome gave me a warning and some time to plan.

Back at the starting line, Joey, in the Hawk, was in the start position in the right lane, revving its motor. A wild-ass little shit, being invincible, he wanted to race.

Not me. I was done for the night. And like me, Crazy Horse drove right on by, letting Joey wind his motor by himself.

"Brr, it's cold out there," Linda said as she hopped in next to me and slammed the door. "We didn't think you guys were ever coming back." Shivering, she reached the red shop rag from my steering wheel, blew her nose on it, and wadded it up in her hands.

I didn't like that a lot.

"How did the race go? You won, didn't you?"

"It was a tie," I lied, staring straight ahead. I wasn't

going to brag and have to eat it later. "Nose to nose at the finish line."

"Wow, he's fast, isn't he?" she said.

"Yeah," I answered. "He's fast, all right."

I drove around the spectators in a lazy arc to head back, and noticed some commotion going on. Joey was out of his car and was yelling some shit at Crazy Horse, calling him out for not racing him. Crazy Horse was calmly explaining to Joey about the slippery track and all, when Joey yelled: "You're nothing but a goddamned chickenshit Indian!"

"That does it," Crazy Horse fumed. "Get ready to get your ass whipped and hang on to your hair."

My mind went directly to what Frank had said: *I hope that kid comes out alive.*

Crazy Horse ordered everyone back out of the car, spun around with gravel flying, and pulled into the left lane.

"Oh boy!" Linda jumped out of my car, ran to the power pole, turned, and pointed the flashlight with both hands.

She flicked the light and they dug in, getting a surprisingly good start. Both were running 4-speeds so they were shifting simultaneously. When the cars went for third, the rear of the Studebaker drifted to the left into Crazy Horse's lane. They collided, sending sparks into the dark sky. The Impala was pulling ahead but was hit again by the Hawk's front fender, making a scraping and grinding sound, causing the lighter Hawk to shoot to the right, into the gravel shoulder that pulled him into the ditch, where he went careening ahead, leaving a rooster tail of rocks and water. *Oh my God, Frank was right.*

Going like hell, he tilted over in the ditch and hit a culvert, cartwheeling frontwards down the ditch over and over, headlights and taillights revolving like a slot machine, with the interior lights flashing on and off, telling me the doors came open at least once. The sound of the car being battered was unforgettable. Suddenly the whole calamity stopped.

Oh shit, could anyone survive what I just saw? I spun around in the gravel, Linda piled in on the run, and I raced towards the wreck. Up ahead, Crazy Horse's headlights seesawed back and forth in the road as he turned to come back to where Joey left the pavement.

I stopped close, left my headlights on, and leaped out. The Hawk was upside down in the ditch with the wheels still spinning and one headlight glowing through the murky water. Freddy was fifty feet out in the field, sitting up and moaning with his head in his hands. Thank God he was alive.

"Linda, go check on Freddy!" I yelled, leaping the ditch, splashing hard on the other side. I yanked on the door handle that was out of the water but it wouldn't open. It was in a bind and the windows were closed. Joey was drowning.

Crazy Horse came on the run, carrying a steel fence post he'd uprooted out of the ditch. I took it and broke out the passenger side window and dropped to my knees in the mud to see Joey lying across the headliner, submerged. I pulled his head out of the water. His face was cold and blue.

"Is he dead?" shrieked Crazy Horse.

"If he's not he will be soon."

Careful-like, we slid Joey out into the muddy field. He was cold like a fish.

"I'm going for a blanket!" I yelled and took a long running jump back over the ditch, yanked open my car door, and ripped my army blanket off the seat.

Back at the Hawk we rolled Joey up in the blanket. The rolling got him coughing and spitting water.

"He's alive!" Crazy Horse said.

"Stay with him! I'm going to the church to call the ambulance."

By then, other cars from our group had arrived. I split the crowd, who seemed dazed and stood motionless, like watching a scene in a movie. I jumped into my '40 and blew up the highway towards the church. Oh so cautious, my demons appeared again. It must have been the excitement and the way I was abusing the '40.

Lights were on in the parsonage. Good. Leaving the motor running, I ran for the porch and pounded on the door with my demons still riding me and leaning into the scene, revved up and curious like they were.

The door opened, and an older gentleman wearing a collar said, "Come in, son. Is something wrong?"

Seeing the collar, the demons retreated into my mind somewhere, in fear of something heavenly.

Hurrying, I said, "There's been an accident. Could I use your phone?"

"Oh my goodness. Sure you can. Is anyone hurt?"

"Yes there is. Two, and I need to call an ambulance."

"Oh my God!" He quick found the number and handed me the phone. "Telephone the police," he said, "and they will relate it to the hospital. That way it will only be one call. It costs a dime to call town, you know."

The preacher gave me his address and I told the dispatcher that we had a driver near unconscious and another shook up and to please hurry with the ambulance. She kept me on the phone until she had relayed the call to a roving squad car and the hospital. I told her to call the towing company with the same information.

"You got it," she said and hung up.

"That will be ten cents." Clearing his throat.

All I had was two pennies, a nickel, and a quarter. "Here's a quarter," I said sarcastically. "Maybe you could put a good word in for me."

He smiled. "Your friends will be in my prayers."

"Thanks." I bounded off the porch, jumped into my '40, and drove hell-bent for the wreck.

Freddy was in the warm Impala, being comforted by nurturing females, so I parked and ran to the Hawk, where Joey was still coughing and spitting blood while gaping at me with a toothless mouth. He seemed dazed. Crazy Horse, keeping steady arms around him, wasn't letting him move, talking to him. We waited like that. It seemed for eternity. Cold and wet, I wondered why we do these things—racing for glory. It didn't seem so glorious all of a sudden.

Headlights showed and I hoped for the ambulance but it was just a car, and it went gawking past with noses pressed to the glass with opinionated righteousness.

They knew what we had been doing out here and some felt we got what we deserved. Guess people forget pretty fast about growing up.

Soon I could see flashing red lights coming from the north and for once it was good news. The policeman pulled up and stopped. He finished with something he was saying on his mic, then exited his car. Passing everyone, he went straight to the Hawk and dropped on his knees in front of Joey. He asked him some questions about how he felt and where he hurt and so forth. Joey gurgled out some words.

The cop turned to me. "Sonny Mitchell, I know you What are you doing way out here?"

"Just a drive in the country, sir," I said. "You think he'll be all right?"

"I hope so," he said, not amused. He knew me and knew what we'd been doing for sure.

The policeman turned to the crowd, asking how the accident occurred. With a lot of hums and haws and so forth the crowd mutually agreed that the Hawk had hit a slippery spot in the road just as the Impala was passing. The other vehicles were out for an evening drive and just happened upon the wreck. Of course the officer didn't believe a damn bit of it but wrote it down anyway.

Joey got a ride to the hospital in an ambulance and Bruce towed the Hawk to the wrecking yard.

When we arrived back at Pop's, my mood was pretty somber and Linda was a basket case. A crowd gathered around my '40 and the talk was about the wreck, and soon the conversation changed to gory details that made their eyes big. I guess some things just don't change. Crashing speed and blood make for big drama. I've been close to it with friends and it's not so cool, I'm telling you.

Linda recovered pretty well on the trip to her house. What we'd been through made me think of things close and important. "Say Hi to Marylyn for me. Okay?"

"I'll pass it on. She'll be real glad to hear it."

I loved the sound of that.

Chapter 15

The next day at Pop's, Bruce's '55 was sitting next to Joe's car, so I parked and went in to find the boys slouched in a booth next to the cigarette machine. It was a slow day at Pop's, so Joe was relaxed and drinking a Coke, listening to Bruce bullshit about something. I plopped down next to Joe. Bruce was telling what he knew about the race at Oakdale Road.

"Sonny could probably fill you in on the first part of the episode," Bruce said. "Right, Sonny?"

"Well, it's pretty simple," I started in. "First, I was racing the Crazy Horse guy and getting my ass kicked while damn near wrecking my car."

Angie brought me a Coke. After a swallow, I went on about Joey wanting to be a hero and how he about killed himself, along with another boy who was with him.

"Did you really get beat?" asked Joe.

"When we crossed the finish line I was ahead, but only because neither of us could get down the track, and the times when things were going good, he was pulling away from me. I know he's got more go; not much, but enough for a couple car lengths, I'd say."

"So you need some more horsepower?" Bruce asked.

"Yeah, I sure do, but I don't want to pay much for it. This racing thing is about over for me, but I ain't taking to this getting beat too well either."

"Joey's Hawk's got a blower on it, and I don't think he's going to need it anymore," said Bruce.

"I know about the blower, but is it available?"

"The car's down in the bullpen, and Joey's dad called from the hospital and said he never wants to see it again. I told him it was totaled and the insurance company would sell it off to a wrecking yard after settling up with him."

"Count me in for the blower and the drive if you think you can get it."

"I was thinking we should buy the whole car together," Bruce said, "and sell off the parts. You'll end up with the blower for free."

"Why do you need me in on the deal?"

"Because you have a bank full of money."

"Okay, Bruce. I'll do it, but it's going to leave me short for a while."

"My heart bleeds for you." He rolled his eyes.

That evening, I made a call to Billy's dorm to ask him what he thought about my blower idea. But first, I brought him up on the happenings around Willamette. He was surprised to hear about the outcome out on Oakdale Road. Not so much about the wreck as about how fast the Impala was. I told him about my plans of mounting the blower on the front of the Olds and asked him what he thought. He said it was a great idea and explained how it would be a simple way to get some more go out of my '40.

As usual, it was easy for Billy. He was close to a mechanical genius. I told him I was looking forward to seeing him on spring break and to start planning something fun for Joe's bachelor party. We said our good-byes.

A week later, Bruce and I were proud owners of a totaled Studebaker Hawk. We spent the weekend at the towing company shop dismantling it. We were thinking the engine, four-speed, and posi-trac rear end were going to fetch some big numbers. It was all first class–like, the leather upholstery and the AM/FM radio setup. I retrieved everything that had anything to do with the blower, including the boost meter.

A few days went by. It was late February, raining, and I was pulling lumber off the green chain. The mill was mostly open—covered, but no walls—so I could see most of the early part of the log-milling process. And I was across a small lot from the sawmill office, which was cut off by the chain-link fence that surrounded the mill property. Through the fence, I could see people coming and going. I'd see the office employees, who had their own parking spaces and offices in the building. They parked in the spaces opposite the office from me, then stepped around and entered on the mill side of the building. The regulars included the owner, of course, Mr. Dunlap, a broad-chested gent of middle age wearing khakis and a baseball hat. He drove a Lincoln. I liked him from a distance. He'd give me a wave if I caught his eye. I enjoyed watching all this action on the business side of the mill.

So it was a big deal that afternoon when a new car showed up in front of the office. It was an eye-popper, a mile long and red—a Pontiac Bonneville that had that new-car, "look at me" look. The driver unloaded. It was Clive, the swing-shift foreman. He was in his thirties, I guessed, and was small and wiry, and strode for the office prouder than shit—looking like he hoped we got a good look at his car and who was driving it. I'd seen him arrive every day but never noticed what he was driving before that day. One could tell about a person by what he drove, and this guy was making some kind of a statement.

Then J. R.'s Buick came up the street and pulled in right between the Pontiac and Mr. Dunlap's Lincoln. I about came out of my shoes. What the hell was J. R. doing there? Was it about me? Was he going to get me fired?

He got out and slammed the door with authority. He was wearing a suit and carried a briefcase under his left arm and hitched up his pants with the other. Pulling his fedora down, he leaned into the rain and headed for the door of the office like he was on a mission. Anyone watching would have noticed him.

While yanking boards, I kept my eye on the door for the half hour he was inside. Then he reappeared through the door, along with Mr. Dunlap. They were so engrossed in their conversation, they continued talking, hunched in the rain. They were a solemn pair, standing there by the door, and whatever they were discussing wasn't good.

I kept pulling lumber, wondering and worrying a little about what might become of the meeting between the old bosses.

Later in the week, the day foreman, Sage, stopped by on his rounds and shoved an envelope into my pocket.

Oh God, I'm fired. It took my breath.

"It's a questionnaire the mill hands out," Sage said, "after a guy's been here a few months—a ritual the old man has done since the beginning."

Whew! Breathing again, I heard him tell me, "He wants to know how you like it here and if you got any complaints and so on. Fill it out and drop it by the office in a day or so. The girl in there is named Sharon and she will look it over for you."

"Thanks, Sage," I said.

After work, I hightailed it for the towing shop, where I found Bruce in front of the bullpen unhooking the wrecker from a smashed-in potato chip truck. He had a bag of Lay's in his hand and was attempting to talk to me with his mouth full of them. The shop was empty, so I pulled the '40 in and lifted the hood. Then I spread all the blower parts I had taken off the Studebaker motor out on the bench. There was space for the pump, but I needed a way to get the crank pulley to fit the Olds. Everything else looked pretty simple.

The following day, I took some of the parts to a machine shop and, with my hood open, explained what I was trying to do. The machinist took measurements off my crankshaft and kept the pulley, saying he'd make me a hub to use the same pulley so I could get power off the crankshaft of the Olds and send it up to the blower. He said he'd have it for me in a week or so, and I thanked him and left.

After work the next day, I reported to the mill office with my filled-out questionnaire. I recognized the girl behind the counter as someone I'd gone to high school with. She was a couple of years older and was good-looking in a secretary way: she wore glasses, was nicely dressed, and had good posture—a father's dream, I thought.

She motioned me to the chair on her side of the counter. "Sonny Mitchell, huh?"

I sat. "That's correct. I've been working here for nearly a year."

"My name is Sharon, Sharon Bell. I think that my sister and you are friends. Her name is Susan."

"That's right," I said with mixed emotions. "I've been getting to know her as of late."

"I remember you in school. Weren't you friends with Billy Wheeler?"

I became more attentive. "Still am. He goes to the university now."

"I really had it for him," she confessed with a blush.

"He's a special guy." I wondered how Billy could have overlooked her—maybe she was a wallflower just now coming into bloom, or maybe Billy was so predisposed with school he missed her. Billy could get so engrossed in something that he was prone to letting something slip by.

She began reading the questionnaire to herself.

Nosey-like, I asked, "What's old Swanson doing around here?"

"Oh, he's our banker—he finances the mill."

"I saw him here Monday and he didn't look real happy."

"The mill is losing money—oh!" She put her hand in front of her mouth. "I shouldn't have said that. Don't you be telling anyone I said that, okay?"

"I won't," I said. I decided to pry a little more since Sharon seemed willing to talk. "I have a special interest in his daughter, Marylyn, so I'm curious about what the old man's up to."

"Oh, yes, Marylyn is a friend of Susan's. She's a wonderful girl—what is your interest, if I may ask?"

"I'm in love with her," I blurted out. My face felt hot.

Sharon put the paper down. Her eyes combed me as she bit down on her pencil, like she was assessing my flannel shirt and my ideas for J. R. Swanson's daughter.

Suddenly, I felt embarrassed standing there in my mill rat getup.

She pulled the pencil from her mouth. "The mill owner, Mr. Dunlap, and his banker, J. R. Swanson, have meetings regularly, trying to figure out where the money is going."

Whew, I must have passed her test.

"This is totally off the record, you know," she said.

"I understand."

"For about two years," she said. "Slowly at first, but it's getting worse now. Whatever it is has us baffled. Everything has looked good to me. The logs come in and the lumber goes out. Well, there's something sick going on here."

"I wish I could help."

"Keep your eyes open, Sonny."

"Yeah, and my mouth shut."

She gave me a smile, then checked off a couple of items on the bottom of my questionnaire. "Looks like we're done here. If you have any problems or anything, don't be afraid to come see me."

"You got it," I said.

Chapter 16

I drove to Pop's out of habit, with the mill problem still eating on me.

Eddy was parked, drinking a Coke in his little Simca car, which was pumping tiny clouds out of its one-inch exhaust pipe. Since he was advertising the warmth of his car, I pulled mine onto the gravel and climbed in with him.

It was a typical weeknight at the restaurant. Cars were parked in the slots with trays attached to their open windows, letting out bits and pieces of rock 'n' roll from the radios, and there was constant chatter from over the new intercom as teenagers were out for the evening. The usual souls were in attendance, along with the clatter of carhops jostling dishes and sprinting through the rain back and forth to the kitchen.

I got the first word in for a change. "What's going on, Eddy?"

"Nothing. I'm thinking of going to the drive-in tonight. It's open during February, you know."

"Yeah, I know. What's on?"

"*Psycho*."

"No shit?"

"Yep."

"You going alone?"

"Are you kidding? You wanna go?"

"Maybe."

"Everyone's talking about the wreck," he said, changing the subject. "Wish I hadn't had to work and miss it."

"I bet you are," I said. "It turned out awful. I guess it could have been worse—Joey and Freddy could have been killed."

"So, if the road was so slippery, why did they go ahead with it?" Eddy asked.

"It was a case of teenage testosterone and male ego," I said. "Joey was stupid enough to want to race on a track that was dangerous and then called Crazy Horse out with an insult, which turned into more than he wanted."

Over my shoulder, I saw Gary's Mercury roll into the lot, windows down. He was so small I could hardly see the little fart in the big car. He was all reared back and slouched, looking cool, wearing some nice duds. He had been working downtown at the men's store selling clothes, so he was coming up in the world. The Mercury fit him to a T—a babe magnet—dropped down with whitewall tires and spinner hubcaps that twinkled from the light reflecting off the million bulbs that lit up the place. Seeing us, he showed off another loop and then landed next to the Simca on Eddy's side. "Well," he said, looking at the little car sarcastic-like, "you guys are living large tonight."

We bullshitted back and forth, the usual bantering, until Gary came up with, "So what's up tonight?"

"Eddy here wants to go see *Psycho*—it's on at the drive-in."

"Let's do it," Gary said. "I've heard it will scare the living shit out of you."

"Well," I said, "we got a problem."

"What's that?"

"We don't have any money," Eddy broke in.

"Horseshit, Sonny's got more money than God," Gary said.

"I gave all my cash to Bruce for car parts and I'm down to 28 cents," I said.

"I got three quarters," said Eddy.

"I've got a dollar," Gary said. "So, since I'm the big money guy, I'll drive and you guys get the trunk."

We piled in with Gary, who swung around by the Huntsmen Tavern, where they'd been selling me beer. I wasn't twenty-one yet, but I guess I was beginning to look enough like it. With the ninety-nine-cent six-pack, we took the Champagne Flight for the drive-in, where a movie cost a buck. So we were looking at a two-dollar evening if everything went well.

A block away, it was possible to see the back of the big screen silhouetted against the night sky. Gary drove past the back gate, thinking there was a chance it wouldn't be guarded. We'd slipped through it without paying before, but tonight they had a sentry—a kid wielding a flashlight like he was defending the homeland.

Gary drove close to the front gate, but out of sight of the ticket booth, and stopped where we could crawl into the trunk unnoticed. Eddy was tall and so was I, making us almost too big for the trunk. We coiled up, contorting with grunts, sharing the space with a jack and a spare tire and some empty beer bottles. It was dusty and smelled of old road dirt from years of being the lonely end of the car.

Gary locked us in with a click familiar to a convict but not to me. I was claustrophobic until I heard the tires rolling on gravel as he pulled up to the ticket booth. The conversation was clear as a bell, as if they were in the trunk with us. "Hi, Marjorie, you're sure looking good tonight." Gary knew every girl in town.

"Oh, Gary," she giggled. "You say that to all the girls."

Eddy let a rip-roaring fart and then tried to contain his laughing. I held my breath, trying to keep from being gassed to death.

Hurry the hell up, Gary, I was thinking.

"How about letting me in free tonight, Marjorie," Gary asked.

"Let's get out of here," I whispered through clinched teeth, loud enough for Gary to hear.

"Just this once, Gary," Marjorie cooed.

"Hurry up. Goddamn it," I wheezed. "I'm suffocating."

Gary turned up his radio to block the commotion in the trunk and we were off to the movies. He let us out in the shadows of the back row. I uncoiled, gasping for fresh air. Eddy was still laughing, so I gave him a shove and told him to get in the backseat. "You're a creep, Eddy."

"Shut up and get in, you guys," Gary said. "If they see you, we'll get kicked out. The cartoon's on. Let's see if Mickey can score with Minnie for a change."

I hooked the speaker on the window and rolled it up, shutting out the winter cold. I hunkered down in the seat, ready to get scared, popped an Oly, and had it up to my mouth when I saw it right in front of me. "Shit," I blurted out. "That's Swanson's Buick parked in front of us."

"So what?" said Gary.

Son of a bitch, I thought.

"Nothing," I said, recovering. "Let's watch the movie."

Through the steamy back window of the Buick, I could make out two silhouettes sitting in the backseat. The one on the right was tall and had long hair—it had to be Marylyn. Being that close sent nice chills up my spine. Here I was twenty-five feet from the Swanson family drinking a beer and smoking a cigarette. *I'm glad old Swanson can't see me*, I thought. He'd have a shit fit for sure.

The Buick's left rear door popped open, flashing on its interior light, confirming for me Marylyn was in the car, bringing me to the edge of my seat. A boy, who I presumed was her brother, Harold, slammed the door and took off on a run for the snack bar.

"I gotta take a leak," I lied. I didn't need to use the bathroom—I just wanted to take a look at the boy and see what he was like. I got out and headed in. I stepped up behind him in line, where he was buying candy.

He turned around to leave, holding his box of Dots like it was precious. "Hey, I've seen you before. You're Sonny Mitchell, the guy who saved my big sis. Wait until I tell them in the car. They'll be surprised."

"Whoa, now, let's keep it a secret," I said, bringing my index finger to my lips. "Just between us, for fun. Okay?"

"Okay," he said, reluctant-like. "But I'll tell Marylyn later," he said, smiling with a mouth full of Dots. "She loves you."

A cloud of warmth settled over me like a blanket with hearts all over it. I wanted to yell hallelujah. "Tell her I asked about her."

"Okay. Could I ride in your hot rod sometime?" he asked.

"Sure," I said.

Harold backed out the swinging door with candy in both hands. Then, with shoelaces untied, he shuffled for the Buick.

I took the other door out so as not to advertise which car I was in. I had no idea if my new friend was loyal to me or not, and I didn't need a showdown with old Swanson at the movie. He'd think for sure I was following them around like some kind of nutcase.

Back in the Mercury, we settled in to watch *Psycho*. Alfred Hitchcock took our minds and led us on a scary-as-hell adventure, with Norman, who worked out of the Bates Motel, murdering young women to the happiness of his dead mother. Figure that one out.

We sat there like stone, with Eddy on the edge of his seat with his head between us, breathing in my ear.

Sometimes he would forget to breathe for a while and then jolt over a scary twist and choke for air.

I wondered what Marylyn thought as she was watching the very same thing at the same time.

Then it was over, and we all breathed again—what a scary rush the ending was.

Gary started the Mercury, bringing me out of Hitchcock's clutches, and lit up his lights, revealing the back of the Buick. Marylyn was still there.

The Buick lost itself in the maze of traffic heading for the exit gate. I rode in silence. I was enjoying what Harold had told me. In fact, it was hard for me to be quiet about it.

"So, Sonny, what did you think of the show?" asked Gary, pulling into Pop's.

"What? Oh," I said. "It was worth going to for sure, and if I'd had the money, I'd probably have paid to see it." I got out of Gary's car.

In the privacy of my car, I howled with pleasure. Harold had brought me back from the doldrums. I felt better than I had in weeks.

Chapter 17

She loves me. The words rocked my brain. What a difference Harold had made in my attitude by cluing me in on his sister's feelings for me. Without her permission, I was sure. Simply a little boy going rogue—innocent with no agenda, just a means of fixing things in his own way. I was smiling—even in the rain.

I was constantly reminded of how two people could love each other. I was envious but very happy for Angie and Joe. They were happy together as she went about the affairs of planning a wedding. March 11 was the last day of school before spring break; the wedding was planned for Saturday the 19th, the day after the bachelor party. Also, Joe was busy looking for employment. I wasn't really worried about Joe. Knowing him, I was sure he would pester someone into a job.

A week went by, and meanwhile, at the mill, J. R. rolled in every other day or so with a reminder of Marylyn swarming all over him. Then he'd tromp into the little office with a concerned look on his face. It was obvious to me the situation was serious, and I wondered if there might be foul play. So I started keeping a constant vigil on the happenings around the place.

From my station at the green chain, I followed the progression of turning timber into lumber, trying to find a leak—a place in the system that didn't quite jibe, where someone could make off with something of value. The process started where log trucks came in with their loads of timber. An independent log scaler—a man who had no stake in the mill—measured a truck's load and documented the board feet it contained.

Then a man driving a log stacker removed the timber and dumped it into the log pond. The floating logs were rounded up by the pond monkey, a man who rode the logs and herded them onto a corral, where they were hooked by a chain that drug them up and into the mill. The first lumber-making tool they encountered was a machine that peeled off the bark as the logs passed by. At this point, the product that the mill bought and paid for had been measured and was safely inside the mill. So far, I couldn't see anything that stank.

From the bark grinding machine, the chain carried the logs out of my sight into the room that housed the giant moving blade. I knew that before each log reached the blade, the sawyer man sized them up and decided on how each individual log should be cut for maximum value. The cut boards then moved on to the edger man, who trimmed off the rough edges, leaving square corners. By this time, the only thing that had been removed were bark chips and sawdust, neither with great value and mostly ending up in the wigwam burner.

I felt that anything of value that could be stripped off or stolen would have to be beyond this point in the process.

I continually rolled all this around in my head, becoming an amateur sleuth in my own mind. I kinda liked having something to keep myself sane from the hours of monotony that have driven grown men wild.

At last, it was Friday. More than a week had gone by since I'd dropped off the blower pulley and hub at the machinist, so after work, I made a beeline for the machine shop. The old fella was there, hunched over a metal lathe with the last inch of cigar clinched in his mouth. He wore coveralls with the stomach area stained with cutting oil and shavings. He was standing deep in filings that he had carved off raw metal, creating parts to make the local industry turn. I stood back quiet-like as he was finishing a cut, but when he saw me, he motioned me over to observe the progress.

When the blade came to the end of the shaft, he flicked off the switch, and the whirring stopped and the old machine came to a halt. "So you're after your hub?" he grunted through the cigar smoke.

"Yeah," I said. "Is it ready?"

He tilted his head towards the front of the shop and hunched off to find the part for me.

I followed him through the maze of machines towards the office. We wound through and stepped over the clutter of shafts and bearings that to me were odds and ends of junk but were obviously raw material to him. My pulley was crowded on his desk, holding down the bill that I was to pay. The amount seemed surprisingly small to me, but according to the scrawl on the paper, it hadn't taken long to accomplish the job. I paid up and he handed over the pieces with his big blackened hands. "Have fun with these now." He grinned.

"Thanks, I plan to."

First, I needed to install the lower blower pulley on the crankshaft to make sure it was going to fit. Then we could line up the blower with the belt and make needed changes, such as hacking a hole in the inner fender area for clearance.

At the towing shop, I caught Bruce closing up and showed him the pulley. We made plans to work on the coupe the following day, which was Saturday.

Bruce helped most of the morning, and we got the pulley installed and ran the boost gauge tube through the firewall and mounted the instrument under the dash. We were ready for Billy's help on the final installation. In a week, he was coming home from college for spring break, and I was looking forward to borrowing his mechanical abilities.

Friday, March 11, was his last day of class, so we had a whole week to position the blower under the hood of my car. And I planned on telling Billy about Marylyn. All of us boys were such a tight group, we had never really shared each other with newcomers. I wasn't sure how he would take it, so I figured I'd bring it up when the time was right.

Friday after work, I waited in my '40 outside the bus station. Billy came walking out of the lobby carrying a suitcase and wearing an overcoat over a sweater. Somehow, he looked different there under the lights—more grown-up or something. No leather jacket or engineer boots might have had something to do with it.

"Get in, college boy," I yelled as I swung the '40 next to the curb. I jumped out and pumped his hand. "Welcome home, Billy."

"It's good to be back in Willamette," he said.

Moving towards my trunk, he let out a whistle. "Your car looks good and the paint matches too."

I dropped his bag in the trunk, then showed him how well the trunk lid fit.

"I got lucky. The guy who did the job was damn serious about making an old Ford look right. You'd like him. He loves cars as much as we do." We jumped in and I pulled out into traffic.

"Man, it's nice to be in a hot rod again," said Billy. "I sure miss my old coupe. College eats money so I had to sell it. I didn't want to give up on it, but there's a lot to learn out there, and I'm digging it."

I felt bad for Billy having to give up his coupe—it had meant everything to him. But like the rest of us, he was moving on.

"I'll be going next year if my job holds out long enough to pay my way. "

"What's the matter with your job?"

I explained to him about the mess the mill was in financially and how it was struggling to keep going.

"Is it the economy?"

"Partly that. And there's money leaking out some-where. It looks fishy, but nobody can figure out what's going on. J. R. Swanson, the banker downtown, finances the mill, and he shows up at the office darn near every day. He spends about an hour with the owner. I guess trying to trace where the money is going."

"Don't they measure all that stuff when it comes and goes?"

"As near as I can figure, yeah. The leak has to be somewhere in the grading and marketing."

Billy mentioned that his folks were planning a trip to the beach the coming weekend and his house would be empty starting Thursday.

"Great," I said. "Perfect for Joe's bachelor party." It was a good place to send Joe off to marriage. We'd had other parties there and had spent a lot of time at the house growing up. Billy's garage was where we'd learned to work on cars, and inside the house was where we saw our first TV. And all the time, Billy's mom and dad treated us like family.

"Sounds good to me," said Billy. "You can't hurt the place. And besides, my folks would do anything for Joe. In fact, I might even tell them. Since I don't have a car and yours is going to be down for a while, what are we going to drive?" Billy asked.

"Dad's pickup," I answered. "I used it the whole time I was fixing my car after the wreck."

Then I got lost in our discussion about the blower project. Billy had a way of getting a person's attention when talking about technical stuff.

"I'm starving for a Pop's burger," Billy said. "I haven't had one since Christmas, and I'm tired of eating baloney."

Saturday morning, I picked up Billy in the pickup, then we buzzed back to my house for the '40. Billy piled in it and followed me out to the towing shop.

Bruce was busy in the yard and Clayton was off for the day, so we had the shop to ourselves. We went right to work with the tools at hand, cutting and welding to make brackets and so on to attach the blower to its new mate, the mighty Olds motor.

Brackets made, Billy warned, "The brackets need to be attached just right so the pulley on the blower aligns perfectly with the one on the motor, or the v-belt will peel off."

Billy donned the welding helmet. "You hold this bracket here just so and I'm gonna weld it."

So with me lining up the two pulleys with the bracket, I shut my eyes while he struck an arc and married the two parts together.

"Looks good to me," I breathed in relief.

So the bracket was mounted. But when we tried bolting the blower on, we were short of space. Though the blower was low enough to miss the hood, it hit the inner fender well. We were scratching our heads on just what to do about it when in walked Clayton. I introduced him to Billy, who had some questions about the lead work Clayton had done on my '40. After they wore that out, I asked Clayton what we should do about the sheet metal problem we were having with the blower installation.

"Take off the front wheel," he said. "I'll get a hammer."

He came back with a couple of hammers and we finished removing the wheel. He took the bigger hammer and began banging on the wheel well until it gave in and began to form a bowl shape. He would beat on it a while and then we would check the fit by propping the cylinder-shaped blower for clearance. Finally, it squeezed into place. Clayton left and we went on with the process. Then we made an Oly carton into a cardboard gasket and sandwiched it between the carburetors and the sheet metal box. Using all-thread bolts, we made an airtight seal. Fortunately, the Hawk had given up enough of the large, flexible hose for us to connect the blower's air outlet to the carbs. Then we simply reinstalled the Studebaker air cleaner assembly to the inlet of the blower.

It was midnight before we fired up the motor with the new blower installed.

"Damn, this thing sounds good," Billy yelled over the whining of the blower.

I gave out a war whoop as I throttled the motor, and the belt didn't fly off, even at higher rpms. So we were satisfied that we had alignment. It was too late to test drive the car, so I locked it in the shop, and we cut out for home in the pickup.

After work on Monday, I picked up Billy at Pop's. After scanning the place, I noticed there was still no Marylyn. The good feeling I'd gotten from Harold was beginning to wane with time, and doubts were beginning to creep back into my young skull.

"Let's go give your car a go and see what it's got," said Billy with a grin.

"I can't wait," I said, coming out of my love-life stupor.

We set out for the towing shop in the pickup, talking all the time about how much the '40 was going to love the extra air brought on by the blower. Once there, Clayton helped us line up the hood so it fit perfectly and closed with a click. I jumped behind the wheel with a confident feeling and took Billy for a test drive around the block, enjoying the new whirring sound coming from the fan in the blower. Back in the shop, I opened the hood, and we went over the brackets and clamps, retightening nuts and screws and so forth.

Satisfied, Billy and I hit the street for the freeway to see how it would run at high speeds. It was raining lightly, so we weren't going to get any low-end acceleration data, but we figured we could see how the blower performed with gradual acceleration at high speeds.

We pulled out onto the interstate going south, and I shifted into second at moderate rpms and then gradually put my foot into it. As we gained rpms, the boost gauge started north and the force of the acceleration planted me into the seat. The blower made a whistling sound as it came on at higher rpms, when normally things were flattened out. At 3,500 rpms it felt like someone lit a fuse, and the afterburners turned and we were flying. Billy had that grin of his going, like speed did to him. The blower was the best of all worlds. It was there when it was needed and then it napped when the driver was going to the store.

Back at the shop, I told Billy I'd meet him at my house. I bailed out and jumped into the pickup. He drove ahead in the '40, giving me a chance to see how it looked in action. Dogging along after him in the pickup, I admired the way my '40 rolled along hugging the ground. When Billy stopped for a sign on 4th Street, he laid out a patch of rubber like a dance step for my benefit.

On our way back to Pop's together in my '40, we made a pact that we'd try to keep the blower a secret as long as we could. It would be best if Crazy Horse stayed ignorant of the fact until he got tired of looking at my rear bumper.

Pulling into Pop's was good again, knowing I had some added horsepower. The feeling was a drug I'd been needing. I kept it at an idle, the blower quiet-like.

Johnny Smith and Archie, both home for the break, were laid back in a Ford sedan that was the loaner car for Johnny's dad's dealership. Angie was just picking up their empty tray, signaling to us they were done eating.

Aha. Now would be a good time to plan the bachelor party because most of the guys were here, except Gary, who was downtown working.

"Tell 'em to follow us, Billy," I said.

"What the hell for?" he asked, rolling down the window.

"We're going down to the men's store to see Gary."

"You going to buy a new tie or something?"

"No, we're going in to find Gary and get this party thing planned out."

Billy jerked his thumb at Johnny and Archie to signal "come with us." They pulled out behind us.

The white Impala was sitting in the end slot again, the windows partly fogged up, with Crazy Horse at the wheel and the rest of the interior overflowing with feminity. I could make out Linda Nelson on the passenger side, with Susan Bell next to Crazy Horse. But with the clouded windows, I couldn't see who was in the backseat.

I gave him a wave as we drove by, hoping that he couldn't hear the blower's whispering like a lion panting.

Soon enough, he was going to hear it roar.

Chapter 18

I entered the men's clothing store with my friends, all of us in our normal duds except for Billy, who was wearing his new college sweater with the big "O" on it.

It was a small joint with suit jackets hung all over one wall, along with big photos of studs showing us what we could look like. There were shirts stacked up and piles of socks and underwear galore. Belts and boots gave the place a leathery, masculine smell. We walked around with our mouths open, looking at a whole new world of the west side of town.

You could buy a white collar here, I thought.

Gary paraded up to us wearing the latest in men's wear—gray suit, pink shirt, a thin black tie, and wingtips dripping with polish. A measuring tape draped around his neck gave him an air of being a professional.

"Jesus, Gary," I said, "you look prettier than a French pimp."

"I wish I could say the same for you guys," he shot back, running his comb through his hair.

"At least we don't look all dorky like you," said Johnny.

"A little culture, my friend." Gary pocketed the comb.

We made a simple plan for the bachelor party: alert anyone who might be a friend of Joe's, now or in the past. Tell them there would be a keg, but to bring anything they'd like to drink.

"Okay, then," Billy said. "It starts at my house Friday night at 7."

"Yep," came from all around.

We all chipped in some cash for the keg and that was about it.

Tuesday came, then Wednesday and Thursday, weekdays of working and shivering in the damp cold of March, with evenings at Pop's. The place was hopping pretty good because of spring break, but still no Marylyn. I daydreamed about her locked in a basement, tormenting over me. I felt like my feelings for her were hopeless. I began to look forward to Joe's party and a good drunk.

Friday came. After work, I grabbed Billy, and with the pickup, we went downtown to the Olympia distributor for the keg. I backed up to the dock, and between Billy and me, we managed the cold, heavy bastard into the bed of the pickup. Circling the block, we found our way onto the gut that we had journeyed together as youths. Out of habit, I turned south from the movie theater, taking us towards the Elks Club, a stately brick building. Mounted above the front door was a bronze statue of a bull elk head, staring at you no matter where you stood.

Then my eyes about popped out—Swanson's red Buick was parked in front, with J. R. and Marylyn's mom climbing out of it. Mrs. Swanson was dressed for a ball and old J. R. was looking good in a fresh suit. As we passed by, he was puffing on a cigar while holding the heavy entry door for his wife.

"Must be something special tonight," I said. "They have some real parties in there. Some last all night, I've heard people say." I drove on.

"Was that old Swanson from the bank?" Billy asked.

Now seemed a good time to tell him. "Yep. He's the father of the girl I'm gonna marry."

"You're gonna what?" He reeled around in the seat, looking at me, astonished.

"Well, there are a few obstacles I have to get over first." I filled Billy in on Marylyn and when I had met her and how we were thrown together the night of the crash.

"So what about the obstacles?"

"Well, her dad squelched the deal."

"Why'd he do that?"

"Well, I guess it's the old blue-collar, white-collar thing," I said. "He doesn't want her to spend her life with a mill rat."

"You aren't going to be a mill worker long, Sonny."

"Yeah, well, he doesn't know that."

"Jeez, I come home for one of my best friend's weddings and find out another one is teetering."

"Everything is changing, Billy. As for me, I'm in the mood to get sloshed."

Billy's house was surrounded by cars—kids' cars, lowered down, most freshly washed for the weekend. I found a space by the front porch and backed the pickup close for unloading.

"This looks like a good place to get drunk," I said to Billy, slamming the truck door.

A couple of eager-looking boys wearing muscle shirts eyed the keg from the porch.

"You guys like lifting?" I asked.

We watched with satisfaction as they grunted the thing through the front door and across the living room, past a crowd of youths who looked on with relish as the keg journeyed to the back porch. A good place—kegs could be messy.

Watching the episode from a big round table close by were most of my closest friends: Johnny, Gary, and Bruce, and of course, the guest of honor, Joe, all grinning and inviting. I drew up a chair next to Joe and said, "Let the party begin."

"The party has been going for an hour already." Gary pointed at some empties and couple of open bottles of some kind of hooch.

"Great things take time," I said. "Billy and I have been busy getting that barrel of beer you just saw go by."

Billy and I settled in, drinking stubbies with the boys over some pre-party bantering, and totally forgot about the beer keg until some commotion from the back porch got my attention.

According to a passerby—with a Santa Claus–looking, frothy beard and carrying a jar of foamy beer—an amply enthusiastic teenage reveler had manned the pump and over-pressurized the keg. The result was a wet floor, and jars and glasses of beer sitting all over the back porch, settling the surf, as the impatient were trying to stare down the foam.

Just when it looked like it was going to be a rather dull affair, with us reminiscing about more festive occasions, the front door burst open and in came Meg Olsen with her sister Denise, older girls I hadn't seen for a while.

I was thrilled at the sight of them. All of us boys were smiling. Girls weren't usually welcome at bachelor parties, but the Olsen's weren't the usual girls. We'd been friends with the Olsen sisters from way back. They grew up in our neighborhood, poor. They were older and good-looking, so they had run with the older boys but hadn't forgotten us.

Meg swaggered up to the table in her usual cocky way and planted a fifth of Cuervo in front of Joe, laid those big red lips of hers on his with a smack, then said, "Well, now, looky what we got here. Little Joey is getting married. It's about time one of you Little Bastards did something productive."

A third girl, who had followed, squeezed herself between the Olsens for a peek at Joe. She was a stranger to me, showing off a pile of purple hair and ample rouge, like she'd come straight from a beauty salon. She wore the apron of a working girl and was carrying a plastic tub. "We're going to take good care of you," she giggled, and gave Joe a pinch on the cheek as she passed by, heading for the kitchen.

Joe's eye's were wide. And so were everyone else's.

After a nod from me, Gary and Johnny gave up their chairs to the Olsens, and leaned in from their positions behind our guests.

"Where's Sharon?" asked Meg, looking around.

"Come on in, Sharon!" Denise hollered towards the door, still open. "It looks friendly in here!"

Sharon Bell entered with caution in her eyes.

"Oh my gosh, Sharon!" I said, surprised. "What are you doing here?"

She looked relieved, seeing someone she knew, and then beamed when she saw Billy sitting next to me at the table. Before I could react with some kind of chivalry, she grabbed a lonely chair and pressed herself between him and me. She offered her hand to Billy as I made the introduction, raising my voice over all the whoopee going on. Billy was liking the introduction too. There was a lot of smiling from our table.

The girl wearing purple hair and an apron returned from the kitchen, steamy water in her tub, and placed it on the floor in front of Joe with a slosh.

"Who in the world is that?" I asked Sharon.

"She's Anna from the Front Street Salon," she said. "We all became friends from frequenting the place. She's a riot. We have a lot of fun down there."

Anna knelt in front of Joe and removed his boots and socks and began washing his feet in the hot water, making Joe's face even redder. His look turned concerned when she flashed tools of her trade from the pockets of her apron: shiny chrome instruments used for cutting and trimming, not unlike what a surgeon would carry in his bag.

Denise filled a shot glass from the bottle of Cuervo and produced a lime, a pocketknife, and a salt shaker from her jacket. Joe was then introduced to the world of tequila shots as he received his first and probably last pedicure.

"How'd you guys find out about the party, anyhow?" I asked.

"We were all down at Anna's shop today and Joe's name came up."

"I'd heard about Joe getting married," said Meg, "so we figured you guys would have a wingding to send him off. So all I had to do was call Angie at Pop's and drag it out of her. You know, about the party and all."

"She told you?" Joe rolled his eyes.

"It wasn't easy," said Meg. "You got quite a girl there."

While others were talking and doing Joe's toenails and such, I was throwing back shots of Cuervo, getting bombed. And my friends' faces warmed with cheer, and the noise level elevated while the alcohol melted away our restraints.

Through the gentle fog that had settled in on me, I noticed Sharon couldn't keep her eyes off Billy. They talked nonstop.

"Billy," she said, "you're a lot different when your nose isn't stuck in a schoolbook. You were so serious in school that you didn't even give me the time of day."

"It couldn't have been that bad, could it?" Billy answered with a slight grin.

"You had that slide rule so far up your ass that you hadn't a clue what was going on around you," she said with a laugh.

Billy weighed back in and on they went, jabbing at each other.

From the back porch came a yell of triumph.

Sharon turned to me. "What was that?"

"They must have finally outsmarted the keg," I said through my numbing lips.

"Oh," she said. "So what's going on with you and Marylyn Swanson?"

"Nothing, unfortunately."

"Have you been to see her? She ain't going to wait forever, you know."

That sobered me a little. "Her dad told me I couldn't see her, and like a dumb shit I didn't argue."

"That's horseshit what that old prick's doing," said Billy. "Why don't you go see her? In fact, why don't we go see her right now." Billy was looking at me with eyes that were softening like he was getting a little wasted himself.

"I don't know," I said. "I'm screwed either way."

"I rather be screwed with her than without her," he said, laughing.

"Let's go," Sharon said.

"Yeah," Billy said. "Her folks are at the Elks getting drunk and won't have a clue. You said those parties last all night."

"Hey, Joe," Billy hollered. "We gotta run an errand, but we'll be right back."

Joe nodded, not taking his eyes off Anna and the operation on his feet.

After a pull up from Sharon, I scooped up a bottle from the table and slid it under my arm for a little more fortification. Even being drunk on my ass, I was worried about going to the Swansons' for a visit.

Chapter 19

Billy drove the pickup with Sharon shivering between us, hugging the heater, something I thought funny since I couldn't have felt the cold if I'd been sitting in an ice bucket. Passing the bottle back and forth, I took two swigs to their one, something I needed for my nerves, I told myself. We entered the Swansons' neighborhood with its big houses.

"Damn, we're in the big-shot neighborhood," Sharon remarked. "These are definitely upper crust, and there's the Swanson house, the upper thrust of the upper crust."

I burst out laughing and then the whole pickup was rocking with it.

We rolled by the big house. A light was on in an upstairs room. "That's Harold's room," I said, trying to serious up. "He's Marylyn's little brother," I slurred. My mouth was numb and my lips were getting big, making it hard to talk.

Billy circled the block, with us giggling like schoolgirls, and drew up to the curb between the street that led to the Elks Club and the Swansons' house.

"I'm parking here so Sharon will be able to see their car coming up the street on the chance the Swansons come home early."

"Don't you want to come with us, Sharon?"

"Hell, no," said Sharon. "I'm not leaving this heater."

"If you see a big red Buick coming," said Billy, "lay on the horn."

"Okay, I've got it," she laughed. "Big car—toot, toot."

Why was everything so funny?

"Be serious, Sharon," I slurred again. "We're on an important mission."

Billy and I stumbled out into the rain and wobbled down the street, which was lit up by fancy streetlights, past pricey homes with manicured lawns. We kitty-cornered across the Swanson front lawn, and sloshed around the garage to the other side of the house, and arrived under the lit-up window of Harold's room. I tried the pebble-window thing like in the movies, but I was so plastered, I couldn't hit my ass with both hands. Billy plinked one dead center first try.

"Why is it I'm always better at these things than you are?" Billy asked.

"I think I've finally found something I can do better than you." I wrapped my arm around his shoulder.

"Oh yeah? What's that?"

"Drinkin'."

The curtain opened, showing Harold's silhouette. He lifted the window and stuck his head out in the rain to see where the rock had come from. He whispered, "Is that you, Sonny?"

"Yeah, where's Marylyn?"

"Keep it down," he said. "You'll wake the whole neighborhood."

I thought it was kind of a grown-up thing to say, coming from a little boy.

"Where's your sister?" I whispered.

"She's taking a bath."

I gasped. Even in my alcoholic-induced state, the vision in my head of Marylyn naked shocked me.

"Open the door and let us in," Billy said.

"No, I can't," he said

"Why?" asked Billy.

"I'm not supposed to open it after dark."

"How we going to get in then?" I asked. "I want to see Marylyn."

"There's a ladder hanging on the side of the woodshed. Get it and you can use the window."

"Harold's a genius!" Billy said. "Let's get the ladder."

Trying to be serious again, I said, "It would be the romantic option, I guess."

We grabbed the ladder off the side of the woodshed and carted it towards the house, stumbling this way and that like Laurel and Hardy. A light came on in the adjacent room and its window slid up with Harold's head popping out of it. "Over here, you guys," he ordered.

Billy shoved the ladder up the siding, raking it with a thump, thump, thump as it peeled the paint off the boards. Then he planted the bottom of the ladder and Harold held the top. I started climbing the slippery rungs, gassed to the point that the normally easy task was a challenge.

Another silhouette, who I presumed was Marylyn, appeared next to Harold. *God, I hope my nose isn't running*, I thought.

"Oh, no," she said, "my hair!" and then vanished.

Oh my God, it's her. What am I doing here? She hates me, I thought through my drunken fog. With all the prodding from Billy and Sharon about coming to visit, I hadn't considered whether Marylyn was going to like it.

I got to the window. Seeing Harold big-eyed, the whole thing got funny to me again and I got to chuckling over my success in reaching the top of the ladder. But then I began wondering how I was going to get into the window. A graceful way would be to extend a leg through and then duck under and in. But because of the shape I was in, this would be impossible without falling backwards off the ladder and killing myself. So I slithered in on my belly, limp as a wet towel. I rolled onto my back—a mistake because the room started to spin. I was spread eagle, holding on to the floor that rotated me in circles. I could see Harold going by like he was watching me ride a merry-go-round.

"What's wrong with you," asked Harold. "Are you okay?"

"I had a martini on the way over. I think it must have been bad." I felt Billy roll up next to me all cold and wet and laughing.

"Hi, I'm Billy." He stood, sizing up the situation, then said to Harold, "You're Harold. Why don't you show me your room?"

"Okay," Harold answered. "I got a new model car," and out the door they went.

The ceiling was still going around in circles when a pair of concerned dark eyes fell on me. The beautiful dark eyes and red lips I had been missing so much.

Marylyn sat next to me on the floor and pulled my head into her lap with warm hands. She held me there, making the room stop going around so I could focus on her face, so beautiful and fresh and feminine.

"Hi, Sonny. It's about time you came to see me," came her voice and her humor.

The shock of being in Marylyn's arms brought me around some, so I felt able to carry on a fairly normal conversation. I wanted her to know why I was sloshed.

"We came from Joe's bachelor party where there was some toasting and I had too much toast, I guess." I thought it was funny but Marylyn just smiled at me. "I've wanted to come sooner," I said, "but I didn't want to disrespect your dad. Now I've done that, and I suppose he'll never forgive me."

"He will have to find out first, and I'm not telling and Harold owes me, so he won't be tattling either. Linda told me about Dad running you off. I suspected as much, but Dad doesn't tell me a lot."

"When I enter the university this fall, hopefully your father will see 'State' written all over me, and he may change his mind about all this."

"He is a stern man," Marylyn said. "But he's not stupid. He knows he can't run my life forever." Marylyn bent down to kiss me. I could feel the warmth of her lips coming close. I rose up to meet them—a horn began beeping like mad and her lips pulled away. Billy came busting through the door with Harold following.

"Your folks are coming," Billy said to Marylyn.

"Oh crap," I said. "I think we better be leaving now."

Billy went out the window like a burglar with a pitchfork after him.

I choked out a hurried good-bye to Marylyn and, charged with adrenaline, stuffed myself through the window onto the ladder, then turned to see Billy running towards my pickup, which was pulling up to the curb as headlights flashed across the lawn on the opposite side of the house. Shit, J. R. was there.

Marylyn's light flicked off, leaving me in darkness at the top of the ladder, bombed out of my mind, fearing nothing at all. The ladder began to slide sideways, scratching along the siding, taking me with it. Harold's head poked out his window, watching me fall away from him. The further I slid, the further he leaned out, until I was afraid he was going to fall too. It was a wonderful feeling flying through the air, riding the ladder drunk as a skunk, until I crashed. Then I figured I was dead for sure. But I'd landed in a scratchy, pokey lilac bush, and I was alive, which I thought was terribly funny.

I rolled out of the bush backwards like a diver leaving a boat and ran, pulling stickers out of my pants, and fell into an abyss, stuck my arms out to catch my fall, and my left hand hit concrete, making a cracking noise. Oh shit, my arm was broken.

Lying there in the dark, not in pain yet but sobered some, a million thoughts went through my mind: *What happened? Where am I? Gotta get to the pickup. And my arm's broken; what about my job?*

I heard the garage door slam. They were home.

My eyes adjusted to the dark. I realized I was in a stairwell leading to the basement. Cradling my broken left arm with my right, I climbed out, then raced for the pickup. Billy was at the wheel and Sharon was in the middle, leaving room for me on the outside. I leapt in, and before I could get my door closed, he slipped away and we were moving off down the street.

"Back to the party?" Billy asked.

"Hospital," I said. "My arm's broken."

"What?" asked Billy. "How do you know it's broke?"

"This ain't my first rodeo," I said.

"Oh, no, does it hurt bad?" Sharon asked.

"It's starting to," I said. "When this antifreeze wears off, it's gonna to hurt bad."

Shortly after we arrived at the hospital's night-nurse station, my arm began to throb like hell. The nurse called my doctor at home to get permission to give me a shot for pain, which pissed me off because I knew he would okay it, and so did she, but she had to do it, I guess.

The doctor didn't answer the phone or his pager. The old fart was deaf and liked to drink, so he wasn't exactly on point most of the time.

"I bet he's at the Elks Club with them other high rollers," said Sharon. "There's that party down there, right?"

The nurse dialed up the Elks, and sure enough, the doctor was there. The nurse held the phone while the bartender went to fetch him. When she got him on the phone, she explained the situation and got his go-ahead to shoot me up with some kind of pain medicine and to take x-rays. He told the nurse that he would be at the hospital shortly.

She said, "Sit down."

So I sat and she came at me with the needle. Thanks to the dope, the pain began to float away.

Sometime after she took x-rays, the doors swung open. The doc was wearing a suit and tie, which was the Elks norm. Red nose and all, he raised the x-ray film to the light and peered at it through his cigarette smoke. He pointed his stubby finger to where the fracture was. "This here is a hairline fracture, so we won't need to set it," he said.

"Well, it hurt like it was broke in half," I said.

"You're lucky this time, Sonny," he said. "Mix the plaster, Harriet."

A bit later, the cast felt good; wet, but nice and warm. Then it became a nuisance, banging into everything on the way out of the hospital and into the pickup. There was no way I could lumber like this. I wondered if Joe could take over my job for me.

"Billy," I said when we were driving away from the hospital, "I'm going to drop you off at the party on my way home. Tell Joe what happened and not to worry—I'll make it to the church on time. And tell him if he can get back from his honeymoon by Monday morning, early, I might be able to get him my job."

"How's that?" he asked.

"Since I can't work, he might as well have my job."

"How you going to pull that off?" asked Sharon.

"Because I know someone who works in the office out there."

"Me?" Sharon asked with raised eyebrows.

"Yep. Joe is on the list, isn't he?"

"He is, but down about the middle."

"Well, just bring him up a little when you get to work in the morning."

Chapter 20

I opened my eyes. It was daylight and everything was lit up but dreary and gray—no color. My left arm was encased in cement. The cast was long, covering my wrist and up over my elbow. I stared at it like it was foreign to me, but it wasn't—I could see my fingers, and my arm began to itch.

And hurt again—everything hurt. My head was throbbing and clogged like it was full of cotton and my stomach felt like I was one day into a bad flu. But then, even with the hangover from hell, through the ugly fog came the memory of lying in Marylyn's arms the night before. That vision wiped away the torment for a moment. I looked at my cast with a slight smile, remembering the calamity of the night before—it was almost funny to me. The memory was truly bittersweet.

"Sonny?" Mom knocked on my door. "Are you awake? Joe's wedding rehearsal is this morning."

"Oh God, I'd forgotten."

Mom and Dad were sitting over breakfast when they

saw my cast and groaned. I told them a short version of how I broke my arm, leaving out most everything but the cement staircase.

"Does it hurt bad?" Mom asked.

"Not too bad, Mom," I lied. I sat and laid the cast on the table before me.

"What about your job, Sonny?" Dad twisted a frown at my arm.

"I'm going to try to get Joe on in my place. I'm taking him to work with me Monday morning and seeing if we can make the switch."

"Oh, that will be nice for Joe," said Mom. "But it doesn't leave them much time for a honeymoon."

"Nice for Joe," Dad repeated, "but you're going to be out of commission for at least six weeks. You'd better sign up for unemployment right away."

"I will Monday, right after I get Joe started at the mill."

After swallowing a piece of toast that tasted like cardboard, I washed down a pain pill with water that tasted like it was from a sweet spring. Mom refilled my glass from the kitchen sink and I drank more. I had a thirst like I'd crossed the Sinai in the summer, so I drained another glass, which gave me the whirlies a little.

"You don't look so good," Mom said. "You don't need to go to the rehearsal."

"But I gotta go—I'm the best man."

"Nothing to it, Sonny," Dad said. "Just stand there, and when the preacher asks for the ring, you deliver."

"Go back to bed for a while, Sonny," said Mom. "I'll call Joe so he won't worry about you, and I'll wake you in plenty of time to get ready for the two o'clock wedding."

I crawled onto the couch across from the oil stove in the living room. Spooky came sniffing my cast, then jumped up and coiled in next to me. With my arm around her, I drifted off, riding the painkiller trail.

"Wake up, sleepyhead," Mom said. "Guess what I found in the mailbox." She was holding something behind her back.

Spooky made a getaway for the stove and Mom sat next to me on the edge of the couch. "It's red and has pretty flowers on it."

She showed it, a small envelope. *Could it be from Marylyn?* I wondered with hope.

"Ooo, it smells so nice," she teased with it close to her nose. "I wonder who it's for." Then reading the front, she said, "Oh, it's to Sonny Mitchell, that boy who's been moping around here lately."

I reached for it, forgetting my cast, and she playfully pulled the envelope back. I used my good arm the second time and stole it from her hand.

She laughed and said as she returned to the kitchen, "There's a bowl of tomato soup waiting for you on the table. You have an hour before you leave for the wedding."

I wrestled the envelope open one-handed, releasing more of the enticing fragrance. I'd smelled this before. It had to have been when I was riding Marylyn home on the bike and my nose was rubbing her neck.

Dearest Sonny, it began, written in a beautiful hand. My heart pounded. *I'm so sorry you broke your arm last night. I hope it doesn't hurt too much. I feel responsible because you should have been welcome to come through the front door. I'm sure that we will get our chance and won't have to meet through open windows, but walk through doors together.*

By the way, Harold and I replaced the ladder on the shed and no one is the wiser.

My best,

Marylyn

It was the most beautiful handful of words I'd ever read. My heart went from pounding to a gentle purr.

But one thing didn't add up—I'd broken my arm late last night and here was a letter that arrived today. How could she find out my arm was broken, write the letter, and then get the letter delivered this morning? I picked up the envelope and discovered there was no stamp or postmark. It must have been hand delivered to our mailbox by someone other than the postman. I put my mind to it. Harold had seen me crash on the ladder, so he probably saw me fall headlong down the basement steps, probably watched us drive away and had figured I was headed for a doctor. Harold's jaw would have been aching to tell Marylyn, so she might have gotten curious and dialed the hospital.

"Hey, Mom!" I hollered. I could see her puttering around the kitchen, dressed for the wedding. "Have you seen a green Volkswagen around here today?"

Stepping into the room, she said, "I've been too busy to look out the window. Why? Is there something wrong?"

"No," I beamed. "I'd better get ready." I was on the mend.

I had a hell of a time with my suit jacket, but with Mom's help, I filled one sleeve with my good arm and carried the other under my suit coat and left for the church lopsided like a one-armed man. I already wasn't liking it and had six weeks to go.

During the ceremony, Angie glowed with happiness, and I could tell by Joe's lopsided grin he wasn't hating it either.

Standing up for Joe made me realize that we were all moving on to the next chapter. For me, the steady rock I'd been standing on since puberty was beginning to change to sand and was leaking out from under me.

An old lady near the front muffled a fart, drawing my eyes to a good-looking girl sitting a pew over—items that in the past would have been exciting to me. But now, like in the dream I'd had, the image of Marylyn in white kept coming back and blowing all other thoughts away.

After the reception, when Joe and Angie pulled away from the curb into their new life, there was a string of soup cans banging on the pavement between the twin pipes. I stood there looking at those tailpipes, which at one time had to be just right: chrome tips perfectly spaced, purring the correct mellow sound. But now, like Joe, they relented to marriage and family and those cans clattering on the asphalt.

Chapter 21

Billy was leaving Sunday, so we had just that night together.

I was getting pretty good at driving with my cast, with my left hand hooked to the steering wheel while shifting with my good one.

I swung into Pop's a little after 7:00, us still in a time warp between being teenage rebels and adults with responsibility. We'd been discussing this at some length since we had left the wedding. Memories blew at us through the same old '40 windshield, but with a different meaning. For the most part, Pop's was entertaining a new crop of pups hell-bent on leaving their mark, which, unknown to them, would be washed away by the first storm following graduation.

The white Impala was holding down its favorite slot at the end of the row at Pop's, filled with a gaggle of the usual. The crowd of teenage girls surrounded the car as Crazy Horse held court with them and the occupants. Now that I'd gotten a chance to be with Marylyn, Crazy

Horse and his harem offered no threat to my ego any longer, so I chugged past, unconcerned, with my blower whispering a confident whistle, passing the swarm, who hardly noticed my car as they continued being engrossed with the charms of the new boy.

My mirror caught a ruckus inside the Impala with arms and bodies flailing around until Susan's door opened, letting Linda Nelson out of the backseat. Like before, she waved us down and entered my car, sliding over Billy's lap and sinking between us, wiggling her tiny butt into my Naugahyde pleats. It was nice to have a defector. Linda was like an open book offering a wealth of information from the other camp. Sometimes, more than needed.

"Whew," she said popping a bubble. "Thank God you guys came along. I had to get out of that rowdy, gyrating, smoked-up mania in that Indian fun house. On top of that, it smells like a French whorehouse with all the perfume and aftershave lotion." She stuck her nose into Billy's neck. "Thank heavens, the smell of man. Oh, by the way," she told Billy, "my name is Linda." She turned to me. "Hey, what happened to your arm?"

"I broke it." Is all I said, letting her begin again.

"I can see that. Where we going?" she said to Billy, cracking a bubble. Linda couldn't stay on track very long.

"Well, first of all, my name is Billy, and I guess we'll go wherever you want us to." He laughed. "We're at your service." Any excuse to drive was okay with us.

"I know who you are. You're Billy Wheeler, friend of the famous Sonny Mitchell here. Well, famous until

Crazy Horse came along and sucked the oxygen out of that conversation."

I didn't like the sound of that very much.

"All they can talk about over there," she said, "is how Crazy Horse is going to kick Sonny's ass out at Otto's come first race of the season."

I didn't like that either. The challenge of it shot a cold quiver up my spine. But I didn't let on. "Where do you want to go, Linda?"

"I wanna do what you guys do. Let's do something cool."

I turned left and entered the highway en route to Billie's Big Boy Burger.

"What makes Crazy Horse think he's such a hot item all of the sudden?" Billy asked.

"He had me out on Oakdale Road that night," I said, kinda glum-like, "and he knows it."

"We'll see about that," Billy said, biting his lip, keeping mum about the blower sleeping under my hood so Linda wouldn't know. She wasn't a snitch, just loose lipped.

"Hey, Sonny," Linda asked, changing the subject. "Have you gotten any love letters lately?"

That perked me up. "How'd you know about that?"

"Do you think it just walked over and jumped into your mailbox all by itself?" She giggled. "I snuck it over there myself."

"I was awful glad to get that letter this morning. It picked me up at a time I was feeling pretty bad."

"Marylyn means whatever was in that envelope, Sonny," Linda said. "I can vouch for that."

"Tell her I miss her awful bad, okay?"

"It's as good as done, Sonny," she said.

After that, we used the road pretty hard, driving back and forth between Billie's and Pop's, listening to Linda pop her gum and gab away at boring subjects, like girls' bouffant hairdos and glitzy nail polish, making me wonder how on earth she found them interesting.

After I let her out back at Pop's, Billy said, "I think it's over."

"What's over?" I asked.

"Spring break," he said. "Sonny, can you drop me off at the depot in the morning?"

"Sure," I said. I would be sad to see him go. Our times together were getting further and further apart.

Monday morning, early, Joe's headlights swept the side of the house. I ran through the rain and one-armed into his car, and we were on our way to the mill.

"How's married life, old man?" I asked over the buzz of the heater.

Joe had a glow about him even in the dark of the car. "It's good, Sonny, it really is."

"Wonderful," I said. "Now all we got to do is get you the job. And I'm warning you, this is going to be out of the ordinary. You are on the list of prospective workers, but you're not at the top, so with Sharon's help juggling the names on the list, we're going to try to slip you ahead. Meanwhile, I'm going to start training you like you're already hired."

"Okay, Sonny."

I showed Joe the office and where to punch in, then in the rain we approached the green chain area with my cast sticking out like an elephant's dick. All eyes were on us. My crew on the chain pointed at me, giving off jabs and wagering on how I'd broken my arm. "Hey, Sonny, what did you go and do this time, take on a lion or something?" Any excuse to plant a joke on someone was good, with the camaraderie and so on with the mill workers. This was good, taking the heat off Joe.

"This here is Joe. He'll be stepping in for me temporarily."

"I suppose we got to train his tender young ass like we did you," came a wisecrack.

I laughed. "Soon as he picks up on this, he'll be outworking all you low-lifers."

I gave Joe my gloves and explained the procedure. The mill came to life, the chain tightened, the first board came to Joe, and he pulled it off okay, just the first in the never-ending parade of green lumber. Using one-armed signals and yelling over the roar of the machinery, I showed him some tricks to make his job easier. Joe caught on fast.

I saw Sharon's car arrive. She parked by the office and made a dash through the rain to the door and disappeared inside.

"Give me your car keys," I yelled to Joe. "I'll be back to get you at the end of the shift." Joe nodded without looking up—he was busy.

Now came the hard part: convincing Sage, my foreman, to let Joe take over for me on the green chain.

I entered the office and found him standing behind the counter shuffling some papers. Sitting behind him at her desk, Sharon looked at me wide eyed.

"What are you doing in here?" Sage asked, giving off a frown. "Aren't you supposed to be working?" His eyes went to my cast. "What happened to you? Who's on the chain?"

That was a lot of questions. I had to think fast. "Joe is, sir," I said. "He's the guy I told you about, and when I realized that I couldn't do my job, I brought him along, and he's out there pulling right now."

"Well, thanks a hell of a lot for letting me know," he said with sarcasm. "There's a protocol for this, you know. A guy can't just walk off the street and begin working here. He has to go through the system before he can be employed."

Sharon pushed up from her desk and broke in. "Excuse me, Sage, but Joe has filled out all the papers and he's on the list already."

"Where is he on the list?"

"Well, he's a ways down but we haven't heard from most of those ahead of him for weeks. If we don't take this guy, it might be a day or two before we can replace Mitchell here."

Sage set his jaw. He was thinking. "I know all that," he said. "We'll try it this time."

Good, I thought. It was a close shave, but it really did make sense to have a man take over instantly so nothing slowed making lumber, and Sage liked making lumber.

"But if someone starts having a shit fit," he said, "Joe will have to get back in line. One thing for sure is, he'll get bumped right away to swing shift. And if we were still running graveyard, he'd find himself burning the midnight oil. By the way, what happened to your arm?"

"I fell down some steps."

His eyes softened. "Yeah, that's what they all say."

He went back to his papers and Sharon gave me a wink.

At the employment office, several military-green desks were hovered over by men with bowties and spectacles. I recognized Fred, the one who got me the job out at the mill in the first place. He waved me back to his desk. I walked past those eyes that were throwing doubts at my cast. This was not starting off so good.

"What's up? Sonny, isn't it?" he said, motioning me to a chair. "Oh," he said, "you've broken your arm."

"I'm afraid so," I said. "I'm going to need a job a one-armed man can do."

"I got bad news for you, Sonny," he said. "We don't have any jobs here, no matter how many arms you have." He went on telling me about the economy and so forth. It didn't sound promising. "Get signed up for unemployment, and I'll keep an eye out for something, but honestly, it doesn't look good right now."

I wasn't shining with happiness when I left.

Still feeling down at the mouth, I picked Joe up in the parking lot at the mill, but seeing Joe smiling brought me back a little.

"Wow," he said. "This is more than flipping burgers. My arms are sore."

"No shit," I said, "but it pays good. Did you hear from Sage today?"

"Yep, I'm starting swing shift tomorrow at 3:00 p.m. Thanks, Sonny. This will really help Angie and me get off to a good start."

So Joe had a job, but of course, I didn't. I felt bad about it too. I felt worn out, and with that and a sudden dose of depression, I went home and crawled onto the couch with Spooky and fell asleep.

A few days later, I was still having a hell of a time, feeling worthless, until Mom said, "You got to get over feeling sorry for yourself. It's not like you. Why don't you go out to Pop's and see if Joe's there? Find out how the job's doing."

"Okay," I said. "It couldn't hurt, I guess."

When I pulled into Pop's, Joe's '50 was parked in front. *Good*, I thought. It would be nice to see Joe.

He was sitting in a far booth with Ingrid, Angie's girl—and now Joe's too—who was coloring in a coloring book. She was pushing three years old and was a cutie and full of energy. This was the first time I'd seen him as a dad, married, and with family.

"Hi, Sonny," Ingrid said. "Wanna color?"

Just like that, I felt better.

"Sure," I said, sliding in. "Give me a blue one. It's my favorite color, you know." I worked in the sky above a crane while Ingrid glazed the bird over with pink, and then she pulled out a red and smeared it all over the bird's beak.

"What's that, honey?" Joe asked.

"Lipstick, silly." She flipped the page and began to redden a hippo.

It was great to see their interaction. "You're taking to this family life pretty well, huh?"

"It's good," he said.

"How's swing shift going?"

"It's okay, but I had a hell of a run-in with the foreman, Clive."

"How's that?"

"My being hired without his knowing it. He was really, really pissed off about it too."

"So why in hell would he care so much?"

"He likes his way around swing-shift time. He flipped out when he saw me pulling boards on the chain. Fortunately, I was so busy with the lumber, I didn't have time to argue and just took his rant. He said he'd get me fired, but so far I'm still working."

It bothered me some that Clive seemed to take such an interest in who worked the swing shift. I asked Joe about this and what he knew about the guy.

"He's a hell of a worker—I'll give him that," Joe said.

"How's that?"

"Well, he likes moving from one operation to the next, helping when he can. He's always jumping on a straddle buggy or a forklift, moving lumber here and there. I've heard that he stays after the shift is over and loads trucks. Oh, by the way, I've noticed that the workers on swing are different than ones you worked with on days."

"What do you mean by that?"

"Well, I was only on day shift once, but on break those guys talked about their families and homes and dreams. But these swing-shift workers only think about getting to the tavern before it closes. They're all like that. They don't give a damn about anything except the next board coming by and quitting time."

"Maybe that's why Clive's so mad," I said. "He doesn't know if you're going to fit into his clan very well."

"He likes to be in control. That's for sure."

"I'm going to call Sharon and see what she knows about Clive," I said.

"Why?" Joe asked.

I told him about the mill's financial difficulties and how J. R. Swanson was connected through his bank.

"Why would you care about what happens to that old fart—he hasn't exactly done you a lot of favors lately."

"Well, you know I'm pretty hooked on his daughter, and I've got a stake in the mill in that I don't mind cashing paychecks."

I stepped into the kitchen at Pop's and dialed the number Sharon had given me.

After a ring or two, she answered.

"Hi, Sharon, this is Sonny. Joe and I are doing some detective work, and I was wondering what you could tell me about Clive."

"Clive is not very nice," she said. "He thinks he's a real ladies' man, but actually, he's a brute who likes to put his hands where they aren't wanted. But he has the owner's ear since he's Mr. Dunlap's nephew."

"Really? How long has he worked for the mill?"

"About two years."

"Isn't that about how long you said things have been going downhill?"

"You think he's got something to do with it?"

"Joe and I are just on a fishing trip—we don't know anything yet. Is there any chance you could find out where he worked before he hired on at Dunlap's?"

"Sure, I think I can find out a lot about Clive. I have his files. Oh, by the way, I was about to call you about some news you might like."

"What's up? I could use some good news."

"Our insurance company audited us this morning, and they want us to put on a night watchman since we aren't running graveyard shift any longer. It doesn't pay as well, but you only need one arm to operate a flashlight."

"I'll take it," I said, excited. "When do I start?"

She told me to come to the office the next day to get a tour around the place with Sage. He'd show me my responsibilities and so on. And I was to start tomorrow night.

I felt like a new man, and it couldn't have come at a better time. With Joe sniffing around during swing and me prowling all night, and with our man, Sharon, on the inside, I was thinking we should be able to smell out the rat, whoever or whatever it was.

I couldn't wait to tell Joe the good news. He and Ingrid were still coloring.

I told him about the night watchman gig and then added, "Sharon filled me in on our man Clive. He's not your nicest human being—maybe just the kind of guy we're looking for. So, anyway, I'm thinking we could play a little Perry Mason and get to the bottom of this."

Joe leaned in interested-like. "You think Clive's involved?" he asked.

"I don't know, but it's some kind of thievery, and almost has to be coming from inside the mill. On the chance that Clive is involved, it's real important to earn his trust, and he may slip up and reveal how he's doing it. When you get back to work, I want you to blend in with the rest of the crowd and not act too smart or anything. I know it will be difficult for you," I said with a wink. "We don't want to let on that we're chums or anything like that."

"But we were together the first day I went to work," said Joe.

"I know, but that was day shift, and like you said, the swing-shift boys couldn't give a shit, so hopefully, they won't remember us together. We'll still be crossing paths at shift's end, so to keep our friendship incognito, we'll want to ignore each other. If it is known that we're conspiring together, whoever it is will shut down for a while or try to get rid of us."

"I guess that's about how Mason would say it—could I be Paul Drake?" he laughed.

"Get serious, Joe. We can catch these crooks."

"Okay, Perry." He grinned.

Chapter 22

It was closing in on eleven and raining when I pulled into the lot my first night working as the mill's watchman— but it was swing shift, so the mill was still running full bore, the whole contraption lit up with yard lights, big and alive against the darkened sky, like a giant monster eating logs and passing lumber. It was big business and a major employer for Willamette, with lots of families depending on it for their livelihood.

But I knew there was something cockeyed that was killing the being, and I was getting more and more determined to find the cause.

Now, however, the mill was about to be put to bed for the night, with only me—the night watchman—to keep it company.

Earlier that day, Sage, my foreman, had given me a map of the property, along with a big black flashlight and a ring of keys, and took me around the site to show me my duties—critical areas that needed an occasional peek, like gates and fuel storage and that sort of thing.

I parked and let myself through the man-gate by the office, stepped in, and set my thermos and flashlight on an empty wooden counter. No one was there, only country-western music twanging from an upright radio standing between a worn leather couch and a coat rack that held my new uniform—a raincoat and plastic fedora. The rubbery coat was big and my cast fit into the sleeve. *Good*, I thought, *I need to keep it dry.* I was happy with my new look. A Dick Tracy look, dashing in my new hat— *how fitting*, I thought. I opened the door and stalked out into the night. My first case and armed to the teeth: a determined look and a flashlight.

The eleven o'clock whistle blew and the place ground to a halt. I was met by a stream of workers leaning into the rain and running for their cars. They ignored me. I was just a silhouette standing in front of a vision of a tavern. They were happy men; their shift was over for another day, leaving them sixteen hours off to waste away their freedom.

And then the quiet came and I was alone.

The only things still on were the scattered lights, covered with green porcelain shades that looked like peasant hats. They illuminated windswept raindrops driven sideways by another coastal storm that had come in from the west. The mill was machine-silent, with only the squeaking of the gate and a comfortless piece of roofing slapping in the wind. According to the security plan Sage had given me, I was to circle the property, checking the outside gates and buildings first, and then explore the central part of the mill for anything peculiar, like a fire hazard or some sort of mischief in the making. I stepped off, following the chain-link fence north, rattling my keys so I wouldn't surprise any critters that only come out in the dark.

I engineered my first duty as night watchman by checking the lock on the north gate. Finding the lock secure, I turned and walked east along the fence until I came to the shop and fuel storage shed. To get enough light off the single overhead bulb so I could see to unlock the door, I had to hunker down under the river that was coming off the corrugated roof. I thought I would drown before I finally one-armed the key into the lock.

Inside, I was met with the familiar smell of petroleum, and since the building was pitch-dark, the fumes seemed amplified as I groped for the light switch. Lit up, the room was like a normal shop, with a high ceiling exposing trusses that held up the metal roof. The structure was similar to the rest of the buildings on site in that, except for the roof and floor, it was mostly wooden. It made sense that if something could be made from wood, it was.

In the center of the cement floor rested a straddle buggy, a machine that totes bundles of lumber from place to place. Man driven, it looked like a spider with wheels and merely straddled the stack of lumber. The driver yanked a lever, activating a hydraulic ram, squeezing the load, and he carted it off to its destination.

The machine's hood was off and a chain hoist hung over it from a rail, in anticipation of lifting the motor, which was partially taken apart. I had seen the straddle buggies in action day after day as they hauled the lumber

I had stacked, so I was interested in what made them go. Inspecting, I found that the motor and drive train were Ford and—by the vintage of the grill out in front—probably built about 1935. A new motor was cradled in a wood box in front of the buggy, ready for installation. Maintenance was crucial to operating something as complex as a sawmill, with so many moving parts expected to run indefinitely day after day. I began to calculate the number of hours the little motor had on it, running three shifts a day. It had pumped its heart out for thousands and thousands of hours without complaining and had finally earned a few hours of respite during repair. With luck and the new motor, the straddle buggy was doomed to slog on for another decade or so.

A window on the mill side of the shop lit up with headlights. This surprised me; it seemed unusual. My watch said 12:15 a.m. Concerned—after all, I was the watchman and a detective on the lookout—I crossed to the window and, squinting through the rain, saw that a flatbed semi-truck had entered the gate to the loading area near the shop. The driver got out. A forklift appeared with a unit of lumber. After a brief discussion with the truck driver, the forklift operator began loading lumber from various locations of the storage area.

I left the shop to get closer, and from the shadows I could see the forklift driver. It was Clive, the swing-shift foreman. Joe said he was a hard worker. He must have stayed late for the chore. It was hard for me to understand how the mill could be in financial trouble with such dedication.

There was no reason to interrupt their loading, so I moved on, checking off my security points one by one, probing deeper into the mill in reverse of the way it operated. I walked past the staging yard, where lumber was readied for shipping, and on to the drying kilns, where I could feel the warmth of the boilers that were fired by sawdust to dry the lumber. Then I passed the grading area and, diverting around puddles in the gravel, came to the green chain. The green chain had been my home for months.

I stood there looking at the empty space, which lacked the grinding noise of chains against gears and metal against wood. The concrete was shiny and worn from men's leather shoes—including mine—men not there now, not yanking or sweating at their posts making lumber.

By the time I circled around and through the property, it had been about two and a half hours. Nothing was normal alone in the dark. I had become nocturnal like a skunk or a raccoon, doing business after hours while civilization slept. My fingers were frozen, but my cast was dry, and inside of it my arm was warm and itched like hell if I thought about it.

I was back where I started. It was time for my fifteen-minute break. I entered the office with my raincoat and hat dripping wet. The room was warm and inviting, with the radio now playing some kind of a nighttime talk show from San Francisco. The host of the radio show was interviewing an author who said he had the answer to what we have all been searching for. With my new job, I was going to have lots of time to reflect and look into my inner self, as suggested by the guest on the radio show.

I hung my rain clothes on the rack, letting the water run onto the floor, grabbed my thermos, and sat down on the friendly looking couch. The coffee in my thermos was a steaming reminder of humanity, something normal that I had been beginning to doubt from being alone at the wrong time of day. Unfortunately, by the time the talk show host got around to explaining what it was we were seeking, my fifteen-minute break was over.

On my third and last round for the night, I came again to the heart of the mill, a big room, out of the weather, and for some reason—perhaps tiredness—it was kind of dreamy looking, and the smell of fresh-cut fir was overwhelming, reminding me of the first time my dad pulled a Christmas tree through the door of our warm living room on a winter's eve.

Like the rest of the mill, this room, with the big blade, was a man's place, with a concrete floor and a corrugated roof held up by big timbers tied together with cold steel. It was the brains of the mill and housed the carriage that carried the dripping logs from the pond into the blade, cutting them into planks. Like the green chain, the place was quiet and man-empty—dead looking. But the controls that ran the mill were there, surrounding the sawyer's chair—an informal perch built into the machine that gave the man who sat in it control of the mill. On the console were levers and buttons and switches, all hand-worn from a million hours of a man's hands taking on the raw logs, which hit the metal blade, giving off a horrific, earsplitting roar, shrieking through the chamber, liberating water and sawdust like a storm from hell. I was mesmerized by it all, and my feet were tired, and no one was around, so I thought, What the hell? I'll take a load off.

I sat down at the sawyer's chair, metal but upholstered green by an amateur, and probably for the umpteenth time, and already ripped. I let my cast lie in my lap, resting my arm. It felt good.

Directly across from me was the empty chair of the ratchet setter, who, during working hours, rode the carriage, adjusting the logs closer to or farther from the blade for optimum usage of the timber. To the right of me was where the off-bearer peeled off the planks with a crow bar as they dropped from the blade, to send them off through the bowels of the mill.

The carnival ride–looking levers were inviting. I took hold of one and hooked another with my cast hand. They were metal—crude and cold—but warmed quickly in my hands as I began to work them like I was running the outfit, driving the carriage that carried the log back and forth through the blade like slicing cheese.

As I got more comfortable in the padded seat, my eyelids got heavy. Then, from far away, I heard a faint noise like a musical note, followed by classical music I recognized as "Ride of the Valkyries" from my cartoon days. From the corner of my eye, I saw an ever-so-slight movement of the chain. The room became fuzzy with steam, and I could hear the clanking of gears pulling chains, and then the music got louder. Through the haze, a skeleton with a tin hat appeared perched across from me on the ratchet setter's chair. The carriage was moving towards the blade, which was beginning to whir, and the music got louder and louder as the carriage flew back and forth faster and faster. The skeleton smiled at me with a mischievous grin.

The off-bearer—a bony creature in a hooded sweatshirt—threw a smirk over his shoulder at me as he crouched, securing the fall-off on each pass until the logs cleared the blade.

All down the line, the machines, including the green chain, were manned by these scantily clothed carcasses with naughty grins, pulling, yanking, and wrenching the raw timber into product.

I was working the levers and flashing signals back and forth to the ratchet setter with my fingers made only of bones. I was tense and alert, trying my hardest to make lumber. I wanted to please, but why was I dead? Why was the machine working and we were all dead?

Suddenly, the music stopped and a claw-like skeletal hand gripped my shoulder, shaking me. It turned fleshy. It was attached to an arm clothed in red flannel and its voice said, "Wake up."

I jumped up and reeled around with my eyes wide to see Mr. Dunlap's face close. He was wearing a bad frown. I had awakened from a dream to a nightmare. *Oh shit, he'll fire me!*

Backing up a step, I said, "Yes, sir; sorry, sir. I just sat down here for a moment."

With a scowl, he said, "Somebody could have run off with the whole goddamn mill or it could have burnt down while you were napping in here. What am I paying you for, anyway?"

"I just sat down for a moment, sir. It won't happen again."

He looked down at my cast. "Hey, aren't you the kid from the green chain?"

"Yeah," I said, glad to change the subject. "I broke my arm and couldn't work, but I got on as night watchman."

"You can pull lumber, I'll say that for you. I've seen you from my office. You the one that saved Swanson's daughter out on the Boulevard?" I felt relieved. I might keep my job after all. "I stopped the car she was in from hitting the train."

"That took some guts," he said. "Swanson finances me—he's a cranky old fart."

"You can say that again." I couldn't believe I'd said that.

"How's that?" he asked.

"He's worried that I have romantic intentions for his daughter."

Smiling, he said, "I can't blame you for that. I've seen her at the bank with J. R. He might get over it. Take care of my mill," he said, then walked away into the darkness.

Chapter 23

Joe and I were on the sneak, amateur detectives living multiple lives, trying to unravel the mystery of the mill's woes without giving away our intentions. On the inside of the mill, we acted like we were unknown to each other. As far as the world around the mill was concerned, we were strangers. Outside the mill, we were still best friends, but we had little time to collaborate because of our schedules.

After a week of graveyard, I still couldn't get used to the routine of the night shift: hurrying home to a fitful sleep when I knew Marylyn and the rest of the world were waking up to daylight and a normal day. It was hard to force sleep just for the sake of it, and I could never sleep enough to get me through the next night without a near miss with a snooze, something I dared not do after my meeting with Mr. Dunlap next to his saw blade. And I missed the sense of sun on my skin and the colors of the day. I felt sorry for my nocturnal peers—the real mill rats, the furry kind that hungered in the night because their diet of something small and vulnerable that had taken a free ride in from the forest during the day had already become squashed and ground to dust, spoiling the little rats' meager meals. Nighttime brought only black and gray and cold, and the sound of rain hammering on the mill's cold steel roof. The sole smell besides raw timber was the coming of rain when the clouds piled up on the coastal mountains, readying for a storm—a natural warning that throws a moist and silent promise into your skull that you're gonna get wet.

Every day, the mill roared at full speed until exactly 11:00 p.m. I punched in and was ready to assume my duties when the whistle blew, grinding the whole affair to a stop, leaving my ears ringing.

By showing up a few minutes before my night shift each night, I'd come to know Clive from a distance. He was slight of build and had steely blue eyes and wore tan khakis over flashy chrome-pointed cowboy boots and a dressy jacket with fancy buttons and the collar always up. But he was not formal and seemed to treat his men respectfully, almost to the point of equals—like a social club and he was the president.

This all intrigued me. He just didn't look like the kind of guy who would waste away his life in a sawmill. The only item in his attire that would give away his profession was the tin hat he wore tipped over to one side, a clue that he might be feeding an ego.

Being the swing-shift foreman, Clive was responsible for the entire mill during his shift. And like Joe said, his crew was motley at best. They were a colorful bunch in the way they dressed, with funny hats and striped shirts, like carney rats and shipwrecked pirates. Their grader wore an old black suitcoat and had an Abe Lincoln beard, making him look like a nineteenth-century missionary bent over his work, constantly hammering the stamp.

One time, near the edger, I met Clive up close— bumping right into him. It was a dark place, a blind corner in an alley, and on foot we crashed pretty hard. Those eyes of his locked on to me like he was quickly judging a side of beef. I snapped a weak apology to his grunt. He moved on in a hurry. I turned to watch him leap onto a forklift and blow away with a load of lumber, just to slam into a pile of boards that had fallen in his path. The way he threw those boards made me wonder what happened when people got in his way.

One midnight caught me near the back gate, checking the lock, when I heard a diesel coming hard down the mill's road. Letting up, its pipes backed off with a Jake brake that I swear could've woken the whole town. It was the same black semi I'd seen from inside the shop before. I was standing in the shadows—quiet, like a detective— and nobody saw me when Clive appeared and opened up, letting him into the freight entrance. Jumping on the running board, he rode along, hanging on the mirror, talking with the driver through the side window as the semi rolled close by me—close enough I could feel the heat off the big motor as it vibrated by me, like it was catching its breath after a hard run.

Clive buzzed around the lot on a forklift, picking up stacks of lumber from different areas and loading them on the trailer, while the driver strapped them to the truck bed.

Because the loads were mixed with different grades of lumber, I figured they were going to a small yard somewhere, retailing to a diverse group of customers. As much as I would have liked to witness wrongdoing, there wasn't anything wrong with what they were doing. Just a devoted employee staying after hours and working for the benefit of his employer.

I met up with Joe at Pop's the following day. It was early and slow, so Joe was sharing a booth with Angie. I sprawled in across from them and clanked my cast on the table. I noticed Angie looking at it, her nose wrinkling. I wondered if it smelled. It was dirty-looking so I pulled it from the table and hid it in my lap.

Angie got me a Coke. I paid her and she dropped the coin into the jukebox. "True Love Ways" came pouring out of the machine like Buddy Holly was still alive and right here with us in Pop's. He'd been dead a year already and it seemed like yesterday that he was killed in that frozen cornfield.

I took a drink, letting the bubbles work. "So how are you and Clive getting on these days? Is he still on your ass?"

"At first he interrogated me all the time on why I wanted to work there and where I'm from and where I worked before and so on. It was like he wanted to know if I fit in."

"So what did you tell him?"

"Mostly, I just played stupid, but when he insisted, I told him I didn't give a damn about trees and lumber and what they make with it—I said I was just in it for the money and wouldn't be hanging around long. He seemed pleased with my lack of interest and ignorance of the whole operation. Since then, he's treated me okay and I'm fitting in, except I go home when the shift is over and most of the other guys head to the Halfway Tavern. I was told Clive has a standing offer to buy any one of us the first beer on our arrival. The bartender knows all the guys, so he just jots down a mark by your name and Clive picks up the check routinely."

"And I bet Clive gets a kickback from the owner routinely too," Angie predicted.

I looked at her, surprised. "What makes you think that?"

"From what you've said about him, the way he treated Joe and all, there is something driving this guy."

"It makes sense," I said with a smile. "We'll be calling you Della from now on." I winked. Angie smiled, liking her new name. "Della Street was the brains behind Perry Mason, you know. No one ever has just one beer. It's a win-win for everybody."

"Clive is no dummy," I said. "We can all agree on that. But he wears something sinister—just a feeling I get when I'm around him. I wonder if he's figured out a way to get some kind of a kickback on lumber."

"Sonny, you might just have something there," Joe said, chewing on a straw. "Whatever is leaking out of the system has to happen as the product is turned into lumber and before it leaves the yard, and that's when Clive is in control of it."

"Good work, both of you," I said. "Let's keep an eye on him. If he is the guilty one, he'll make a mistake sometime, and we'll nab his ass."

When I left for work that night, I was carrying Dad's binoculars. It couldn't hurt since I knew I'd been lucky being up close the last time the semi arrived, but it was dangerous to be that near. If they caught me snooping, it could scare them off, or Clive could catch me watching and come after me with a board—either way, I could lose my job and maybe get my bell rung pretty good too— well, that was if he was somehow stealing and liked not getting caught. As midnight approached, I was perched high on a stack of lumber in the yard, watching through the binoculars as Clive welcomed the black semi through the gate. The diesel truck idled past some stacks of lumber in the yard and stopped under a yard light that illuminated a sign lettered on its door: Lewis Farms, Silverton, Oregon.

Hm, I thought. A farm truck hauling lumber? Was the driver a farm kid backhauling boards on his hay truck? If he was running farm plates, this was a little shady. The trucks that came and went during daylight hours wore commercial plates. According to the drivers, who would come around and bullshit with us while waiting to load, permits were hard to get and expensive. Farm license plates were cheap and meant the truck was supposed to be used to transport only farm products to and from the farm, and what the kid was hauling was a hell of a lot more lumber than needed on a farm.

To make sure my suspicions were correct, I had to get closer.

I dropped out of my blind and snuck in, covered by shadows, from one stack to the next until I could see the semi's license plate. Sure enough, it had a big "F" for farm on it.

I got a pretty good look at the kid from there. He looked rural, with his cowboy hat pulled down, and was farm-like, not truck driver–like. Truck drivers wore uniforms or bibs, clean with polished Wellington boots. This kid wore Wranglers and a ranger-like coat to keep off the rain.

After forklifting the load, Clive and the kid exchanged papers and, with some talk I couldn't hear, said what looked like good-byes. Clive let the semi back out through the gate it'd come in. After he padlocked the gate, he walked across the lot to the office, where he spent a few minutes before leaving in his Pontiac around 1:00 a.m.

I was pumped up about what I'd observed—for the first time since I'd suspected something bad was afoot, I'd found something irregular. Maybe we really could solve the mystery, saving the mill along with a pile of cash for J. R., and it might steer him around to my way of thinking about his daughter and me. I looked forward to seeing Joe and comparing notes.

The next day at Pop's, Saturday, I sat down with Joe for what was getting to be our daily war meeting.

I told him about the black truck and how Clive loaded it every night after dark. And how he and the truckdriver looked pretty chummy to me.

"What are you saying?" Joe asked. "Is Clive in cahoots with the black semi-truck?'

"It could be something like that," I said. "The truck is a connection between Clive and the outside world. Clive loads it himself, and it hauls lumber out of the yard at an odd time, running license plates that are a little less than legal."

"So," Joe speculated, "what you're saying is, someone on the outside is getting more than he's paying for, and if so, Clive is getting compensated like Angie predicted—getting a kickback?"

Hearing her name mentioned, Angie poked her head out from the kitchen. "Hey, anyone for pie? I'm getting ready to pull a marionberry out of the oven."

"I am," I said. "But first I'm going to call Sharon and see what she can tell us about Clive."

Sharon's voice came on the line. "Hi, Sonny. What's up?"

"Joe and I are doing some more detective work and we need some info, and we were wondering if you like berry pie."

"Well, that's quite a sentence coming from a mill rat like you. I like pie, and what can I help you with as far as private-eye stuff?"

"Why don't you come out to Pop's and you can enjoy some pie à la mode while Paul Drake and I question you," I said.

In a few minutes, Sharon came through the front door. "I like pie," she said again as she dropped into the seat next to me. "And the Hardy Boys are about to solve the riddle, huh?"

"Well," Joe said, "we have some ideas we'd like to pass by you to see what you think."

"Shoot."

I went first, telling her that we were thinking it was an inside job and probably had something to do with grading the lumber. I explained that it had to be an elaborate scheme that probably involved more than one employee and someone profiting from the outside.

"Do you have anyone in mind?" Sharon asked as she was about to take a bite of pie.

"Clive."

Sharon's eyes popped. She put her fork down. "You really think so?"

"We are convinced that he's involved somehow," I said.

"You really think he's got something to do with it?"

"He might have the mill in his heart, but we're thinking he's filling his pockets with the mill's money," said Joe.

"What makes you so sure?" asked Sharon.

I told Sharon what we had noticed about Clive and his habits. His swing-shift men that he kept an eye on and that he liked to control and so on, and how he loaded that black semi with farm plates every night by himself.

"Oh, that's the Lewis guy," she said, "who hauls out one load a day to a retail store up north called Econo-Lumber. It's a mixed load of boards: utility and low-grade lumber used by ranchers for fencing and such. They've been good customers and pay like clockwork."

"Oh crap," I said. "Just when we thought we had something. So why does the truck come after hours?"

I asked. "And why can he do it without commercial plates?"

"Because he's backhauling, and its after dark, so no one notices, I guess. He delivers hay to dairies in southern Oregon, and by the time he gets back empty, it's late."

"So how long has this Econo-Lumber been buying from the mill?" I asked.

"As I recall, shortly after I came to work—about two years."

"About the same time as Clive showed up?" I asked.

"Right-o," she answered raising her eyebrows.

Maybe we were still on track. "So, let's say Clive is loading valuable lumber on that semi, along with the culls. Who else would have to know about it and go along with it?"

"The swing-shift grader keeps track of the number of stacks of different grades of lumber. If something was wrong, his reports and our sales wouldn't jibe."

"What do you know about him?" I asked.

"He came on right after Clive got here. Right before the problem started."

"Right-o again," Joe popped in. "And this grader guy is the only person on swing shift that Clive doesn't wallow all over—he'll just throw him a nod occasionally."

"He's the one who looks like Abe Lincoln, right?" I asked. "What else do you know about him, Joe?"

"Well," said Joe, "he does look like Lincoln—preacher-like, wearing a black beard and no mustache. He huddles in front of the stacks sporting a black, long-tailed coat and wears payday pants, black of course, and swings that grading stamp like he's judging souls or something."

"How can an employee of the mill be the judge of what it's selling?" I asked. "It's seems to me that the grader could be partial to the mill's benefit."

"The grade of the lumber is there for everyone to see," Sharon said. She then explained that it would be obvious if the mill started overgrading in favor of itself, and the mill's reputation would be damaged, so it's up to the grader to do the best possible job in an unbiased way. She said there were several grades depending on each board's load capacity and its number of knots and other blemishes. Select is cabinet quality and then it drops to number 1, which is at least 75 percent clear, and then down to 2, and then 3. The lowest grade is called "utility." Sharon added, "Usually, anything under number 2 isn't stamped because it won't make basic construction quality anyway."

"We need to get a close look at the lumber that's going on the midnight semi," I said, "and that will be up to me because Joe can't leave his work area without alarming Clive. I'm going to have to spy in close and follow the boards from the grading station until they're loaded.

"Sharon, could you ferret out some information about the grader to see how far back his relationship goes with Clive? Is there any chance you could find out where he worked before he hired on at Dunlap's? Or could you get in trouble for doing it?"

"Sure, I think I can find out a lot about Clive. I have his files. I look at everyone's file periodically to update their insurance policies, among other things, so I'm perfectly in my right to rummage around."

As I scraped the last tiny morsel of pie off my plate, I thanked Sharon and told her she would be hearing from me, probably soon.

Sharon left, but not before she thanked me for the pie and said, "I hope you get the son of a bitch."

Joe was excited with all the progress we'd made, and I was feeling like we were closing in on the rat.

"Good-bye, Perry," Joe laughed.

"See ya, Paul," I joked and then left for home.

Chapter 24

Sunday found me in deep thought. My brain kept grinding away on how Clive could be stealing from his uncle by shipping expensive lumber in the guise of junk. What kind of guy would rip off his own uncle? I didn't know the price difference between utility and select grades, but I suspected it was large.

Monday night, the black semi showed up right on time, and from the shadows, I spied on Clive forklifting lumber from the cheap grade area onto the front of the semi's trailer. Then, as the cowboy kid strapped it down, Clive began loading more cheap stuff on the rear of the trailer, leaving the center empty. Hm? I leaned into my binoculars, watching as Clive disappeared into the maze of stacks at the other end of the yard, the area where the select and other expensive grades were kept. Sure enough, he returned with a stack and loaded it in the middle of the trailer, followed by three more, and the cowboy was loaded. Aha! So this was it. He was smuggling valuable lumber out disguised as junk.

Excited thoughts flew through my head so fast I couldn't breathe regularly. What did I do now? Who were we going to tell and would they believe us? What would J. R.'s reaction be when he found out?

One thing was for certain: I had to be sure.

So after Clive splashed out the driveway in his Pontiac, I walked my flashlight to the staging area to look for fresh tire tracks left in the glaze of fine sawdust that swirled out from the mill. Sure enough, the warmest tracks led to the select pile and disappeared into the web of tire prints heading for the loading area where the black semi had been.

The rest of the night passed with my mind abuzz with a feeling of triumph. I saw the same thing happen again the next few nights. Finally, at 7:00 a.m. on Friday, finished for the night and still jubilant, I went to the office to clock out. Sharon was just coming in to start her day.

Before I could tell her my success, she said, "I think I have something for you guys. How about pie tomorrow afternoon? Four o'clock?"

"Yep."

Saturday morning, with a feeling of accomplishment—I'd seen Clive repeat the process with the black semi for the fifth night in a row—I fell into a deep sleep. I felt good when I rolled out at 3:30, my morning. With giddy anticipation, I drove to Pop's to meet Sharon and Joe for pie.

Yum. The smell of berry pie engulfed me as I entered the restaurant. It was still in the oven cooking and giving off fumes that made my salivary glands throb. Sharon was waiting in a booth. "Hi, Sharon. What did you find out?" I asked as I plopped down.

"Well, it seems this isn't Clive and the grader's first dance together."

"What do you mean by that?" I asked.

"Before they arrived here," she said, "they both worked in the same sawmill. It was also a small outfit owned by a family that had been operating it for years."

"So what happened to that mill?" I asked.

"I'm getting to that," she replied with a satisfied look on her face. "I looked up their phone number in an old sawmill publication that was in the office."

"And?" Joe said, sitting on the edge of his seat.

"And a lady working in a beauty shop answered. She said she gets calls occasionally asking for the mill and that she has had the phone number for about two years now."

"That two-year thing seems to be a pattern," I muttered.

"So then I called the chamber in Gresham, and they told me the mill filed for bankruptcy in the summer of '57."

"Wow," I said, "a little over two years ago."

"I'll be damned," said Joe.

"I'll second that," I said. "This is all coming together now. Clive is our man for sure." I told them about Clive sneaking the select lumber onto the middle of the cowboy kid's load the previous nights. "With the help of the man in black swinging the stamp and the owner of Econo-Lumber, he just sucks the blood until the beast is dead."

"I can't believe he'd do it to his own uncle," said Joe.

"You told us he wasn't very nice," I said, looking at Sharon.

She nodded. "So what are you guys going to do about it?"

"Tell Dunlap," said Joe. "It's his mill."

"He would never believe us," Sharon said. "He would tell Clive and then they would have a grand laugh and we would all be fired."

"Oh, no," I said, "I never thought of that." It was maddening being so close to something that I couldn't do a damned thing about. I'd been going through a lot of it lately, and now here it was again. The letdown made my arm itch where I couldn't scratch it.

"I guess we could go to the police," I said.

"What if they don't believe us?" said Joe.

"There's one way to find out. Grab your smokes, Paul," I said. "Let's go."

"I hope old Duffy ain't working today," said Joe.

"Yeah, me too." We'd steered clear of the bald-headed, fat son of a bitch since our encounter with him during that hot summer with the cowgirls.

I parked the '40 across the street from City Hall. Duffy's car wasn't in front, so, relieved, we went in. The lady cop at the front desk told us to wait out in the lobby for the policeman on duty.

A car squealed to a stop in front of the building, the door blew open, and there was Duffy. Oh shit, just our luck. Joe groaned. Duffy looked older and stooped some, and what hair he had was white, and his skin was loose on his face. Unfortunately, his mannerisms were the same—his cocky swagger. He hadn't changed.

"What are you doing here?" he spat, looking down at my cast. I knew he wanted to ask about it, but his ego wouldn't let him look concerned. And I wasn't offering.

I started in, explaining the crime right there in the hallway. He stood looking at me with narrowed eyes, picking his teeth, obviously not moved by the story. "You talking Dunlap's Mill?" he grunted.

"Yeah," Joe said.

"That's out of the city limits—you'll have to see the county for that." He turned and strutted into his office, slamming the door behind him, and that was that.

It was nice to part company with the old prick, even if we hadn't gotten anywhere on our quest.

A half an hour later, we were roosted on another bench that was familiar from colorful episodes growing up, in the county courthouse sheriff's office. Finally, a desk cop–looking guy with a stiff shirt and a sunless face invited us into his office. He slung his hand towards a couple of folding chairs, offering us a seat. Leaning back in his creaky, sprung office chair, he threw his feet up on the desk of papers and took a curious look at my cast. "So what can I do for you young men today?"

This time we got further into our story and allegations before the deputy stopped us.

"You guys know what you're saying?"

"Yes, we do," I said. "We work there and have been watching the mill go downhill for some time."

"You can't go around accusing someone of something out of the blue—you have to have proof. You got any evidence?"

I looked at Joe and got one of his "this isn't going so well" looks.

"Well, no," I said. "Don't you have detectives for that?" My arm began to itch.

He laughed. "With the recession going on, we barely have force enough to keep people from killing each other without going out on every limb looking for something to do."

"There hasn't been a murder in this town," I said, "since Annie Joe what's her name murdered herself five years ago."

His face reddened. "That's right. We do a hell of a job with what we have, and like I said, you need proof if you're going to come in here with a story like you just told." He dropped his feet and his eyes went to the stack of papers. We were excused. I stepped off the concrete steps towards my car feeling deflated. "Jeez, Joe, we're in a bad way. We know what's going on out there, but we can't do anything about it if they don't believe us."

"And we don't even know how to get the evidence," said Joe.

We got in my car and circled around town, feeling downtrodden like a couple of generals without an army. Being a normal Saturday, the street in front of the movie house was clogged with mother-driven taxis with horns, come to pick up their kids, who were gathered under the marquee. Posted on the sign was *The Unforgiven*, which like most Westerns, I figured, brought out the man in every junior high tough kid who rode a velvet-covered theater seat.

I slowed for the crowd.

"Hey, are you Sonny Mitchell?" called out a raucous female movie gaper of about fourteen.

She jumped on the running board. "Is this your famous car?"

Suddenly, my '40 was swamped with teenage madness. They swarmed my car with confidence fueled by the safety of a crowd.

"That's him," I heard a boy say. "It's the fastest car in town too."

It was Marylyn's brother, Harold, riding Joe's side. "I saw him break his arm!" He looked proud as punch the way he eyed my cast, like he was about to enlighten the girl about how that happened. I didn't think that the whole town needed to know how I'd broken my arm, so I moved to another subject.

"How did you know my car's fast?" I asked him.

"My sis told me," he said, confiding-like. "She loves you."

Man, that shot a nice tingle up my spine, but just like at the snack bar, I didn't let it show.

Harold's statement was apparently too much for the girl on my side, because she just gazed at Harold with her mouth open. She was digging old Harold.

"Marylyn probably doesn't want you to blab it all over town, does she, Harold?" I said.

"You can't tell about her. She's a girl, you know," Harold said, rolling his eyes.

"Hey," he said, "how about me signing your cast?"

"Okay, I guess. Do you have a pen?"

"No. I hadn't thought of that," Harold said.

"I got you covered," Joe said. He pulled a fist full of crayons from his jacket pocket. "I've been using these lately."

"Red!" Harold said. Why was it everyone liked red, I wondered. They were always the first gone in a Crayola box. I threw my arm across Joe's lap for him, and leaning in, Harold scrawled his name in big letters up my cast. By then, a girl next to Harold reached a blue one off Joe and began writing her name, carefully, like she was signing an important document.

Everyone was yelling for a crayon—wanting in on it. Horns honked behind us, so I eased my car over to the curb and settled in for autographs. They lined up on my side of the car, and one by one left their marks on my cast. They were young and naive and had big, innocent eyes, and they took the ordeal seriously and were rigorous with the pains they took in their signatures. When they were done, I had a Freddy, a Ruth, two Lindas, and some more. And one I hadn't noticed: "White Rats."

"Hey, Harold. Who are the White Rats?"

"We are." He motioned to some boys circled around him and wearing pouts and Elvis hair. "We got things to do, you know, Sonny. Let's ride," Harold ordered, and he and his gang saddled up and sped off hard on the pedals.

"That looks a little familiar," said Joe.

"How do you mean?"

"That was us just a few years ago."

"Yeah. I kind of envy them."

"And they envy you. How does it feel to be a celebrity?" Joe asked almost seriously.

I pulled out into the now-deserted street with my cast of many colors hooked into the steering wheel. "Well, for one thing, I'm not one. And if I was, maybe I could get someone to listen to us about our findings out at the mill."

Then I got an idea. "Wait a minute, Joe. There is one guy who might be willing to help us."

"Who?"

"Sheriff Buster Cleveland."

Buster had been the sheriff during our time of growing up in his county, and we'd become acquainted mostly by us being bad and him chasing us for it.

"Buster? He's retired—why would he want to get into it?" Joe asked.

"That's just it, Joe, because he probably doesn't have a hell of a lot on his plate. I heard his wife passed away recently, so he's probably up there with his dog just waiting to die."

"Let's go and find out," said Joe. We'd been to Buster's ranch before. In fact, unknown to us, we were having beers in his driveway when he and his wife unexpectedly arrived home. It was a nervous affair, to say the least.

After a ten-minute ride out of town, we arrived at the end of Buster's long and winding driveway. It was just getting dark and raining. The open gate that guarded the place leaned haphazardly against the fence, seeming worn and useless. I drove in on the gravel, dodging potholes, towards the house, a ranch style with a feather of smoke coming out the chimney.

Good, I thought, *he's home*. I pulled up near the light that was burning over the porch and shut off the motor. On the steps, Buster's bloodhound got up and stretched. He was a dog of many years, which was evident by his graying hair and clouded eyes. He wasn't a watchdog, in that he didn't make a sound as we approached the etched-glass window in the front door. I knocked.

Someone inside turned down the volume on a TV or radio, and then a shadow moved behind the glass. Buster Cleveland, with a cigar hanging from his mouth, opened the door wearing a bathrobe and slippers. He was unshaven and looked tired, but at the sight of us, his eyes came to life. "Hello, boys." He grunted. "What can I do for you?"

"Hi, Sheriff. I'm Sonny Mitchell and this here is Joe Harden."

"Oh, yes. I recognize you fellows. It's been a while. Come on in."

With the dog following, we stepped into an entryway that led to a living room that smelled of smoke and leather. It was home to a huge rock fireplace and wild animal heads everywhere on the walls. They threw us cautious looks as we sat down on the couch.

Buster, with a slight smile, said, "The way I remember it, you guys have a taste for beer, right?"

"Sure," we both answered at once.

Buster went to the kitchen.

Joe and I exchanged looks of encouragement. This was starting off pretty good.

Buster returned with a cold six-pack of Lucky Lager. I smiled at Joe, who gave me a wink. It must have been on sale. Buster opened three and set the rest on the coffee table. We weren't just having one. That was good, in that it told me he was going to give us some time.

Over beers, Joe and I laid out what was on our minds, how the mill was in trouble and what we knew about Clive and how exasperating it had been not getting the law to intercede and bring the culprits to justice.

Buster relit his cigar and listened, all the time scratching his dog's ears and taking in every detail of what we told him. He'd nod at times, like he was generally interested in what we said.

When I finished, Buster set his beer down and looked at me with eyes showing he was thinking. "From what you have told me here, I'd have to say Clive is a real dipshit. Thank God they don't come like him very often. I know old Dunlap, and you're right about one thing— he would never admit that one of his own family is a crook, so it won't do any good to go to him until you got the jerk behind bars." Buster went on to tell us that, from what we said, he figured Clive and the grader guy were shuffling the papers and degrading some of the expensive product for cheap stuff and getting a kickback from the lumberyard. "That's all fine and good," he said, dropping his cigar butt into his ashtray, "but you're going to have to prove it if you expect anyone to take you seriously."

"So how are we going to do that?" I asked.

"Well, for starters, I'd follow the truck and make sure where he's delivering to. Make sure he isn't unloading anywhere except the Econo-Lumber store. Then I'd take pictures of lumber showing Dunlap's stamp on it sitting on the Econo-Lumber's lot. Then compare them with your girl's paper work in the mill's office, and if it doesn't jibe, you have a start," he said, pulling a new cigar from his shirt pocket.

"As this moves along, I think we're going to need some more of your help, Sheriff," I said. "Would you help us out? Joe and I are new at this sort of thing."

He lit up a wooden match with his fingernail and then looked at me with a sparkle in his eyes I hadn't seen till then. "I'll be right here—it doesn't look like I'm going anywhere." Looking down at his dog, he handed me his card, which still had the star embossed above his home phone number.

Buster was cool. Sipping that beer with him in his world by the fire and under those trophies was humbling, and I was liking him for it. As we walked for the door, I thanked him. "We'll be in touch and probably soon."

Buster let us out and the old dog stayed in.

On the way back to town, Joe and I talked.

"That old coot really leaves an impression on you, don't he?" said Joe.

"Who'd ever thought we'd end up partnering with him—and on real live case. Ain't life great, Joe?"

"Sure is. And you never know where it may take you."

"Yeah," I said. "He's done real well for himself too. I don't know how big his ranch is, but I'd love having one like it someday."

"You'd look good sitting on that porch up there in a cowboy hat."

"Big ten-gallon one," I laughed.

"So what do you think? Who's going to follow the semi-truck to see where it goes?"

"How about you and Angie take my pickup Monday night after you get off. You'll have time to pick her up and be back at the mill when the cowboy kid pulls out with his load. No one will recognize the old Chevy. Follow the semi to see where it goes. Call it a moonlight ride."

"I like that," Joe said. "And Angie's pretty excited about all this detective work. Ingrid can stay with her grandma. "

Chapter 25

Monday at midnight, Joe and Angie were hidden out across the street in an unfinished suburb, and I was smiling to myself as the black semi pulled into the yard right on time. So much had happened since I'd first seen the cowboy kid and his truck—it was like I was somehow in control now. The pieces were coming together, and I was digging it. I was hiding close this time, cramped between lumber stacks, not scary close, not close enough to make out words, but neighborly close.

I could see the freckles on the kid's face and his innocent eyes looking at Clive as he handed him an envelope. Clive clammed onto it, rubbing it with both hands as if measuring the content without opening it. It was cash for sure, I figured. I'd probably just witnessed the payoff—the smoking gun. A bonus I was ecstatic about; like I said, everything was falling into place now. But I was surprised the kid might be involved.

After loading the lumber, Clive let the truck out the gate at 12:25 and, after his usual time in the office, left the property in his Pontiac about 12:45 a.m. I spent the rest of the night doing my job in the mill, wondering how Joe's trip was going.

The next afternoon, I got up early, about 2:00 p.m., excited by what I'd seen and eager to see how Joe's midnight ride went. I caught up with Joe at Pop's before he went to work at the mill. I pulled in the same time he did and parked by his '50.

The sun broke through the clouds and it was pleasant. We stood out there. I plopped one foot up on Joe's bumper and laid my cast on the hood. The hood was warm from the motor, warming my cast, making my arm feel good." So tell me how it went for you last night. Did you follow the truck?"

"Yep," Joe said. "We pulled out behind him just like we'd planned. He headed straight for the freeway, turned north, and trucked through Salem, then took the exit to Highway 99E until he turned off and took the highway right into Molalla."

"So he didn't stop anywhere along the way?" I asked.

"Nope. He entered town and motored right down the main street and turned into a driveway adjacent to the Econo-Lumber yard, got out of his truck, keyed open the gate, and unloaded the lumber himself, using the yard's forklift."

"So he has he own key?" I said. "That's interesting. He knows his way around the place then."

"Yeah. That's what I thought," Joe said. "One thing, though."

"What's that?"

"He unloaded the entire load in no particular order—just willy-nilly, like his job was to get it off the truck, leaving the organizing of stacks for someone else."

"What's that mean, Joe?"

"I'm thinking the cowboy kid doesn't know about the different qualities and the worth of it all," said Joe. "Like he's not included in anything to do with the running of Econo-Lumber."

"So what your saying is, he's probably not in on the scheme?" I asked.

"I'm thinking he's just an innocent kid picking up some extra work."

"I kind of hope you're right about him," I said. "I admire his work ethic."

"Speaking of work," Joe said, "anything new happen at the mill last night?"

"Yeah," I said. "Something big. I saw our cowboy kid driver hand Clive an envelope."

"Payoff, you think?" Joe said excited-like.

"Looks like it," I said hopefully.

The fact that the kid unloaded the entire delivery at Econo-Lumber was important to the case. So I figured that since we knew that, it would be easy to compare the paperwork in the office with the photos we were going to take, and prove that Clive, with the help of his friend the grader, was turning in false inventory numbers to the office. So Dunlap assumed all the lumber going to Econo was cull, when in reality, parts of the loads included select. Clive was shipping good lumber for bad, racketeering the mill and his uncle. And with seeing the fat envelope in

Clive's greedy hands, I knew he was getting the kickback we had assumed.

The sun disappeared behind some clouds, but it didn't dim our enthusiasm. "Let's go in," I said. "I'll buy you a quick Coke you can drink before work."

The door had barely slammed behind us when Angie appeared, grinning. She beat us to the booth. "How'd we do?" she whispered with a giggle.

Sitting down, I said, "Good. You guys did real good."

"I love the espionage and intrigue of it all," she beamed. "Being incognito and sneaky is fun and romantic," she said, looking over at Joe, who was blushing.

"Hey, Angie," I said, "you got a camera. How about you loaning it out to us."

"I do have a Brownie," she said. "What you want it for?"

"Joe and I need to take some pictures," I said.

"Yeah. What of?"

"We're going back to Econo-Lumber tomorrow to photograph lumber. We gotta have proof that is where the boards end up. Is it hard to run a Brownie?"

"It's already loaded with film, so just point and click."

Angie knew Joe and I didn't know the first thing about photography. Our kind never walked around with a camera strapped on like the brainiac kids at school did.

The following morning, Joe and I, armed with a loaded Brownie, went to visit Econo-Lumber. We buzzed up the freeway in my old pickup—driving it, thinking we might want to bring back a board or two for evidence. Turning off, we followed the two-lane through farms and small towns until we hit the outskirts of Molalla. It was a quaint little town situated in the hills of the Cascade Range, backed up by Mt. Hood, snow covered and daunting.

"Turn right here." Joe pointed to the Econo-Lumber sign.

We drove into the lot like normal shoppers and parked beside some pickups hauling cow dogs guarding hay bales, showing their teeth and daring us to come close. Joe and I stepped carefully between the dogs into the lumber area, rubbernecking around at stacks, looking out for boards showing off the Dunlap stamp.

A fellow wearing mirrored sunglasses and riding a forklift intercepted us. "What can I find for you fellas today?" he asked, grinning through a one-toothed mouth of tobacco.

"We're looking for some good fir that we can saw up for furniture boards," Joe said.

"Down at the end and over two rows you find the select," he said, spitting. "When you find what you need, just whistle, and I'll come load it for you." He revved his motor and roared off, looking for more happy customers.

We walked across the gravel lot towards the high-grade lumber area, looking for our brand, and we didn't have to go far to find it. We came face to face with several stacks of prime select lumber with the familiar Dunlap stamp staring at us. "Bingo," said Joe.

"This lumber left Dunlap's recorded as cull or low-grade stuff, " I said. "I'll betcha the grader simply writes down numbers in his daily log, altering the grades on a few stacks, and when he turns in his records after his shift, no one is the wiser."

"Yeah," Joe said. "It leaves Dunlap's as crap and transforms itself into royalty on the way."

"Yep," I said. "Then Econo-Lumber sells it for big bucks and Clive gets an envelope full of cash."

"And then Clive pays off the grader and everyone's happy," said Joe.

"Pull that Brownie out of your pocket," I said, "and see if you can fire off some shots before the forklift jockey gets wise."

Click, wind, click, wind. Joe looked like he knew what he was doing.

"Now get a close one of the stamp with the Econo Lumber sign in the background."

He clicked off some pictures of the units showing how clear the lumber was with the Dunlap stamp. We picked out a couple of eight-foot two-by-sixes that showed the stamp well and headed inside the store to pay.

The checker, a girl of about eighteen with auburn-colored hair, looked us over with soft blue eyes. She wasn't like a glamour girl and her teeth were uneven, but she wasn't hard to look at, if you know what I mean. But she couldn't hold a candle to Marylyn.

"Nice boards you all picked out." She had a southern accent she was using on us.

"Yeah. We're building furniture for Joe here. He just got married."

"Oh, how sweet," she said. "I have a boyfriend. He has his own truck. It's diesel, ya know, and he hauls hay with it."

That got my attention. "Oh yeah? What color is it?"

"Black as ink," she said. "And he hauls lumber at night. He's a hard worker and we're saving up to get hitched."

"Does he haul the lumber here?" I asked.

"Yep. Hauls out of one place—loads about midnight down south and delivers here in the middle of the night."

"That's great," I said. "Sounds like you got a good man there."

She smiled at that. "You all come back now, hear?"

Carrying the boards, I said, "Did you hear that? Her boyfriend's got to be our semi driver."

"So do you think he's in on the scheme with Clive?" Joe asked.

"Nah," I answered. "Clive wouldn't cut him in. Like we were thinking before, the boy's just got a nice backhaul, I'd say.

Back in Willamette, I dropped Joe off at Pop's and then hurried the film downtown to the drug store before it closed for the day. Buster had said to get one each, but I was thinking it would be good to have multiple copies made of each photo: one set for Buster, one set for Joe, and the other for me, for safekeeping.

A girl wearing an apron took the roll. "I'd like three copies each, and could you make 'em big?" I asked.

"Okay," she said through a shiny set of braces. "They'll be large, eight by tens. Come back in a couple days,"

"Is there any chance I could get them sooner? I'm in kind of a hurry for them."

"Oh, why?" she said. "Are they pictures of that hot rod you drive?"

"No. In fact they're real boring pictures. How'd you know about my hot rod?"

"I saw you with Marylyn Swanson in that picture on the front of the paper. She's a cheerleader at school. I bet she really loves you for the way you saved her."

"I wish it were that simple."

"Come back tomorrow after lunch," she said with a smile. "Since you're a hero and all, I'll slip the roll in front of the rest."

I felt my face redden. "Thanks."

I drove back to Pop's, where I used the phone to call Buster.

"Buster," he answered.

"Hi, Sheriff. This is Sonny Mitchell—I got an update here on our progress."

"Oh, good. What have you got so far?"

Keeping the best for last, I told him about Joe's night trip to Molalla and our day trip with the camera.

"Did you keep the receipt?"

"Yep, two boards, the date, and the amount." Then I dropped the good part on him. "Hey, Buster," I said. "I watched the truck driver hand over an envelope to Clive."

There was silence and then Buster let out. "Aha, that's key if it's a payoff."

"Clive held the thing like it was precious," I said.

"Call me back when you get the pictures developed and we'll set up a time for a visit."

"I'll do it. Good-bye, Buster."

I hauled ass for home to see if I could sleep the few hours I had before work.

The next afternoon, which was Wednesday, I was met at the drug store by a different checker and she narrowed her eyes, probably wondering how my pictures raised to the top of the pile.

I paid up and left, carrying them under my coat to protect them from the mist of a clearing-up shower and from the eyes of the curious. I got in my car and slammed the door. Safe behind the wheel, I flipped through them, becoming ecstatic. The pictures were terrific, considering who took them—good enough that I could make out the Dunlap stamps and the Econo-Lumber sign swelled up in the background. I added them to the envelope of mill papers under the seat.

At home, I phoned Buster and told him how the photos came out.

"That's good," he said. "Come out about three today and bring the mill papers and the pictures."

Because of his work schedule, Joe couldn't go along. I didn't like that, and I knew Joe wouldn't either, but it was Buster's call.

I drove the pickup so I could show him the boards.

"Come in, Sonny. You like coffee?"

With a hot mug in hand, I showed the sheriff the photos. He looked them over real careful-like.

"These should work," he said finally. "Nice job in getting the Econo-Lumber sign in the background. Let me see the mill papers."

I handed them over—the whole stack. Sharon had given me copies dating back thirty days, just like Buster asked for. He took them in his big hands like they were precious documents.

"So, Sheriff, when we going to do it?" I asked. "I'd sure like to be rid of this cast before we do anything exciting."

"Can't wait," he said. "If this investigation gets out before we spring it on him, he'll take a trip to Mexico and not come back. We'll do it Monday night. That should give me enough time to go over these pages with a fine-tooth comb." Buster was unwavering. It was like he'd done this before, which he probably had. He knew just what he was doing.

I wasn't so sure about any of it, but his confidence was rubbing off on me, so I was all in. "So *how* are we going to do it?" I asked.

"Clive gets done loading the semi-truck about 12:30, right?"

"Yeah, pretty close to that every night," I said.

"You let me in the gate soon as he's finished loading, and we wait and watch until we see him go into the office. Then, at 12:45 on the dot, your friend Joe is going to march into the sheriff's office with this here note I'm writing. It will tell the officer on duty a short explanation of what we're doing and to get a deputy to the mill office as quick as possible."

"Do you think they'll do it? Joe and I didn't have much luck down there."

"They'll come a-running," Buster said. "My name will be on the note."

"Then what?" I asked.

"We'll just follow him into the office when he's alone and leaving for home, and hit him with it, and hopefully he'll panic and confess and we'll have him."

"What about Clive's partner the grader guy, and the guy at Econo? What are we going to do about them?"

"The paperwork will prove they were in on it," Buster said. "They'll be dealt with as soon as we get Clive."

"Monday night, huh?"

"Be sure to tell Joe how important it is to show up at the sheriff's office on time."

"Okay," I said. "We'll be ready." *How do I get ready for something like this?*

Stepping out the door, I turned back and said, "Oh, by the way, Sheriff, what if he doesn't panic?"

"It's the chance we'll have to take."

Chapter 26

Later that evening, before my shift, I was inside Pop's having a burger and thinking of what Clive might do when the sheriff came knocking.

Suddenly, Eddy came crashing through the door all excited about racing. "It's going to be out at Otto's," he said, dropping into the booth across from me. "The word is Saturday night, just you and Crazy Horse."

"Just the two of us? Are you sure about this, Eddy?"

"Yeah, everyone in the valley is talking about it."

"Everyone?"

"Well, most people, I guess," Eddy said.

Eddy was exaggerating but I kinda liked it.

Damn, I was wishing the race thing would wait. Racing needed thinking and planning, and right then I was up to my eyeballs in concentration over Clive and dealing with him. But I knew better. Things could get busy. So I figured I'd better get Crazy Horse off my back and then get ready for the visit with Clive on Monday night.

"See if you can get Joe to be the starter, Eddy," I said. "He has a good swift flag timed always the same, and doesn't get all flustered like some do when things turn serious." I could have asked Joe myself, but Eddy liked being part of it.

"Good idea," he said.

I left Eddy and pulled out through the parking lot, noticing the Impala was in its usual place and that the volume from the crowd around it had turned up in amps. The little fickle shits taunted me with insults over the smallest infractions, like, "Where's your hubcaps, Sonny, going racing?" They'd thrown in with the new kid, convinced he had the faster car.

I wasn't sure about that, but we were about to find out.

That part was the same old thing. Who had the fastest car? That was the only thing that hadn't changed.

It seemed I was constantly reminded that things were different for me at the drive-in and everywhere else on the circuit, but at Pop's it was obvious because, at one time, we ruled the place. I missed it. I had known everyone and they knew me, and if not me, they knew my car and were afraid of it. Most of my friends had left, leaving ghosts that drifted through parked cars I didn't recognize, waving at me as I throttled by.

Linda Nelson, always my ally, jumped in my car and gave me the scoop from the enemy camp. "He thinks he's faster, Sonny." And she brought me up to date on things with Marylyn. "Her dad has her practically under house arrest."

"Tell her I'll be seeing her soon," I said, wondering what I meant.

It wasn't lost on Linda either. "How's that, Sonny?"

"I don't know. I just got a feeling in my bones," I said. "Something is going to break loose. This isn't going to go on like this forever." I had no idea what was coming— maybe it was a premonition.

Saturday afternoon, with the intent of getting my car ready for racing, I turned in to Frank's Mobil and rolled right into the empty lube bay.

"What's going on?" asked Frank, wiping his hands on a red shop rag.

"It's time to go racing," I said. "I need to adjust the valves."

"That ought to be a lot of fun with one hand."

"Yeah, Frank," I said. "It's a bitch wrenching with one arm."

"Not so good for racing either maybe, huh?"

"I'm getting pretty good at driving like this," I said. "My shifting arm is good, so I just hook the wheel with the other and get after it."

Frank helped me roll my mounted cheater slicks off the upper rack, and with a little air, I set their pressure for maximum bite and filled the front tires for easy rolling.

Then I pumped ethyl into the tank until the gauge met the half-full marker. I didn't want to haul around any more gas than necessary, because of weight, but I didn't want to short myself either.

The last genuine racing I had done was the night I raced a Corvette and then ran out of gas with Marylyn.

Eddy came putting in to the station in his Simca. He was wearing his usually frantic expression. "Nine o'clock at Otto's," he said.

"What's at nine o'clock?" I asked, knowing damn well what he meant.

Ignoring the question, he said, "It's early. What ya want to do?"

"Let's go for a ride," I said. I backed the '40 into the bay and got in with Eddy.

"Let's go have a burger," he said.

"Good idea," I said, "I'm starving."

Entering Pop's parking lot, I suddenly realized the wallpaper had changed. The Impala wasn't there. A cold feeling shot down my spine, turning my balls to ice. Crazy Horse was somewhere tuning. It wasn't just me who was serious—had he been deadpanning all along and tonight I was going to meet the real Crazy Horse? Suddenly, I wasn't hungry. "Take me back to the '40," I said. "I want to look it over again before the race."

Back at Frank's, Eddy bumped me on the shoulder and said, "I'll see you out at Otto's. Good luck, Sonny."

Frank was gone, and I was left alone with my car, and with my demons, who were pestering me through my side window.

I had some time. I planned to arrive at the race a little late, giving Crazy Horse a chance to get unnerved a little. I checked everything again, the oil and the water and the blower belt, making sure she was ready for a hell of a test.

The clock in the office said 8:15. It was time to go. I fired up the motor and it sounded good—crisp-like, building my confidence. I backed out and let the motor warm while I locked the station. Back in the '40, I took a drag on my cigarette, pulled the shifter into low, and drove.

It was getting dark out and freezing-ass cold. I wondered if there would be much of a crowd. With the heater buzzing, I took off through the hills of North Willamette in a roundabout way of getting to Otto's, giving me time to settle my nerves. My '40 wanted to run—as if I couldn't hold it back. It was like a colt doing a warm-up lap, and when I'd give it the goose, it roared with instant throttle response, like it was raring to leap out in front.

I passed wild cherry trees in blossom, and leaves were forming on the oaks, saying, "Listen, time traveler, you better catch up; we're moving on with this."

Shifting down, I dropped out of the hills a mile west of the outlaw drag strip known as Otto's, pulled over and uncorked my lake pipes. On the road again, I let my pipes cackle going by the gravel pit, where it felt like just a short time ago Sheriff Cleveland hid out, masterminding the capture of the Little Bastards. How ironic, I thought—now Buster and I were cohorts in a criminal investigation..

Otto's farm buildings appeared next to the stretch of two-lane blacktop running south, and fields and pastures that were dotted with trees and brush. The drag strip— a gearhead playground.

About 9:15, I pulled up to a hell of a crowd, a gaggle of the younger set milling around the starting line—a fresh spray-can line painted across the highway. Small red flares cast shadows on the faces of the smokers, and the light from my headlights reflected off the glass bottles that held the beer that helped fuel the event. The festive part of the drag race was in full spin. There were some familiar faces from my past, but most were strangers to me. The crowd was yelling and hollering and rooting on their favorites—the beer had been doing its share to rev them up. Only, tonight it wasn't about several cars vying to be heroes according to speed, but just two cars in a grudge race: Crazy Horse and me. Like Eddy said at Pop's, "the biggest race of all time." Maybe it was, for our town anyway. To me, the awe of it all was beginning to fade, swallowed up by life's changes.

I rolled up near the starting line with my pipes bellowing out music only a car freak could appreciate. The spectators, who were warming in their cars, flipped on their headlights to illuminate the track. Joe was standing on the starting line, his face shining in the cold air. It was good to see him holding the flags—a green one for staging and a red one to start the race. Joe motioned me up with the flip of the green flag he held in his right hand. When I arrived in the pre-stage area, he walked over to my window. "You want anything special tonight, Sonny?" he asked as he wiped his nose with the front of his t-shirt.

"No, just fair and square, Joe," I answered. "Oh, and zip up your jacket before you freeze to death."

"It's not cold where I'm standing," he said with a grin, then pushed off from my door to do business. More crowd poured out of their warm cars, craving the full dose of power given off by tires and the screaming of motors, producing way more than Detroit dreamed of.

The Impala rolled up next me, and then with a noise like a roar from a wild animal, he laid out a smoke-belching burnout across the line. It was a carbon copy of the spectacle I'd performed the summer before, beating a rattled T-Bird racer from Portland.

I held my ground and waited for him to back up through the smoke.

When the smoke cleared, Crazy Horse was at the line, waiting for me to warm my tires. I hooked my cast into the steering wheel, laid into the throttle, and dumped the clutch. The sound coming from the pipes from my big Oldsmobile motor filled my car with a roar as I blew across the starting line. Then the smoke from the burning rubber came through the cracks in the floor. The smell and the g's forcing me back in the seat were intoxicating. My demons were egging me on. *Don't let up*, they taunted. They wanted to lay rubber all the way to Willamette. I came to my senses and rolled to a stop at half-track. I opened my door to let the smoke clear as I brought my floor shift into reverse and began backing through the haze, which looked like the aftermath of a battle.

The crowd was delirious from the effect of our ground-pounding burnouts. I backed across the starting line to where Crazy Horse was waiting in the other lane. My heart pounded; my demons rooted me on with their shrill little voices.

Joe turned inhuman then, became a machine in the way he signaled with a slight movement of the green flag calling me ahead to the line. I eased the clutch out and began rolling ahead. Suddenly, I was caught off guard by a vision entering the corner of my eye like a dream. It was Marylyn looking at me through the lingering tire smoke. She was standing behind a row of Crazy Horse fans who were shivering out encouragement to their superhero. Her face was pale and she had a hankie in her hand and a look of hope on her face. Then poof, she was gone.

What was happening? Was I going insane over all this? Or was it her ghost, or my demons tricking me?

Joe was frantically motioning me to close in next to the Impala, which was already staged and revving, ready to go. I was out of whack with the surprise sighting of Marylyn, or her ghost, or whatever it was. I was supposed to be concentrating on the flag, and my mind was racing after Marylyn. I was confused, and the simple steps of braking, clutching, and feathering the throttle became foreign to me.

Suddenly, Joe's red flag was in the air and the Impala launched. Then I left the line, and as I went by Joe, he had a "what the hell?" look on his face. This brought me back, but it was too late. Crazy Horse shot out four car links ahead of me, and I had to follow those taillights for a quarter-mile of getting beat. I was beaten, but on the bright side, I realized that in the high end of every gear, I had pulled on him. He got me by two car lengths. After crossing the painted finish line, we slowed and made U-turns, and I followed him out of respect for his victory. From where I was, the starting line looked like a lit-up border crossing in the middle of nowhere.

I hadn't had to return to the line as the loser since Bruce beat me out on Muddy Creek Road when we were juniors. I hadn't liked it real well, and I noticed the feeling hadn't grown a lot better. The good news was that we were going best out of three, so I still had a chance.

On his return, Crazy Horse stopped at the starting line to take in the glory from his fans and admirers. They crowded around his car, which was illuminated by the headlights. I had to sit back in my car and wait, with the demons needling and heckling me, bouncing all over hell with their eyes shooting sparks as they taunted me for losing. I waited in agony for the spectacle to end.

Finally, Crazy Horse made a U-turn to line up again, letting me by to do the same.

I got quiet looks of disbelief from Eddy and the older veterans, who had been there during the drag wars of the past. I felt bad that I'd let them down over dropping the ball at the starting line, so with discipline, I looked straight ahead, making sure I didn't see any ghosts, and methodically approached the line for round two.

Crazy Horse abandoned the long burnout ritual in favor of old-dog normal start, which was fine with me. He staged first. Joe brought me in with the green flag, and then lowered both flags to his ankles in a crouch, signaling us to bring our rpms up.

I entered the zone in my mind—the zone where I went to be alone, lonely like I was supposed to be. No demons, no nothing, just the flag and my tachometer. I could see Joe's muscles tighten in his neck as they flexed in anticipation.

Then the flags jetted north, and I was gone with a roar. Crazy Horse got off good with his grill on my door. We were almost even, side-by-side through most of first, but when my blower got charged with that cool night air, I crept ahead like it was a walk in the park. Second gear was the same. He got back a little ground in the low end of each gear, but as my tach began to climb, I put some more real estate between us. In high, I knew I was toying with him.

I didn't want him to get discouraged and wimp out on the third and final race, so as we neared the finish line, I slowly let up on the throttle. I wanted the world to know, and for Angie's sake, I wanted those teenybopper punks of Crazy Horse's to ingest a little crow along with their cherry Cokes.

When we returned to the starting area, it was a whole new ballgame. The Crazy Horse worshippers were more subdued, and my camp had come to life with thumbs up and so on. It was a good feeling. It was then I remembered why I had raced for all these years. I smiled to myself. I was back.

The Impala staged first again, for the third and final race. Joe started to wave me ahead then he cocked his head to one side and stopped cold.

A shadow wiped over my rearview mirror and then my passenger door opened. It was Marylyn. I was flabbergasted.

She jumped in and slammed the door. "Sonny, I have to do this. It's time we did things together." She had a mischievous look on her face as she grabbed hold of my wrist with her cold blue hand.

"I thought you were a ghost out there," I told her.

The word ghost brought the demons from hiding. They wadded up on the dash opposite Marylyn, big eyed with curiosity. They didn't know what to think.

"Sorry about that," she told me. "Linda told me about the big race and I wasn't going to miss it for the world."

"What about your dad?"

"They left for the weekend, and I got a babysitter to watch Harold for tonight and here I am." Grinning again.

"We don't have to do this together," I said. "It's dangerous—you might get hurt."

"I love you, Sonny," she said, looking intense. "Now let's beat this kid."

I couldn't pull my eyes away from her, she was so beautiful.

"Concentrate, Sonny." Her mouth curled with a determined look.

The little demons scurried away in fright. Marylyn had overpowered them.

"Okay. Hold on and brace yourself," I said.

She settled back in a frozen stare, as if she was approaching the top of a roller coaster.

I looked at Joe, put Marylyn and everything else out of my mind.

Crazy Horse and I got off the line together, and then I pulled on him in every gear. When I crossed the stripe, I didn't know how far back he was, but his headlights were small.

I backed off the throttle and turned the heater fan to high, just in time for Marylyn to collapse into me. She had been more wound up by the race than I knew.

In my mirror I saw the Impala's headlights swipe the highway and turn red. He was headed back.

I swung off at a wide spot in the road and turned perpendicular to the road. The sound of my tires rolling in the gravel woke Marylyn. She sat straight up. "Why are we stopping?"

I shut off the motor and opened my door. "I'm going to cap the lake plugs."

I jumped out into the night, shutting the door behind me. When I finished with the plugs I took a look at where we were. It was cold out but quiet. Heavenly quiet. The highway, just a two-lane road, went both ways. I could return to victory, but up ahead the highway looked like a blue ribbon all lit up by the moon and the city lights of Willamette and my future.

I jumped back in the warm car and pulled Marylyn close to me. I started the motor, pulled the shifter into low, hit the throttle, and drove straight ahead.

"We won." Marylyn said. "Aren't we going back?"

"No," I said. "We're not going back. That was my last race."

"Where are we going then?" Surprised.

"Forward. Look, Marylyn, the road is straight. There's nothing in our way."

"It will be wonderful," she said, huddling into me, "but what about my dad?"

"I'm working on that."

Marylyn got close and, with giggles and squeezes, hammered home the fact that we were in love.

"What time is it?" she asked.

"It's almost 11:00. Why?"

"Uh-oh! Harold's sitter has to be home by 11:00!"

With some handy driving, I pulled up to the Swanson residence on time. The babysitter, a neighbor girl of about fourteen, came out the front door. She waved to Marylyn with her mitten-covered hand and skipped off for home.

In the fuzzy light given off by the porch, Marylyn opened her coat as she turned towards me. Her hands, warm now, were under my jacket and around me, pulling me from behind the steering wheel, close now, engulfing me with the fragrance I'd been craving for. She swung her leg over my lap and straddled me on her knees and moved her face into my neck with a shiver, her breaths coming faster. She wiggled in, not for warmth but from passion. Her breasts rose and fell, throbbing against my t-shirt. I wrapped my arms around her. She was firm but soft, and feminine, her lips I'd been yearning for kissing my neck and moving up and now on mine. Full and wet and burning—I pulled her sweater up and unhooked her bra and let it fall, setting her free—oh God, she was hot and I was on fire. I threw my face into her bosom, kissing and sucking. Marylyn reared her head back and shrieked as she pressed her soul into my face. Then pulling back, her hands on my shoulders, her chest heaving, she stared at me with eyes dancing with fire. Both hands went for my belt, pulling it loose. Still looking into my eyes, she found the top button of my Levi's and unfastened it, then pop, pop, pop the others relented as she ripped them open with her fingers.

Bang, bang, bang came from a shadow through the steam on Marylyn's window.

My heart stopped. She pulled down her sweater and swung off.

"Oh God. It's Daddy," trying to whisper.

"We're in trouble." I said, trying to hold my breath.

"We're dead. He'll kill us." Marylyn shuddered

The sweat on my face froze and my heart almost exploded—thinking of Bonnie and Clyde's riddled bodies lying dead in that V8 Ford somewhere in Louisiana. I should run, or drive off with Marylyn, maybe to Mexico or—the door handle squeaked, turning in the silence, then the door flew open. It was Harold. Whew. I breathed again.

He looked odd standing there in front of the light with the steam swirling around him as it exited the car. I could have hugged him.

"Sis. Mommy just called from a pay phone in Bridgeport. They're on their way home."

Oh God, I thought as I sat there deflating like a leaky tire. What next?

"You're full of it, Harold," Marylyn said, composing herself. "They're not due home until tomorrow."

"No, really. Daddy got sick and they'll be driving in any second. What you doing in there anyway?" he said, cocking his head.

Marylyn shut the door on Harold and turned with a weak smile and a kissed me, tender this time. "This is good-bye for now, Sonny, but not for long. I love you." She turned and opened the door.

"But you forgot this, " I said, holding her bra just as the door clicked shut.

I'll have to be careful with this, I thought as I slipped it into my pocket.

I wiped steam from the windshield with my red shop rag and drove, getting some distance between J. R.'s house and me. Then, overcome with emotion, I pulled to the side of the street and stopped. I sat there for a moment letting my mind go. Then, full of bliss, I pulled out for home. I was on top of the world, floating above, sitting on a little cloud with stars twinkling at me. I could see Willamette below and my little coupe all shiny and blue scooting along in traffic through downtown. The streets were lit up with lights decorated for Christmas, and bells and music all festive for the occasion. I was hallucinating and knew it. I was in the clutches of love and I let it all in.

From above I saw my '40 pull up to our house, all decorated and wonderful. Everything was wonderful. I laughed and laughed, knowing I'd lost touch with reality. Effortlessly, I swooped down to our door, not like a paratrooper but more like Peter Pan. Spooky, younger looking and smiling, welcomed me inside.

I sat down on my bed. It was soft and warm. I was in ecstasy. Marylyn loved me, I'd beaten Crazy Horse, and Clive was going to give in tomorrow, making me a hero to J. R. What could go wrong?

I collapsed.

Chapter 27

I woke up Sunday with a grin on my face, thinking of the previous evening. It just couldn't have been better—Marylyn coming after me and telling me she loved me. Beating Crazy Horse wasn't bad either. I was happy. Even if we were apart again, I knew it was only temporary.

I threw out, and stood up to see the lumber pictures taken at Econo-Lumber staring at me from the top of my dresser. My mind wrenched back to the mystery at the mill and the plan to solve it. What if Clive ran? He looked to be in good shape. Could I catch him, and then what? What if he wanted to go for a joy ride after we hit him with the evidence? He might run, and it would be in that big-ass Pontiac, which he claimed was fast. It might be a long-legged race, so I had to change back to my high-speed gears, and I had to do it today. I could smell coffee coming from the kitchen.

Steering with the cast and munching on toast between shifts, I drove for Zig's Towing. Good. Bruce's Chevy was parked in front. I pulled through the gate, right up to the shop door, and barged into the office. "Bruce, we gotta change my gears back."

"What's the hurry?" he said, chewing on a donut. "Heard you beat Crazy Horse last night."

"Yeah. He needed beating. It was that blower that did it."

"You going to pull it off too?"

"Nah," I said. "I might be needing it. Is the shop empty?"

"Pull your car in and I'll help you change 'em."

It's nice to have friends, I thought, *especially when you only have one good arm*. The change took us all morning. Finished, I filled the housing with ninety-weight oil, thanked Bruce, and drove for Pop's.

"Hi, Joe." He was sitting in the normal booth, coloring with Ingrid again.

"Hi, Ingrid. How's my favorite artist doing?" Ingrid was working on an elephant with pink ears. She smiled and rolled her eyes at me.

"What's the plan?" Joe asked as I was sliding in.

"Buster and I are going to drop it on him at work."

"When?"

"Tomorrow night, right after the black semi leaves. We're going to trap him inside his office and pull the rug out from under him."

Ingrid was doing the lips on the elephant.

"Wow," said Joe. "I can't wait."

"You ain't going."

Joe's mouth dropped like the air went out of him.

"Why not? I want to see the look on his face when the world slips out from under him."

"Sorry, Joe," I said. "You have a job to do, and you're the only one who can do it."

"What's that?" I told Joe what Buster had for him. He seemed let down, but I told him his job was absolutely important for the nab to go down right, and the timing was crucial. He nodded. Joe was okay with it.

"Take Buster's note here," I said, handing him the envelope, "to the sheriff's office at exactly 12:40 Monday night. Make sure it gets into the hands of the night officer, and make sure he reads it. Tell him it's from Buster Cleveland."

"Why don't I do that sooner, and then I can come with you when you arrest Clive?"

"Because," I said, feeling bad for Joe, "then the law would go out to the mill sniffing around and probably scare Clive off. It's all got to come down simultaneously."

"Okay, Sonny. You got it."

Monday at 10:45 p.m., I arrived at the mill at my usual time. The brass padlock shined my headlights back at me as I approached the man-gate on the mill side of the parking lot gate. To my left, I could see the office through the chain-link fence. Parked next to it was Clive's Pontiac, sitting in its usual space. *So far so good*, I thought. My heart jumped a little.

I grabbed my copies of the pictures and the papers from Sharon from off my car seat and stuffed them into my pocket. I swung open my door into weather that was terribly bitter, with windblown raindrops that cut like razor blades. Hunched over with my lunch bucket, I splashed for the office, where I punched in and snatched my gear like a routine night at the mill.

The mill ground to a halt with the usual rush for the gate. I timed my watch schedule so I'd be close to the loading area at the back of the mill when the semi arrived. The kid pulled up to the loading gate right at 12:00 p.m. He was punctual. So was Clive. He rolled up on the forklift and opened the loading gate, letting the truck through. I watched as Clive started loading. Just like always, he placed bundles of select in the middle of the trailer, with the junk on each end.

Satisfied that everything was going as planned, I hurried back through the mill to let the sheriff in the man-gate.

Buster was waiting in his black two-door Chevy. I threw him a wave, and he got out of his car wearing an ivory-colored Stetson over a tan rain jacket, making him look ranger-like. He walked straight for the gate and entered and followed me to a dry place in the main building, where we huddled together behind a straddle buggy, with a clear view of the office door.

Buster said, "We'll jump him soon as he goes into the office."

Buster had a sure-as-shit look on his face as he leaned into the wind, looking for Clive to appear. It was rubbing off on me. I wouldn't say I was cocky, but I could see why some people liked to be lawmen. They had a lot of power over people. And it looked like it was gonna be easy. "Okay, Sheriff," I said.

I heard the semi start up, and moments later, Clive came driving up to the office on the forklift. He leaped off and walked in carrying an envelope.

The sheriff crept towards the office with me behind him. Then he reared back and crashed through the door with the authority of someone to be reckoned with—Joe Friday couldn't have done it better. I followed with all the resolve I could muster. Clive was standing behind the counter facing us with a fistful of papers in one hand and a pencil in the other.

Buster slammed his big police flashlight down on the counter. Clive's jaw dropped. "What you doing, Clive? Adjusting the numbers a little?" Buster demanded.

Clive's eyes got big—but he covered quickly, composing himself.

"Who the hell are you?" he growled. And then he turned on me. "You're the night watchman—throw this old fool out and get back to work."

"I'm Sheriff Buster Cleveland, retired, and I'm arresting you for fraud, racketeering, and embezzlement."

"You can't do that—you just said you're retired," Clive laughed.

"You've just been arrested," Buster stated. "In the name of Buster Cleveland, citizen of Willamette County." He threw me a look.

I slapped the photos down in front of Clive, the one with the Econo-Lumber sign on top. And then the stack of invoices that had Econo and Dunlap all over them. The evidence was on the counter looking right at Clive. Clive spread out the blow-ups like he was showing his hands, and then his eyes shot to the invoices. "What's this?" Clive sneered, bold but with a crack in his voice.

"As we speak, your friend, the grader, is being apprehended for aiding and abetting," Buster lied, "and your cohort in Molalla will be getting a visit as well." Pulling handcuffs from his coat pocket, Buster said, "You can come peacefully or the other way, it's up to you."

Clive looked again at the pictures taken at the Econo-Lumber yard, then his eyes swiveled to the shipping papers and invoices. With a flash, he changed his demeanor.

Looking down quiet-like, he said, "I guess you've got me." His lower lip stuck out with remorse. He seemed beaten.

This was even easier than I thought.

"I'll get my things," he said and turned and entered his office. The door clicked shut after him.

Buster gave me a wink as he pulled out a cigar. "Get my car, Sonny," he said. "The deputy will be here shortly, and we'll turn Clive over, and that will be that."

"Okay." I smiled and loped for his car. I was relieved it went so well. I'd gotten about halfway to the employee parking main gate when I heard a car door squeak open behind me. Sliding to a stop, I turned and looked back to see the interior light illuminate Clive as he threw what looked like a briefcase into his car. Diving in behind it, he slammed the door. The motor fired up and raced as I beat it back to the office. "He bailed out the window," I yelled as I opened the door.

Buster's cigar fell out of his mouth. "Get my car, and I'll meet you out on the street."

As I ran for Buster's car, I heard the Pontiac throwing gravel and then the peeling of tires as they hit the pavement. I ripped open Buster's door—no keys! Shit, now what?

My '40 sat close under a light by the man-gate, looking as good as ever. I didn't want to take it because I knew chasing after Clive could be hard on it.

Oh well. I legged for it, turned the key, and the motor roared to life.

Chapter 28

Slipping and sliding, my tires spun through the wet bark and gravel as I flew out of the parking lot to get Buster. Seeing him standing there in the middle of the mill road and leaning into the wind, I figured he'd know where Clive was off to.

I wasn't disappointed. When I slid to a stop, Buster bailed in, saying, "His lights just disappeared into that housing development across River Street."

I feathered the throttle, looking for traction as my car fishtailed up the slimy street.

"He must think he's going to shake us," said Buster. "The son of bitch is in a hurry too. Must have the big motor."

"Yeah, a Bonneville," I said. "He's been bragging about how fast it is."

"We might find out," Buster said. "I assume this old Ford is fast too?"

"It scoots pretty good," I said.

I roared over the bridge at Kane's Creek, and then with a quick glance blew through the stop sign on River and entered the new housing development past a No Outlet sign.

"We could trap him in here," I said as I throttled down.

"Shut off your headlights," Buster said. "We'll prowl around."

I flicked them off and was surprised at how dark it got. Just some lonely street lights in the rain.

"Soon as he feels penned," said Buster, "he'll make a run for it and make like a rocket for the freeway. You said Sublimity, right?" He relit his cigar.

"Yeah," I said. "That's what the mill records show."

"Okay," Buster said, clinching his cigar, "what he'll do—I'm guessing now—is head for home after the sack of money he has rat-holed. Then he's going to try to make his grand escape, so we need to head him off before he can get home."

"You sure?" I was impressed by Buster's theory.

"Yep," he grunted, sitting up and searching.

That was funny. How could Buster be getting funny at a time like this? I idled along quiet-like, past unfinished houses with no lights, creeping over freshly paved streets. I turned a corner.

"There he goes!" hollered Buster.

"I see him," I said. The Bonneville's big ass disappeared around a corner onto a side street.

We played a cat and mouse game, switching streets and catching glimpses of the Pontiac from time to time. We kept him south of us, ever herding him towards a blind street without an exit. Suddenly, we reached the last street next to a canal, offering no way out except the way we came, and Clive was making a U-turn at the end of the block.

"We got him now, Buster."

"Maybe," Buster said.

Feeling good about it, I pulled into a driveway and backed into the middle of the street, blocking his only escape route, figuring he'd give up. The Pontiac stopped under a streetlight and looked menacing as hell, with its big chrome bumper mirroring at us. I began to worry a little.

"What do you think he's going to do, Sheriff?"

"Well, it would be nice if he throws in the towel."

Clive threw his headlights on and then the front of his car rose with acceleration. Steam boiling from his rear fender wells, he launched towards us.

"He's coming at us!" I yelled. "He's going to run into us."

"No, he ain't," Buster said, cool as shit. "Sit tight."

I wasn't so cool as Clive came bearing down on us with all four of those quad headlights on bright. If he t-boned us, which is what it looked like was coming, he'd kill Buster for sure and maybe me.

I slipped my shifter into reverse and had my motor revved, ready to get out of his way, but at the last possible second he wrenched the wheel and left the street, mowing down some shrubs and a fence, bouncing across the owners' front yard. Making for the street, he uprooted a fifty-five-gallon burn barrel, which came tumbling at me, crashing into the right front of my '40, bouncing up and breaking the windshield on Buster's side, giving it a crushed-ice look. I winced as I pulled back into the driveway behind us, slamming the shifter into low and hitting the gas. I raced after Clive.

Sure enough, he turned right on River Street and headed hell-bent for the Boulevard. I yanked on my headlights, and the good news was I still had one that worked. The burn barrel back in the development must have taken out the other one. I floored it and gained on him midway through some turns and straight stretches, but it would have been impossible to get him stopped safely around so much sleeping humanity, so I just stayed glued to his ass.

I was pushing eighty when headlights appeared up ahead. At our speed, we closed on them quickly—passing, I glimpsed the curious look on the driver's face under a cop's hat—a cop in a county black and white. Then, checking my rear view mirror, I saw he was cramping a U-turn already, and with red lights blinking and a siren, he joined the chase—after me, though, I guessed. "I suppose I'm going to get a ticket now," I said to Buster.

"No, that's Joe's deputy coming to help us out," answered Buster.

"He's a little late," I said. "You think we should pull over and let the officer take over?"

"Shit, no," Buster said. "That Pontiac would have that Chevy for lunch. The only chance we got of catching our man is in this hot rod Ford."

Clive ran the stop sign and entered the Boulevard sideways, straightened out, and accelerated towards the freeway.

Buster was sitting up close to the windshield, squinting through the cracks in the smashed glass, hanging on to what he could. I could see his grinning face out of the corner of my eye. The old fart was loving this.

Clive throttled the Boulevard, and then with brakes, he steered right for the freeway entrance.

"Like you called it, Sheriff," I shouted. "He's heading home."

Clive hammered the throttle up the ramp, with us right on his tail. It was one of those circular affairs and easy for my car, which hugged the pavement, but his car swayed way over with the tangent. The Pontiac was fast, but it handled like a boat.

"This old hot rod corners, don't it?" hollered Buster over the pipes.

"I had some help with that from an old circle-racing whiskey tripper," I yelled back.

"Musta known what he was doing," Buster said, nodding at me with a grin .

"Yep," I said, flooring the throttle. The Pontiac was a long-distance runner, with a speedometer that went clear to the glove box. My speedometer was pegged at a 100 only because that was as far as the numbers went. I guess that's all Henry Ford figured I'd need. To stay with Clive, my tachometer was bouncing off 6,500 rpm. I had an old sheriff with me and a cop behind me with his flashing lights getting smaller and fading, and I was doing 130 down the highway. What could go wrong? Most anything, I guessed.

I began to worry which car would take the punishment and which would get tired and give up. We flew past a car or two like they were standing still. Oncoming headlights flashed by us like airplanes, followed by taillights that looked like shooting stars.

About twelve miles out of Willamette, I followed as Clive veered off an exit for Highway 48 and ran the stop sign, hitting the gas for the east. The narrow, paved highway was dark, with trees and brush lining both sides. I pointed my car down the road like I was following a bullet down a gun barrel.

"We need to get him stopped out here," said Buster, "somewhere before we let him get into town."

"How we going to do that?" We were yelling back and forth, going like hell on the Pontiac's ass.

"See if you can get up beside him and crowd him over, but watch out now," Buster warned. "The closer he gets to home, the more desperate he'll get to lose us."

I began to creep up on the Pontiac, but suddenly it dropped over a rise and I lost his taillights. I buried the throttle in fear I was losing him, but when I crested the hill, he was right in front of me. I slammed on the brakes just in time. Had he wanted me to smash into him? Could that be his strategy? He had the advantage in that the back of his car was guarded by a trunk so big and long a guy could haul plywood in it, and all I had out in front was a tin grille and my radiator.

Maybe I should slow down.

He goosed the Pontiac, and my demons came cheering back, dancing all over in my car, grinning at me and egging me to blow caution to the wind, in control of me maybe. I stomped on the throttle and we were in full flight again, and I was gaining on the Pontiac, until we got so close I was reading B-O-N-N-E-V-I-L-L-E in big letters. Clive pounced on the brakes; I couldn't stop and crashed into the back of his car. I heard the rake of my fan going through the radiator, and then smelled antifreeze and steam escaping through the louvers in my hood, spraying all over my windshield. I couldn't see much except that Clive's car looked undamaged, as if I'd picked on something way bigger than I'd thought. My cowardly little demons had disappeared with the crash. My motor was still running hard, but it wasn't going to last long.

"Well, that didn't work," Buster said. "You got any ideas?"

"Yeah," I said. "I'm going to hit him again."

"You're going to what?"

"In the sweet spot. I'll show you. We need a corner."

"There's one coming up," hollered Buster, knowing every road within miles of Willamette.

Sure enough, Clive was entering a left-hand corner, and with full throttle, I crept up on his right rear, careful not to get into the gravel. Just as he was cornering to the left, I gave him a shove on his bumper, and just like Clayton said it would, the Pontiac began to go into a spin. But instead of rolling off to the left and out of my way, it was sliding sideways in front of my car.

"Hit him! Hit him!" shrieked my demons, and I stomped the throttle, slamming into the side of the Pontiac, shattering Clive's side window. His passenger door blew open, flipping on his interior light, revealing him clamming onto his steering wheel and looking straight at me with terror in those eyes of his, like he was staring at death itself—or was he looking at the demons dancing on my shoulders, taunting him out of meanness and daring me to stay on the gas.

Clive and I were locked together, me t-boning him down the middle of the highway at 100 mph. I knew Clive still had his foot on the throttle too, because I could hear his rear wheels clawing into the asphalt. With some traction, the Pontiac inched its way forward, grinding metal against metal with a sound like in a shipyard. The Pontiac finally shook free and catapulted across the oncoming lane, crashing into the borrow pit, flipping end over end like an acrobat doing somersaults.

I hit the brakes, stopped, and ground my transmission into reverse and stomped on the gas backwards. "You think he's dead, Sheriff?" I asked, worried as hell.

"No one could survive what he just went through," said Buster.

Oh God, I must have killed him then. Backing up the highway fast, my motor began squalling with the stench of burning oil, slowing my '40, choking the life out of it.

And then it died like I'd shut off the key. It had seized up. I'd killed it too.

I jumped out and ran through the smoke and steam towards the upside-down headlights and wheels still spinning on Clive's car. He was staggering off towards the trees—good. He wasn't dead; in fact, he was running away. I overtook him with a headlong tackle. He didn't fight.

With my good arm, I pulled him to his feet, and with a little shove, he stumbled back towards the road. Buster cuffed him to the door handle of the Pontiac.

"That ought to hold him," Buster managed to say, out of breath from the excitement but grinning.

Buster leaned back on the Pontiac, cool as shit, happy with the catch. So was I—it was over now. We'd done what we wanted, caught Clive, and now he would roll over, and we'd have the other two, and the mill would be saved, and J. R. would be happy, and Marylyn—

A siren broke the silence, followed by red lights flashing, reflecting off the trees and the dark spring sky.

Moments later, a Willamette County deputy came screeching up in a squad car, lathering from a long run, followed by a state trooper. The cops jumped from their cars, guns drawn like they were coming up on a bank robbery.

"Hey, is that you, Sheriff?" hollered the deputy. "Need an ambulance?"

"No, just a tow truck," Buster said. "Call Zig's, wouldja?"

They shook hands like old friends.

"This is Sonny Mitchell here, Deputy," said Buster. "You might know of him."

"Yes, he has quite a résumé down at the office. Good mostly."

That sounded good.

"So what took you so long?" kidded Buster.

"Sorry about that, Sheriff. That little Ford is hard to keep up with. We got orders on the radio to look up this way, that you were probably on your way to Sublimity, so after you outrun us, we chanced Highway 48 and here we are."

"You would have never caught up to us. If he," pointing at Clive, "would have stayed on the interstate, we'd be in Seattle by now."

"This the bad guy?" he asked Buster.

Clive was staring at me with those eyes of his, only with feelings now. Feelings of hate.

"Yep," said Buster. "I guess he's your property now."

While everyone was getting caught up on the details, I slipped into the Pontiac and came out with Clive's leather briefcase. I handed it to Buster, who in turn passed it on to the trooper.

"There should be enough evidence in here to confirm what we already know and put this guy in the slammer for a long time," Buster said.

Chapter 29

While Buster and the two cops were doing business with Clive, I stepped over to visit with my '40. It was a sad affair. The front fenders and grill were destroyed, and the hood was pushed back in a grotesque way, revealing the motor, once proud and feared, but now injured, cooked, maybe beyond repair. Water and antifreeze were running from the radiator, mixing with oil on the pavement, giving off the smell of a machine way overused.

Another set of headlights appeared on the rise and a car came puffing up. A Plymouth sedan, fairly new and plain as it could get, yet all business-looking, like maybe a government car. Could have been the FBI driving a car like that. Boy, that got my attention. How'd they get here so fast?

It shut off close to the Pontiac, and its door swung open, revealing a man dressed in an overcoat and wearing a fedora with one of those plastic covers that look like a lady's shower cap. He could have been some kind of agent until he got close. He introduced himself with a tip of his hat, which carried a card in the band: Press. He was from the newspaper. That was a letdown.

He was a tall, skinny guy and had that underpaid look about him.

"Jeez, Sonny, did you do all this?"

When had my name become household down at the paper? I was mixed about that.

"Your car don't look so good," he said, scratching his head sarcastic-like.

"Oh, no shit, really?" I said. He pissed me off. His attitude matched his wardrobe, worn; at least, he was wearing on me. I noticed he looked hurt with that. "Sorry about that," I said letting him off. "I've had a busy night."

He asked some questions about how the whole thing came about, and I gave him some short answers that he considered—always licking his pencil lead before jotting down the information in his little notebook. "Hey, it's quit raining," he said. "I'm going to fire off some pictures while I got the chance. Stay right there." He went back to his car and dragged out a big fancy camera and began popping bulbs at me and the vehicular chaos I was standing in.

He ran out of film, or just figured he was done, threw his camera strap over his shoulder, and wandered off to talk with Buster and the two cops, who were comparing notes over the hood of one of the squad cars.

346

Finished there, he whipped his car around like he was afraid someone might horn in on his story, and tore off back to town to report the scoop.

Buster, seeing me alone, stepped over to console me. He threw his arm around my shoulder. "Sorry about your car, Sonny."

"Thanks, Sheriff," I said. "I guess it would have been your car messed up if your keys had been in it."

"I wish it had been," he said. "But we'd never have caught him in my car. You going to be okay?" He pulled me a little closer—looking like he cared. He smelled of some kind of cologne and cigar smoke. Man smells. Who would have thought he could help, but the comfort he offered did help. He was good at it, like he'd been around a lot of misery—sorrow was no stranger to him.

"Yeah, sure, Sheriff. Thanks for believing in Joe and me, and helping catch the rat."

"You're pretty good at this sort of thing," he said. "Ever think about being a lawman?"

"Nope, the county couldn't buy me cars often enough."

"I'll go along with that," he said. "You're hard on cars." Smiling then. "I'm getting a ride back with the deputy, to make sure Clive gets locked up okay."

Right before he got in his car, he waved and yelled, "Come by and see me!"

"I will," I said. His invitation hadn't fallen on deaf ears. The old sheriff and I had become friends, and I planned on checking in on him to remind him of it.

The squad cars made U-turns and drove off towards the interstate.

It got quiet, with only the noise of a lonely owl, and began to rain again. I wondered where in the hell Bruce was. Finally, there were headlights, and then I heard the sound of his motor. I sure was looking forward to seeing him. He pulled up to me and rattled down the window. He had a rider. Joe was with him. It was good to see Joe.

"Now what have you gone and done?" Bruce said as they piled out.

"Nice to see you guys too," I said with sarcasm. "And how'd you get here, Joe?"

"I was just in the neighborhood, and well, really I was still at the sheriff's office when they relayed your call to Bruce, so I hustled out to the Boulevard and caught a ride. You okay?"

"Yeah, I'm fine, but my car ain't so good."

"I guess it could be worse. You guys could have been crushed in that thing," Bruce said, nodding at my '40. "You could be dead now."

"It's worse, Bruce. The motor is shot. I burnt it up chasing this Pontiac down."

"So what happened?" asked Joe.

"He didn't go down easy," I said. "I'll tell you about it on our way home."

I don't remember much about towing my '40 back to town, except I rode in the middle, close to the heater. There were questions from Bruce and Joe about what happened and all, and then I remember the buzz of the heater and things got sleepy and fuzzy-like. I was worn out.

I woke with Bruce slowing for the Willamette exit.

"Do you want to take your car back to the yard?" Bruce asked.

"No," I said. "Let's leave it at my house—I'm not sure what I'm going to do about it yet. I'm tired—I think I'll sleep on it tonight."

I must have really been wiped out, because when I woke up, Spooky wasn't there. I'd never slept through her wake up routine before.

I heard Dad talking with Mom in the kitchen, and it was daylight out. He never came home for lunch. Had I slept the whole day away? I'd never done that either. Mom was standing over him with her hand on his shoulder, both reading the paper. Hearing me, their eyes left the newspaper and fell on me with a "who are you?" look.

I sat down, and without taking her eyes off me, Mom handed me a glass of Kool-Aid and half of her ham sandwich. Spooky appeared for her share of the ham. I passed her a sample as Dad slid the paper to me—**HOT ROD DRIVER CATCHES THIEF** was headlined big above a half-page picture of my '40 sitting in front of Clive's inverted Pontiac. Wow, what a picture, and that's why Dad was home—because of what was in the paper, and he'd probably seen my car out front. He came home to check on me. That was nice.

I began to read, hoping the skinny-ass reporter got it right.

CATCHED THIEF

WILLAMETTE—Sonny Mitchell, with speed in his veins, is at it again. Early this morning, Mitchell, a 1959 graduate of Willamette High and a current employee of Dunlap Sawmill, with the aid of retired Willamette County Sheriff Buster Cleveland, apprehended Clive Bursell, foreman, also employed at Dunlap Sawmill. A 50-mile high-speed chase and ensuing crash yielded the capture of Bursell on Route 48 east of Salem. According to a Willamette County sheriff, records showing a trail of embezzlement were seized at the scene. Mr. Bursell was arrested and charged with racketeering, along with other crimes, and transported to the Willamette County Jail.

Good, I thought. I wonder how smug Clive is now. The article went on to explain the details of the investigation and who was involved, including Joe Harden, who, the article said, was also an employee of the mill. I was glad Joe was in the article—it wouldn't hurt his status at the mill, for sure.

"Are you okay, Sonny?" Mom asked. Her lower lip had that quiver going.

"I'm okay," I said. "My car is pretty badly damaged, though."

"How did all this happen?" Dad asked. He was serious, like he was glad I was there in the safety of our house and breathing.

I brought them up to date—I could tell the story seemed to transfix them, the way they became absorbed in it. As the story moved along, only their facial expressions changed—from curiosity to disgust to fear, and then relief.

"I'm sorry about scaring you like this," I said to them.

"You've always done what's right," Mom said. "We're proud of you, Sonny." My folks were looking at each other then, the way they did sometimes.

"I'm going to look at my car in the daylight." Leaving them alone, I stepped out into the rain with Spooky. My '40 was even worse than I remembered, sitting there wet and whipped-looking, with the front all crushed like it was.

I stood there like it was a viewing down at the morgue. My car hadn't deserved what I'd done to it again. I peered through the driver's side window at the broken glass on the floor, when suddenly my demons were looking back at me. Not grinning now but sad, with tears running down their little faces. They must have felt terrible about my car. Were they in the car waiting for me? No, they were sitting on my shoulders, a reflection in the glass, and when I moved they went away. I waved good-bye to them and then looked around to see if anyone had seen me. I felt foolish.

As if the mood had changed, the sun came out, bright like it does between showers, offering a rainbow.

I heard a car coming up the street behind me.

I turned to see the massive chrome grill of J. R.'s red Buick reflecting the sun back at me. It was like God or the devil himself had just appeared, and I was about to find out which.

He pulled in behind my car and stopped just as the sun disappeared again and the rain came back with a vengeance, like maybe a warning of what was about to happen. I stood there, not feeling the rain splashing off me, with Spooky at my side, ready in her mind to protect me.

He left the motor running, powering yard-long wipers, pumping rain off the windshield, and approached me carrying a rolled-up newspaper and leaning into the storm. I faced off with him on the sidewalk, not offering him space on our property.

He looked at me through the rain, which was pleating his face. His eyes were bloodshot and water was dripping off his nose. "Sonny, I'm here to thank you again. The last time you saved my daughter, and now I guess you've saved my tired old ass." He stopped talking and screwed his face up like he was searching for the right words. "Sonny, I forgot where I came from. I was raised in a place that makes yours look like a king's estate." He waved the paper towards our house. "I come up hard and I didn't want to look back and I didn't want my family to know. That's why I'm who I've been. But it's all changed for me now."

Where is he going with all this? He ain't getting off easy, I challenged myself. I'd been waiting for this moment for a long time, and I wasn't going to help him along. I thought he owed it to Marylyn to have to swim in his own soup, so I looked him straight in the eye and didn't blink.

He pulled out a monogrammed handkerchief and blew his nose. He went on, "I've been terrible to you. Uh, what I meant was ... is, I apologize for it—what I've done, you know—I haven't been very popular around my house with practically locking up Marylyn, who's been pining away for you. I've been such a hard-ass that even her mother won't hardly talk to me since all this happened."

I'll be damned; he's apologizing. I never thought he had it in him.

"I'm real sorry, Sonny. I'm real sorry, and I'd be honored if you would come to our house for dinner Sunday. Would ya?" he stuck out his hand.

And I took it.

Acknowledgments

My editor, C. Lill Ahrens, appeared soon after I'd written *Swerve* once. I will be forever grateful for her devotion to the book. She was a great sleuth in her continuous scrutiny of the project. She pushed me without mercy, time and time again to dig deep. "It's good, Jim, but it can be better."

Thank you, Lill.

My girlfriend and love of my life, Kathie Whitmire, encouraged me with enthusiasm and patience.

Thank you, Kathie.

Designer Tom Heffron. The wonderful graphic images throughout the book.

Thank you, Tom.

Artist James Owen. The fine depiction of Sonny's '40 Ford.

Thank you, James.

Advance Praise for

The Little Bastards 2

Change is a major theme in this splendid novel, and the manner in which Jim Lindsay reveals it is mesmerizing. Friends, family, challenges, errors, habits, accidents, loss— all of these elements mutate us and we become people. Jim Lindsay has captured that as well as any other writer. His is a remarkable achievement. Highly Recommended.

—Grady Harp, Amazon Top 50 Reviewer

Jim Lindsay's handsome bad-boy character Sonny Mitchell returns in *Swerve!*, the riveting sequel to *The Little Bastards*. The book picks up right where the last one left off, with Sonny a hero and pining after a girl on the other side of the tracks. His prose is smooth and very easy to read. You'll feel like you're right there in Sonny's world. Hold on, you're in for a thrill ride.

—Pam Gossiaux, author, Mrs. Chartwell series

Lindsay is an author of considerable warmth and charm and has a knack in weaving an engaging story, particularly if you grew up in the same era as Sonny. There is something to be said about those nostalgic moments when you might long for the past and ask yourself what happened to this guy or gal or perhaps relive some of the escapades similar to those described in the novel. What really caught my eye in the novel is the manner in which Lindsay skillfully paints a picture of the pulse of the 1950s and his ability to generate strong mental pictures of Sonny's experiences during the critical years of his life, which is so essential in producing a believable and affecting novel.

—Norm Goldman, publisher, Book Pleasures.com

About the Author

Jim Lindsay was born in Corvallis, Oregon, in 1947. He was raised on a farm that sustained him, his parents, and his brother, Bob. After eight years of education in a two-room grade school, he attended and graduated from Albany Union High School.

A stint in the Navy Reserve and a year and a half of college were followed by 42 years of farming. He has two children, Caralee and Jake, and a girlfriend, Kathie. Jim became a writer late in life, but not without enthusiasm. *Swerve: The Little Bastards 2* is a sequel to the novel *The Little Bastards*.

He lives with his dog, Ruby, on the same farm where he was raised. He's a hot rodder, drag racer, and lifetime member of the Bonneville 200 MPH Club.

CPSIA information can be obtained
at www.ICGtesting.com
Printed in the USA
FFHW020910061218
49765928-54240FF